THE GOOD SOLDIER

NIR YANIV

PRAISE FOR THE GOOD SOLDIER

"*Drawing on a tradition of anti-war fiction and his own military experience, Nir Yaniv meshes together classical American gung-ho SF with the delightful absurdism of European literature to create an unforgettable far-future fable for our times. Think* M.A.S.H. *in space, and you'll come closest to capturing the spirit of* The Good Soldier, *but you'll have to enmesh yourself in the (mis)adventures of Idiot-First-Class Fux and company of the good ship Spitz to find out for yourself. This is one explosive novel you do not want to miss!*"

LAVIE TIDHAR, AWARD-WINNING AUTHOR OF
CENTRAL STATION AND *NEOM*

"*In this amiable satire of the gung-ho heroics of military sci-fi, Yaniv (coauthor of* The Tel Aviv Dossier) *sets a seeming simpleton against an immense empire, and the contest is hardly fair . . . (A)n amusing alternative to the usual run of martial marvels and battle-tested warriors. Military SF fans will enjoy this gentle roasting.*"

PUBLISHERS WEEKLY

SHADOWPAW
PRESS

NIR YANIV

THE GOOD
SOLDIER

THE GOOD SOLDIER
By Nir Yaniv

Shadowpaw Press
Regina, Saskatchewan, Canada
www.shadowpawpress.com

Trade Paperback ISBN: 978-1-989398-82-1
Ebook ISBN: 978-1-989398-83-8

Front cover created by Nir Yaniv

Shadowpaw Press is grateful for
the financial support of Creative Saskatchewan.

PART ONE

THE GREGARIOUS GREENHORN

FUX IS DRAFTED

He delivered distraction, devastation, and disorder. He dealt desperation, depression, and destruction. He carried chaos and confusion and peddled perversions and perturbations. Many of his contemporaries ceaselessly cursed his name. Others, patient souls that they were, put up with him. But more than a few, strangely enough, seemed to like him. In times of war, a common soldier may find joy in either being a fanatic or, as most do, in any available distraction. To such satisfaction-seekers, his stupefying subsistence spectacularly hit the spot.

All in all, he probably meant well.

INTRODUCTION TO *THE GOOD SOLDIER,* AN
ANONYMOUS MANUSCRIPT POPULAR ON
BOHEMIA IV

PRE-PRIVATE FUX of Bohemia IV demonstrated his questionable qualities in a most splendid and satisfactory manner less than a minute after setting foot upon the imperial light frigate UPS *Spitz*. The incident, an airlock disruption or commotion or some such, resulted in a momentary all-ship red alert, a few light injuries, and, so rumour had it, the demise of a forklift.

This feat, Lieutenant Lipton pointed out when word of it reached the Officers' mess, must have been a record of some kind, to which young Ensign Berserker hotly replied that it was no laughing matter, this being another sign of a deranged and traitorous mind typical of the inhabitants of Bohemia IV; to which Lieutenant Lipton said, "Shut up, Berserker," to everyone else's satisfaction.

"The captain will hear of this," mumbled the humiliated ensign, only to be told among bursts of laughter, "And *you* will be the one to tell her?"

Lieutenant Lipton's thirty years of age made him somewhat too old for his lowly rank, yet his authority reached far beyond it. Or so it would have seemed to anyone careless enough to take the ship's command manifesto at face value. In it, Lipton was registered as acting top vehicular life-support officer, in charge of the ship's entire air systems crew. This lofty position was somewhat limited, though, by the fact that said crew consisted of no one but its commanding officer. The airlocks were officially under his jurisdiction, though not under his direct command. This meant that while he had no influence or say on the matter, every airlock-related incident was to appear in his personal file, gleefully maintained by the political division. Therefore, regretfully, Lieutenant Lipton had to conduct an investigation in person.

He embarked upon this task without delay, unless one counts waiting for the shift to end, a repair crew to be sent to airlock D, some shaken recruits to be put in the infirmary, and the brig to gain one new Pre-Private occupant. A few more minutes were spent locating the airlock shift leader, one Corporal Kohl, who was eventually found painting the upside curve of an otherwise abandoned service corridor.

The UPS Spitz was old but not old enough to require anything as ancient as paint. Almost every surface inside the ship was made of self-repairing opaque mesh. This, however, wasn't reflected in the regulations, which required applying a fresh coat of paint every hundred standard shifts. No paint or brushes were in existence anywhere upon the ship, but such trifles failed to prevent Corporal Kohl from smudging the wall with vaguely foul-smelling dabs of liquid. Regulations demanded a light-blue colour, but it was hard to see in the dim light whether the corporal's goo complied with this instruction. This, too, might require an investigation at some point. But not right now.

"Corporal," said Lipton. "Report."

"Sir," the corporal said, inflicting some more wetness onto the wall, which promptly rejected it. "I'm applying a new coat of light-blue paint to the . . ."

"The airlock, Kohl. What happened in the airlock?"

"Sir!" said Corporal Kohl and stood to attention. "One of them draftees, sir. Leaned on the emergency lever. Saw it happening with my own eyes, sir."

The corporal's broom-like moustache seemed to be standing to attention, too, in accordance with the gravity of the situation but in defiance of any other kind of gravity. This was especially notable since, by now, the ship was under acceleration on its way out of the Bohemia star system. In other times, this might have been amusing, but airlock breaches were serious business. They could endanger not only the lives of a few draftees but also the career of a promising young officer.

"A draftee?" said the promising young officer. "And no one tried to stop him?"

"I'd've done so but had twenty newbies in the airlock, sir, at least five between him and me. I was just telling 'em the basics."

The corporal's right foot, Lipton noticed, was right in the middle of the puddle of whatever it was that the wall had rejected, and the liquid was slowly but determinedly climbing up the man's cardboard shoe and paper uniform.

"The basics," Lipton repeated, fascinated by this display of capillarity. By now, the corporal's uniform had absorbed so much liquid that it was on the verge of disintegrating.

"The basics, sir," the corporal said, oblivious to all this. "As in, if it's blue, it's engine systems, don't touch it, yellow's air systems, don't touch it, green—"

This mention of naval regulations shook Lieutenant Lipton out of his capillary curiosity and put his mind back to the matter at hand. "And the lever?" he asked.

"'Course, sir," the corporal said, his moustache quivering with indignation. "First thing I said, 'This lever here is airlock-override, don't touch it! No matter what you do, don't touch that lever!' Then this draftee went and pulled it, and the sirens ran off, and the air ran out, and—"

"How come no one flew out into space, then?" Lipton

felt an unintentional smile climbing up his face. No one died, after all. The incident was probably nothing more than a freak accident. No one would be punished, most importantly, not himself.

"We would've, for sure, only we were still packing supplies in there. Had a forklift in the airlock. Smashed right into the outer door and got stuck in it."

"Ah," said Lipton. "The forklift." So the rumours were true. He was fighting his own smile and losing.

"Bit of luck there, really, sir."

This true statement wiped the stubborn smile off Lipton's face. He couldn't afford to be even slightly suspected of agreeing with it. "Oh?" he said. "Are you implying that the decommission of mission-critical Navy equipment is 'a bit of luck,' Corporal?" This was the speech expected of him in such circumstances. He hoped the corporal would have the presence of mind not to answer.

"Better than losing a man, sir?"

So much for presence of mind. This was getting too politically dangerous. Lieutenant Lipton had to steer the conversation away.

"Did you see this man *actually* do it?" he said. "Did he just lean on the lever or actually pull it?"

"I . . . I don't know. We can check the logs, sir."

Lieutenant Lipton raised his eyebrow at this and rather pointedly said nothing at all.

"However," Corporal Kohl added hurriedly, "the local logcams were probably certainly damaged by decompression, sir, because, eh, because everything was flying around like crazy, and something must have hit—"

"A full report on my desk within the hour, Corporal," the

lieutenant said harshly; but a faint smile, visible only to his interlocutor, belied this entirely.

"Sir, yes, sir!" the corporal said, barely avoiding a sigh of relief.

Lieutenant Lipton turned and, hoping that his now carefully severe facial expression was readable by the corridor's single working logcam, forcefully marched away. Just as he crossed the grey metal exit hatch, he heard a very satisfying yelp from behind, a sure mark that Corporal Kohl had just made an important liquid discovery. Being out of the logcam's field of vision, he allowed himself a brief, thin smile.

His next stop was the brig, in which the culprit was stowed until further notice. The adjacent guard station was better lit than most of the rest of the ship. Too much so, in fact. The harsh light painfully reflected off the oddly cheerful blue walls, bright-green pipes, and rainbow-coloured contraptions, a display of tastelessness that would have been out of place even in a kindergarten. Perhaps, Lipton thought, this was a sophisticated way of breaking the detainees' spirits. Or maybe it was just an accident. A rather fitting word, Lipton now discovered, since among the blissfully bored brig personnel now sat a nasty surprise in the form of Ensign Berserker.

"What are you doing here, Ensign?" Lieutenant Lipton asked dryly. He never felt comfortable around Berserker, partly because of the latter's political zeal but mostly because other than that, and a certain age difference, the two men resembled each other to a very uncomfortable degree. Both were thin, pale, yellow-haired, blue of eyes, and sharp of nose. Those features coincidentally resembled High Command's idea of The Ideal

Crewmember Type III (Caucasian), as shown in every naval manual in existence, to Lipton's great discomfort and Berserker's obvious delight. If this wasn't enough, the similarity between them was of such a degree that many of their colleagues inquired whether they were related, mostly as brothers but once, to Lipton's unrelenting dismay, as father and son.

"I was told by Command to participate in this inquiry as your orderly so as to learn how it's done, sir," said Berserker. The shadow of his nose, black and sharp in the harsh light, cut an unflattering shape across his face. Especially when he was moving his lips. Lipton hoped that his own face did not suffer the same fate.

"Ah," he said, forcefully keeping his face as passive as possible.

"Therefore, in accordance with Command's instructions, I would . . ."

"Yes," said Lipton. He was familiar with said Command and was, therefore, silently cursing the bastard's cautiousness, laziness, and, to be frank, very existence. He was absolutely opposed to having any orderly whatsoever, as in his experience, those were either outright dangerous or merely in constant need of supervision. He was also absolutely opposed to having any Berserker whatsoever in any capacity whatsoever. He suspected that this uncomfortable pairing was some sort of punishment. It probably had to do with his recent romantic entanglement with Commander Aruhu and especially its unfortunate ending, which the lieutenant preferred not to be reminded of.

He looked at the ensign. Objecting to his presence would not end well. He noticed, though, somewhat gleefully, that the younger man, barely more than a teenager, really, had started developing a potbelly.

Maybe, if his face gets a bit puffier, too, the resemblance won't be as striking. No matter. Not now.

"Very well," he said. "Open the door and stand in the corner and be quiet."

Berserker obeyed swiftly and efficiently and with an unbecoming smile.

The interrogation room was not much larger than Lieutenant Lipton's tiny quarters and mercifully monochromatic, a relatively inoffensive grey. At its centre, in between various bits of furniture made entirely of metal beams, peacefully sat that prime example of a prime suspect, the record-breaking draftee.

A rather stocky man, the lieutenant noticed upon entering the room, the brig-master and Ensign Berserker in his wake. *Definitely a troublemaker,* he thought. The round face and disarrayed hair, both vaguely red, refused to give away the man's age, which could have been anywhere between forty and sixty years of mischief. The misfit was sitting on one of the interrogatory chairs, his left arm raised in the air and handcuffed to the interrogatory table, still in its zero-grav position, and thus bolted up on the wall. He was wearing the most infuriatingly innocent expression the lieutenant had ever seen, accompanied by a torn and misused orange Bohemia IV prison uniform and a blue Bohemia IV police officer cap which was almost certainly stolen.

"What's this?" said the lieutenant. "Can't you dress him in something less disgusting?"

"Well—" the brig-master said.

"I dutifully report, sir," said the apparition, "that these

are the honourable and traditional garbs of my people, the good folk of Bohemia, of which I'm very proud, and so I've asked not to be parted with them." His accent, Lipton noticed, was rather strange, rolling the Rs and stressing the Ss.

"A subversive element if I ever saw one," said Ensign Berserker.

"Shut up," the lieutenant said, not bothering to look back at his unwanted subordinate, and sat in one of the other chairs, facing the subject. He sighed, but quietly. "Full name."

"Joseph Fux, sir," said the interrogatee, "of one hundred ninety-seven Vodik Street in the district of Vinohrady in the city of Praha in the county of Czek in the state of Bohemia, apartment number five, third floor on the left."

For a moment, no one spoke.

"Well," said the lieutenant and paused again to think.

"Well," echoed the brig-master.

"A purveyor of quality purebred dogs and mutts," Fux added helpfully. "You ask, we find, no questions asked, no returns whatsoever."

"Dogs?" the brig-master said.

"Ancient pre-imperial Terran animals," said Lieutenant Lipton absentmindedly. He found Fux to be a rather curious person and, therefore, a possible source of entertainment, a thing quite uncommon in the daily, dreary naval life. But then, there was the nasty business with the airlock . . .

Lipton inhaled, forcing himself to focus on the matter at hand. "So, Joseph Fux," he said, slowly and deliberately, "can you please explain to us why—"

"A religious pervert for sure, sir," said Ensign Berserker.

"What?"

"The nickname 'Joseph,' sir, is well known for referencing obsolete yet dangerous belief systems, common among undeveloped cultures such as—"

"Oh, for the love of—" said Lieutenant Lipton, cutting himself short just in time.

"Yes?" said Ensign Berserker, smelling blood. "For the love of who, pray tell?"

"Did I just hear you using religious terminology, Ensign?"

"What? I—"

"*Pray*, Ensign? Would you like to elaborate on that? Who exactly would you be *praying* to?"

"No, I mean, it's just a manner of speaking—"

"Speaking, Ensign, being the one thing you were instructed to avoid. By a superior officer. Are we clear?"

Ensign Berserker shut his mouth and nodded obediently, but his face betrayed his feelings.

Through all this, Fux's bulge-eyed innocence and infuriating smile remained constant and, despite Berserker's best efforts to compete, slowly got on Lipton's nerves.

"Right," Lipton said.

"This," said Fux before Lipton could go any further with his inquiries, "reminds me of a funny thing that happened a while ago."

"No it doesn't," Lipton said.

"It was back in my home city of Praha," continued Fux, nodding appreciatively toward the lieutenant, "a few streets down from my place, not far from the Vlt, which happens to be our river, of which we are very proud."

"Be quiet!" said Lipton, somewhat louder than he

intended. "If you want to tell us a story," he added, "start with this one: why did you pull that lever?"

"Lever, sir?"

"The one you pulled. Don't try to—"

"Oh, the handle. It was unintentional," said Fux, smiling beneficently upon his interrogator. "The honourable Corporal Kohl explained over and over how dangerous it is to touch anything in the locker room, and so I was determined to obey his wish."

"The *airlock*," said Ensign Berserker.

"Yes, the locker room, sir," said Fux, nodding. "And so, in order to make sure that I did not touch anything, I hung onto this handle, which was very conveniently located for that very purpose."

"Said handle, in United Planets Ships of the *Neukölln* class, utilizing the standard naval air-exchange chamber Mark IV, being the airlock's manual override emergency lever," explained Ensign Berserker, determined to demonstrate his surplus knowledge even in the face of the enemy, or at least in the face of a handcuffed subversive and religiously perverted element, whichever came first.

The lieutenant turned his head, gave the ensign a brief look of contempt, then returned his gaze to the peacefully smiling detainee. "Are you pretending to be an idiot?" he said.

"No, sir," said Ensign Berserker.

Lipton demonstrated a considerable amount of restraint by simply remaining seated, closing his eyes, inhaling, exhaling. Eventually, he said, "Are you pretending to be an idiot, *Fux?*"

"No, sir," said Fux. "Absolutely not, sir."

"Right. So—"

"I am *confirmed* to be an idiot, sir."

"Excuse me?"

"Sir, I am confirmed by the municipal police of the city of Praha in the county of Czek in the state of—"

"Will you stop with the geography and get to it?"

"Bohemia," continued Fux, unperturbed, "to be a complete idiot, second-class, sir."

"Confirmed, you say."

"Registered, sir. It's even written on my identification card. Sir."

"Give it to me."

"The card, sir?"

"Yes, the card, Fux."

"Unfortunately, sir, during the mysterious trouble in the locker room, it was somehow—"

"Enough," said Lieutenant Lipton. He rose from his chair. "Brig-Master, put this man in the shower. Set it to high pressure and uniform selection to naval draftee. Then send him to the infirmary for checkout and processing."

"Yes, sir."

"Ensign!"

"Sir!" said Berserker, standing at attention.

"Write an essay of fifteen hundred words to summarize what you've learned from this interrogation," said the lieutenant. Noticing the evil smile creeping onto the ensign's face, he added, "Limiting yourself to describing the detainee only." He greatly enjoyed the ensign's change of expression, especially after further commenting, as an afterthought, "Within the hour."

The ensign was about to protest, but the detainee was

quicker. "Thank you for your kindness and understanding, sir," he said, gazing amiably at the lieutenant. "If there is ever anything that you need, please do not hesitate to ask." This was followed by a rather indiscreet wink.

"Take him away, Brig-Master," said Lipton and quickly walked out so as to make sure that the dangerous line of conversation employed by Fux came to an end and did not, as he suspected, become a matter of record for the political division.

On the way back to his cabin, he thought to himself, *If that's a second-class idiot, I wonder what it takes to make a first-class one?*

And thus was Fux enlisted to the Imperial Naval Forces of the United Planets.

2

FUX IS CURED

The Controller is the best machine ever invented. It protects us from bad people and also from becoming bad people. It is the reason we have, for the first time in history, true world peace.

CITIZEN OF THE GALAXY, AN IMPERIAL BOARD
OF EDUCATION PUBLICATION FOR CITIZENS
AGED EIGHT TO TWELVE

A BIT LATER, elsewhere upon the good old light frigate *UPS Spitz*, Lieutenant Commander Doctor Nightingale was having a very good time. This was achieved by the flawless execution of an elaborate plan: first, she wisely procured fifty grams of excellent Hašek from the city hospital of Praha; then, she craftily conveyed to Engine Master Chief Maguro that she could use a willing companion for inhaling the said substance, and perhaps some other recreational activities;

and finally, she arranged an extended off-shift period, and her own cabin, for all this to take place in.

To her pleasant surprise, both substance and partner surpassed her rather immodest expectations. Now, bathed in the soft glow of an improvised lighting fixture, lying in her modified acceleration bunk, illegally converted to a plush double bed using assorted military-mesh fabrics, she was quietly congratulating herself. This, she thought, was perfection. This was the best you could get out of this Navy life. This made it all tolerable. This train of thought, however, was soon brought to an unexpected stop by a nasty chirp from the com.

"Override, reject, otherwise occupied, contact only by end of watch," groaned Doctor Nightingale breathlessly. She put down the Hašek jar and smiled at Maguro, who was on the verge of causing her some serious pleasure.

"Voice pattern identified, connecting your call," the com sang. "Thank you."

"Override, disconnect!"

"Ma'am! Ma'am! Are you there?" the com shouted with the voice of Medical Ensign Grippe, whose single task for the next five hours was to quietly occupy the infirmary doing absolutely nothing.

Nightingale had made a point of clearing the infirmary's schedule in advance, right after dealing with the new draftees. She had personally verified that all of them went through initial political recalibration and cell sampling, plus hasty anti-shock treatments related to some bizarre incident in airlock D. She'd also verified that Ensign Grippe understood her direct and exact instructions, with special stress on not letting anyone into the infirmary for any reason whatso-

ever. This, as she had joyfully explained in the highly fiction-
alized infirmary log, was due to an important medical
equipment maintenance procedure involving dangerous
chemical elements.

"I'm busy," she said, turned on her side, reached the com,
and clicked its large and friendly RESET button. The existence of this control was the only good thing about the awful
military-issue com units — they could be turned off. As
opposed to her birth-installed neural connection, for
instance, always online but utterly useless upon a Navy
vessel or anywhere other than old Terra itself. She felt a brief
pang of longing for the good old days when no physical
device was needed for any kind of connection, everything
happened within one's head, and communication was not
something you spent any time thinking about, except for the
usual mandatory political correctness. This feeling did not
last long, however, firstly because it brought with it some less
favourable memories, and secondly because of Grippe's
voice, crying, "It's an emergency, ma'am!" through the unaffected, traitorous com.

"What the Space, Grippe? I told you to stay put!" she
said, reaching for the com again.

"Ma'am," said Grippe, just as she was screwing out the
com's round back. "We have a," he continued as she was
unplugging the power unit; then, just before dying, the com
emitted one final word. "Patient!"

For a long moment, there was nothing but silence. Then
Maguro slowly, from his position on the other side of the
bunk, started moving toward her.

"Crap," said Nightingale, then gently but firmly pushed
him away. "We'll continue this some other time."

She went into the shower and emerged five seconds later, her dark skin dry, clean, and mostly covered by her official light-blue paper med uniform. On her way out, she commented, "Good job, Master Chief. I'll see you later. Don't finish the Hašek."

SHE SAILED into the infirmary like a frigate of old, guided by a well-known lighthouse straight into a reef to run aground. Said obstacle was immediately in evidence, snoring peacefully on one of the medichairs. The atrociously ineffective navigational aid, in the skinny, lanky, wide-eyed form of Medical Ensign Grippe, was nervously circling the patient and hitting controls at random. On the back wall, the main controller machine, a great metal and polycardboard contraption covered with entwining pipes, dials, lights, wires, and whatnot, was whining softly to itself.

"Stand aside," she said.

"Yes, ma'am!" the ensign said and obeyed. His gaze kept moving nervously between his superior, the patient, and the controller.

Nightingale glanced at the medichair's telemetry, conveniently projected on the ceiling above it. Then she checked the medichair itself and verified that, despite some odds and ends and cables and tubes emanating from it, it wasn't any more dysfunctional than usual. Then she turned to the patient and quickly concluded that the medical condition from which he was suffering was, as she'd suspected, a deep and undisturbed sleep.

"What's going on here?" she said.

"Ma'am, the was patient identified as Pre-Private Fux, serial number—"

"What's going on here?"

"He got here from the brig on Lieutenant Lipton's orders to be checked and processed immediately," said Grippe. "I told them we were closed, but the brig-master was like, 'You take him right now, or I go straight to Nightingale's room and see how busy she is,' and I knew that you didn't want anyone to know about you and Master Chief Maguro, so—"

"Crap," said Nightingale, feeling the blood rushing to her face.

"I mean, eh," the ensign continued miserably, "I, like, I don't even know Master Chief Maguro. I was just—"

"Enough," she said. "So. What happened then?"

The ensign stared at the snoring patient, who was wearing a dark-purple standard uniform and a weird blue cap. "Then," he said and cleared his throat, "then I put him in the chair for overall checkout and initial recalibration."

"Is he ours or theirs?"

"Ours," the ensign said. "The Infantry got their draftees right away."

"Of course, they did," said Nightingale. Regulations gave the Mobile Infantry the first choice of new draftees, leaving the Navy to deal with the leftovers. In the long run, it didn't matter. In the short run, here she was, dealing with the consequences.

"So," the ensign continued, "his checkout was just fine. I ran it twice just to be sure."

"Yes?"

"So I, well, I—"

"Yes?"

"I, like, I put him to sleep, I took the necessary cell samples, and I—"

"You gave him the pill."

"Yes, ma'am," said Grippe, now sweating despite the infirmary's cold atmosphere.

"So far," said Nightingale, "this is standard procedure, even if one remembers that I specifically prohibited you from supplying anyone with any medication or substance or treatment whatsoever."

"But, ma'am, the brig-master said that Lieutenant Lipton said that he must get the pill, and he must—"

"Yes, yes. And what happened then?"

"Nothing, ma'am."

"Nothing?"

"Nothing at all, ma'am, I swear."

"Nothing at all, Grippe, does not count as an emergency."

"No, ma'am."

"So?"

"So, I checked the telemetry, and it's like the pill never got to him, never even reached his stomach, no influence, nothing. The controller received, like, zero data from him. I checked three times."

"And?"

"And so I . . . I . . ."

"Yes?"

"I gave him another pill."

"In a way, I deserve this," the doctor said after a short yet ominous silence. "Step aside, Grippe."

"Yes, ma'am."

Nightingale briskly walked toward the convoluted

contraption covering the back wall of the infirmary. She swiftly and expertly pulled something and nudged something else, and the controller stopped whining, beeped once, said "entering sleep mode" in a somewhat resentful tone of voice, and turned itself off.

"Now, Ensign," she said, "we will have a short and painful lesson regarding what you should already know. What is the full name of the controller?"

"But, ma'am—"

"'But, ma'am' me one more time, and I'll put you on plumbing duty for a month. Answer the question."

Nightingale was at least a head shorter than the ensign, but that didn't prevent her from looming menacingly over him. She knew that the gaze of her deep-black eyes could easily intimidate almost anyone on board. She practised and perfected a certain menacing demeanour for just that purpose, with great success. And indeed. Grippe promptly and nervously retreated.

"Well?"

"The Behavioural Optimizer-Controller Mark XII," he said.

"Which means?"

"It analyses and corrects the political fitness and behaviour of individuals who—"

"And how do we achieve said analysis, Grippe?"

"By . . . eh, by inserting Analysis Nano-Agents into the body via the digestive system, encapsulated in a pill, " said Grippe, quoting the manual, "transmitting constant information to the controller, ma'am." He pointed at the device, then thought better of it.

"And now, Ensign, what is the most important factor in

ensuring the success of said agents in performing their duties?"

"Like, for them not to be recognized by the white blood cells, ma'am?"

"And therefore —"

"And therefore, their quantity and configuration should be set in advance to proper—"

"Proper indeed," said Nightingale. "And so, assuming you did quantify the agents to begin with—" the ensign nodded but managed to keep his mouth shut, "it appears that you gave him twice the calculated dosage."

The ensign nodded again.

"What, then, would be the result of doubling the analysis pill dosage, Grippe?"

"Like . . . the white blood cells . . . will, like, notice?"

"And so?"

"Like, this isn't good?" hazarded the ensign.

"Let me explain it to you in a way that you will not find in the manual," said Nightingale. "By giving this person— what's his name, again?"

"Pre-Private Fux, ma'am."

"So, by giving this Fux person a double dosage, you have wasted a perfectly good pill, that's one. Also, by giving this Fux person a double dosage, you risked alerting Command of a special situation here, that's two."

The ensign shuddered. He knew pretty well what a *special situation* could mean.

"Also, most importantly, by giving this Fux person a double dosage, you have effectively made him immune to the analysis nano-agents, that's three."

The ensign merely stood in his place and said nothing,

miserably staring at her. Then he made an attempt at mumbling something.

"What's that, Grippe? Anything else?"

"So," the ensign said. "So, like, they also wanted him to be recalibrated. So . . ."

"Are you trying to tell me that you've attempted to give a full initial recalibration, which you are absolutely unfit and unauthorized to do, to a patient whom you've just immunized against the analysis pill?"

"I thought, like," mumbled the ensign, "I mean, like, I was told to, I mean, like, the orders were very clear, like, that is—"

"And to think that for this, Grippe, I've given up a lucrative position in a top medical faculty, on Terra, no less," Nightingale said. "On the grounds of everyone around me being insufferably stupid. For *this*."

"Is this why you joined the Navy?"

"No," she said, her mind painfully skipping over that particular sad memory, and especially who turned out to be stupid after all. "And it's none of your business," she added. "Now, as long as the controller is off, let's get things straight here."

The ensign nodded hesitantly. Even he was not dumb enough to ignore the analysis agents in his very own blood.

"This conversation never happened," Nightingale said, "else both you and I are done for."

"Yes, ma'am."

"We'll tell them that this Fux person has some rare condition. I'll take care of that. We've had uncalibrated people before; all we need to do is to instruct them properly. The relevant manual is somewhere in our public folder, no password needed. Get it and deliver the instructions to the patient. Other than that, just say nothing and pretend to be stupid. Shouldn't be hard for you."

"Yes, ma'am. Should I put him in the recalibration bin? Or send him to the correctional closet?"

"After what happened here, do you think that either is going to work? No, we're going to go manual; recalibrate him right here with the main controller."

"Yes, ma'am."

"Now, let's pull the damned thing out of its sleep."

"The patient?"

"When I said 'pretend to be stupid,' Ensign, I did not mean *that* stupid, that's one. Also, especially not when talking to *me*, that's two. Also, not the patient, Grippe, the *controller*, that's three. Turn the controller on."

"But, ma'am," said Grippe, "the emergency."

"What about it?"

"It's not the patient, ma'am."

"Not the patient? Not the immune, un-calibratable draftee that you've just created for us, Grippe?"

"Ma'am, It's the controller."

"Excuse me?"

"So, the patient may be immune to the—"

"Definitely immune, Grippe."

"Yeah, so the patient is, like, definitely immune to the controller, but the controller isn't definitely immune to the patient."

"What did I just say about being stupid, Grippe?"

"I swear!"

"I'm losing my patience, Ensign."

Grippe stepped back toward the controller, pushed

something, and nudged something else, and the machine buzzed into life, clicked and hummed a bit, then started whining.

"Well?" said Nightingale.

"Listen."

She did. Above the gentle snoring of the patient, the hiss of the air circulation, and the ever-present humming of the ship, she heard the controller's regular mournful stream of semi-consciousness. Each and every medical officer was trained and ordered to be attentive at all times to this blabber, on pain of losing one's rank. Each and every medical officer found ways to utterly ignore this blabber, on pain of losing one's mind.

"Apartment number five, third floor on the left," the machine mumbled, paused, then pleasantly added, "I didn't touch anything; it was conveniently located for that very purpose."

"Well?" said Nightingale.

"Does that seem normal to you?" said Grippe.

"This dog is totally purebred, and its lineage is completely and reliably absolutely authentic," the machine said.

"That is, indeed, slightly abnormal," said Nightingale, "but I wouldn't call it—"

"It is *perfectly* normal," the machine said, raising its voice, "in accordance with the honourable tradition of the good folk of Bohemia."

There followed a short hush, which ended with the doctor uttering, "Crap."

"There is no need for profanity," the machine said, "I am perfectly capable of—"

"Turn it off, Grippe."

"I wouldn't recommend this course of action," the machine said, "as I find it quite disrespectful toward—"

Ensign Grippe turned something and pushed something else. The machine hiccuped and managed to add, "It wasn't my fault," before turning itself off.

There followed a moment of blessed silence, into which the still-sleeping patient emitted a loud snore.

"Ensign," said Nightingale, "call Lieutenant Lipton and tell him to come here at once. Say that it came directly from me and that you don't know why."

"Ma'am?"

"Do it," she said. As he was fishing in his pockets for his com, she added, "This is going to be a long shift."

THE GOOD DOCTOR WAS, as usual, too right for her own good. The long shift was not limited to the infirmary, though, since a few moments later, every wall, floor, ceiling, and table inside the ship started projecting a rather vocal informatica. This eye-watering, ear-shattering presentation consisted of the recycling of one Corporal Kohl. The poor bastard kept his dignity until the very last moment, right after being pushed into the green bio-reclamation chamber. Shortly, the awkward silence was replaced by muffled screams. They continued for quite some time, even as the nearby reclamation container, a deliberately transparent receptacle, started filling with green-brown ooze. All this was accompanied by a mechanical voice, dryly reading a summary of the crime, it being the usual gross negligence, and then of the punishment, it being the usual horrible death. It finished with the obvious lesson: never make any mistakes. Or, as everyone else saw it, never get logged.

"Even though he grossly betrayed us, his fellow brothers and sisters, Corporal Kohl's last contribution is an important one," the voice intoned. "His bodily fluids and essential substances shall sustain us in our ongoing fight for justice. Remember: thou shall not waste!"

The projected image accompanied this by focusing on the brown-green ooze.

"Crap," Nightingale said. "As if we're not busy enough as it is."

The gruesome display on the wall was replaced by the usual political curriculum presented by the ship's officially-beloved political officer.

Ensign Grippe was smart enough to remain quiet through all this. Executions, common as they were, were still a serious matter. Especially for the infirmary, which had to deal with their residues. Now, under Nightingale's scrutinizing gaze, the ensign busied himself with Fux. Luckily, the patient required nothing more complicated than light sedation until the powers above decided what was to be done with him.

And thus was Fux politically cured, albeit in a somewhat theoretical fashion.

3

FUX IS REASSIGNED

Among those forbidden titles, pay special attention to The Person in the Flying Fortress, *a deliberately controversial fake history book in which the state of Columbia, named* Amerigga *after some obscure Florentean explorer, wins a fictional conflict dubbed* The Second World War. *This is obviously a metaphor for the Grand Clash, which famously begat our empire and caused the cowardly escape of the renegade old princedoms of Europe outwards to the furthest corners of space.*

The following keywords are to be fed to all on-board Behavioural Controllers: "World War," "Axis," "Allies," "1939," and "1945" (the years, old-count, of the beginning and end of the fake "World War," as opposed to 1814 old-count, first year of the Grand Clash, and 1972 old-count, marking its end and year one of our true world peace), "Pearl Harbour," "Normandie," "Iwo Jima," "Hiroshima," and "Nagasaki"

(designating major "historical" battles), "Little Boy,"
"Fat Man," and every person mentioned by name in
the aforementioned book.

As per standing orders, any person flagged by the
Behavioural Controller is deemed politically incorrect
and should be promptly recalibrated.

NATIONAL HOLIDAY GUIDANCE, YEAR OF OUR
PEACE 335, UNITED PLANETS IMPERIAL NAVY
POLIDIV CENTRAL, TERRA

COMMANDER KAPUST, the vessel's top-ranking political officer, official chief political authority, head of the political division, and so on and so forth, was annoyed. This, as unanimously agreed by all those who served with him over the years, as well as his wife and his mother, both estranged, was his usual disposition. He hated the Navy's nefarious nincompoops and the Infantry's infuriating imbeciles. He detested war, peace, space, planets, plants, pets, and people. The latter two he felt to be rather similar in nature, including, as he had already witnessed during his long service, a troublesome tendency to defile one's carpet. He loved hard politics and hard liquor, both efficient methods of rejecting his fellow officers, the sight of whom he found hard to bear.

At this particular moment, stuffed uncomfortably between his tiny chair and his tiny desk in his tiny cabin, he was darkly thinking that among said officers, none were as bothersome as the two standing before him. Those consisted of Lieutenant Commander Doctor Nightingale, whose authority over the ship's politi-medical equipment was suspiciously unwavering despite his most earnest schemes, and Lieutenant Lipton, whose ideological correctness log was too good to be true and who therefore was most likely a spy.

Their histories, however, were mere trifles when compared to their looks. Contemporary political manuals stressed that people of all genders and races were born equal and equally enjoyed the right to be governed by their betters. But Commander Kapust, who was brought up in an ancient and conservative fashion, could not bring himself to believe that. He tended to be intimidated by anyone non-male, non-white, and, in his heart of hearts, anyone he suspected to be either more male or more white than himself. Together, Nightingale and Lipton filled all these requirements in a rather disturbing way. The fact that both looked suspiciously similar to the politically ideal crewmember types for their respective skin tones did not help one bit.

Getting rid of these two would not be easy. If it was merely about the nasty airlock incident that had just cost them an expensive forklift and that stupid Corporal Kohl, he could have deflected it easily. But it was far worse than that. *Damn.*

In the corner stood the rest of the UPS *Spitz* political division, namely, the overzealous Ensign Berserker. This reinforcement did not improve the commander's mood in the slightest. He had recently been made aware of a troubling rumour that the ensign and Lieutenant Lipton were somehow related. He couldn't see any similarity between those two, as Berserker was, while obviously a nuisance, at least a properly loyal and law-abiding young man, and Lipton was anything but. *Could the ensign's behaviour be a sham, a front, a deception? Could he be the lieutenant's eyes* and ears in the political division? Could he, by extension, be serving other forces on board? Maybe even the captain? Oh, no.

But that had to wait for later.

"Who is this Fux person anyway?" Kapust asked. "Do we have anything on him?"

"He says he's a purveyor of dogs," said Lieutenant Lipton, conveying a smile without bothering with the actual facial expression.

"I did not ask about, ahem, ancient Terran mythology," Kapust said. "Or is this what you take to be a joke, Lieutenant?"

"Not at all, sir," Lipton said. "It is merely what he told us. If there is any other information available, it was not made accessible to me."

Pushing it right back at me, eh? Kapust thought. *We shall see about that.* "Fine," he said aloud and tapped his desk. The latter, having listened in on the conversation as was its usual habit, was already projecting Fux's official history as received from the Bohemian police.

To whom this may concern,

Please find below our detailed report in regards to one Fux, Joseph, recently transferred from the Kundera Correctional Facility to the custody of the United Planets Imperial Fighting Forces, may they vanquish all our enemies forever!

Fux, Joseph, male, Caucasian, height 169 centimetres, weight 92 kilograms, hair red, age unknown, address

*unknown (self-claimed address incorrect), relatives
unknown (classified), previous records unknown.
Reason for unavailability of previous records: recent
damage to the Vinohrady district public records
facility during the empire's honourable and justified
reclamation of the city of Praha by force.*

*Police record summary: small-time crook and occa-
sional vagrant.*

List of 38 recent arrests follows.

*Arrest #38: Drunkenness, political incorrectness,
insulting a police officer. Remarks: caused some
unrest among other detainees while being processed,
released due to lack of prosecutors. Note: aforementioned police officer quit shortly afterward, where-
abouts unknown.*

*Arrest #37: Bar fight in the flower district. Suspected
connection to illegal gambling ring of pig- and
chicken-racing tournaments. Released due to lack of
evidence, as related chicken escaped custody.*

*Arrest #36: Civilian complaint in regard to the distri-
bution of fake canine spare parts . . .*

Kapust let the rest of the list roll quickly. At the bottom,
there was a short note:

Regarding subject's mandatory attempted recalibra-

*tion treatment at the Kundera Correctional Facility,
see additional information in Appendix X, classified.*

Take him, and good riddance.

Sincerely,
Sgt. K. Čapek
Municipal Police HQ, Praha, Bohemia IV

"Ludicrous," Kapust said. "Who is this Čapek person? I would arrest *him* in a heartbeat."

"Well, that's not an entirely unheard-of history among our recruits, sir," said Lieutenant Lipton, who insolently leaned over the desk and read its contents without asking for permission.

"We make our new citizens better than they have ever been!" said Ensign Berserker from his corner.

Do you think I'm going to be fooled by this cheap display of loyalty? Kapust thought. *We shall see about that.* "Be quiet," he said aloud. The ensign stood to attention and forcefully shut his mouth into a thin line.

"What's in this Appendix X, then?" Lipton asked.

"That's, ahem, above your clearance level," Kapust said. The insufferable lieutenant gave him a shrewd glance. He probably guessed that Kapust himself didn't have that clearance either. *Damn him.* "In any case, I believe the given information is sufficient," he added. "We know where he came from and that he's a troublemaker."

"Be that as it may," said Lipton, "it doesn't help us with our current problem."

"Ah," said Commander Kapust. "The *problem.* Yes." He

gave the cocky lieutenant a nasty stare. This, alas, seemed to have no effect whatsoever.

"Yes," Lipton said. Both he and that bloody Doctor Nightingale stared blankly at the superior political officer. *Bastards.*

"And so, I'm expected to believe in this nonsensical tale of yours," Kapust said, gazing at some point in the air between the two offending officers, "and accept without question the fact that the, ahem, the political stability of this ship is endangered by the decommissioning of my main controller."

"The controller is not one individual's property but rather belongs to the people as a whole," said Ensign Berserker. "It is an instrument of the state's sovereignty, by virtue of—"

"Atten-*shun!*" Command Kapust shouted. He gave the uncomfortably overstretched ensign a nasty sidelong stare and added, "When I'm interested in passages from 'My Capital Struggle,' I'll be sure to ask you."

The merciful silence that followed this declaration did not, alas, last long. "Sir," said the insufferable Nightingale, "we are now working double shifts retrofitting a replacement unit. However, that is not the main problem on our hands right now."

"Ahem," said the commander, "*I* shall be the one to determine what consists of a problem and how important it might be."

"Sir, with the utmost respect, sir," said that slippery character, Lipton, "I would like to offer for your consideration the issue of a given person, Pre-Private Fux, sir, who contaminates every controller that comes in touch with him."

"Ludicrous," said Kupust. "No citizen of the United Planets is capable of anything of the sort."

"I respectfully remind you, sir," said Lipton in a manner totally devoid of deference, "that Bohemia IV was only recently assimilated into our great federation, and therefore some of its citizens have spent most of their lives, and in particular their formative years, in a manner entirely alien to the natural way of life we all enjoy and cherish under the wise authority of the benign ruler."

Before Kapust could answer this outrageously presumptuous line of thought, the Nightingale woman interfered. "Sir," she said, "we have empirical proof that this particular person, Pre-Private Fux, causes damage to any controller he comes in touch with, that's one. Also, we have determined that a controller which succumbed to such an issue is beyond our current ability to repair, that's two. Also, we—"

Kapust, who had previously experienced some of the medical officer's frustrating enumerated logic, hurried to put a stop to it before it grew beyond his control. "Enough!" he said. "Save your one-two-threes for your underlings, officer!"

"Sir—"

"And as for this treacherous native of that disgusting Bohemia IV place, you might as well recalibrate him before it's too late."

"Sir," the doctor said, "regardless of any academic discussion of the social and political history of Bohemia IV, which I am sure is a matter more suited to you than to us simple officers —" the warning glance she gave Lipton did not escape Kapust's watchful eye— "we have already tried this. That's how we have empirical proof that Pre-Private Fux cannot go through recalibration for the same reasons stated before: the med-politic equipment has no influence over him."

This will not end well for any of us, thought Commander Kapust gloomily, *and especially not for me, not after that brothel on Puddabest Station.*

Puddabest, originally a mining station orbiting the desolate Ugnr III, had long been famous for being a fun place to spend a vacation.

Fun, Kapust thought bitterly and stared longingly at the cabinet on the far wall behind his guests, in which a bottle of excellent Bohemian brandy was waiting in vain for his caressing touch. *What kind of a name is* Puddabest, *anyway?* he thought. *How is that a proper name for a city? Bloody miners. Bloody civilians. Traitors, the lot of them. Oh, what's the use?*

He was about to suggest recycling the idiot, but this was like hitting a microbe with a bomb. Also, this kind of measure would have to involve the captain. No one wanted that. Least of all, Commander Kapust.

"Having caused this situation by your careless behaviour," he said cautiously, "have you got any operational suggestions regarding possible ways of, ahem, of resolving this matter?"

"Yes, sir," said Lipton promptly. "Reassign Fux to the Mobile Infantry, effective immediately."

Kapust glanced at his desk, over which a list of current personnel was already projected, then back at the smug Lieutenant Lipton. "The Infantry already got their fifteen draftees," he said contemptuously. "And we have our five, and this Fux is one of them."

"We could ask for a replacement," Lipton said, a bit less cocky now.

"Of course," said Commander Kapust. "And I assume that Colonel Havock, ahem, will merely say, 'Yes, sir, of course, sir, right away, sir,' as is his custom."

"Well, I—"

"Have you ever *met* Colonel Havock, you crackpot?"

"Er—"

"Sir," that Nightingale woman interfered, "It can be done in an . . . alternative . . . way."

"In the same way, I presume, that the alternative to my working controller is having a non-working controller?"

"In fact," said the impertinent medical officer, "almost precisely like that, yes."

In his corner, Berserker opened his mouth, no doubt in order to utter some sanctimonious stupidity. "Be quiet, Ensign," Commander Kapust said, but without much conviction. He wanted that brandy really badly now. And also for everyone else to be gone from his cabin. And hopefully from his life. He turned again toward the intrusive officers. "Well?"

"Sir," said Lieutenant Lipton and pointedly glanced toward the shameful ensign in his corner.

"Ensign Berserker," Commander Kapust said, "march on the double to the officers' mess and find out whether the second-shift lunch is ready."

"Sir!" the ensign said. "Lunch will be ready, as per fleet standing protocol, it being a Wednesday, only by O-five-hund—"

"Find out whether *lunch* is *ready!*" the commander shouted, applying all of his considerable girth into that effort.

"And what they have for an appetizer, main course, and *dessert!* On the *double!*"

The ensign ran outside. The door hissed in his wake.

Kapust turned back to the other two. "Well?"

"We can go over the medical records," said the insolent Nightingale, "and find someone who, after further medical analysis, seems to be unfit for serving in the Mobile Infantry, sir."

Commander Kapust, well aware that this kind of conversation could only take place in the absence of a properly functional controller, sighed. "Well," he said, "I shall leave this delicate task in your most, ahem, *capable* hands."

Nightingale and Lipton nodded. Neither smiled. Not visibly, anyway.

"Get out," said Commander Kapust. Then he added, in complete and utter contrast to every logical conclusion which could be drawn from the previous discussion, "and make sure that I never hear of that Fux person again."

HAVING SUCCESSFULLY REPELLED the outrageous onslaught of his fellow officers, Commander Kapust, determined to postpone the ceremonious opening of his precious bottle of brandy till after lunch, promptly consumed half of it. Now, slightly for his personal dignity and mostly for his personal knowledge of the captain's approach toward alcohol, he was applying his intellect to the pressing question of how to avoid detection. This was not going well. For the past few minutes, he had been gradually failing to resist his only idea: complete dismissal of the issue in favour of a joyful early trip to the officers' mess.

Kapust was so immersed in this demanding mental activity that he did not notice anything unusual in his surroundings until the door to his cabin suddenly shrieked and disappeared. In its stead, there appeared nothing but null and void and the looming figure of Colonel Havock, commander of the 91st Mobile Infantry regiment.

"Ahem," said Kapust, but the colonel wouldn't have any of it. Briskly stepping into the cabin, he went straight to the tiny desk and smashed his fist into it.

It took Kapust, who almost fell off his chair, a moment to recover. "You can't," he said, noticing that something was rather off with the colonel's appearance, though failing to grasp what it might be, "just barge into—"

"Inadequate brain patterns!" the colonel shouted, stretching to his full height and thus almost touching the ceiling. "Inadequate bloody brain patterns!"

"Excuse me?" said Kapust, disturbed less by the colonel's words, which seemed to be utterly incomprehensible, and more by his figure, which seemed to be utterly askew.

"Nobody's brain is inadequate for the Mobile Infantry!" Colonel Havock shouted. "You hear me? Nobody!"

"Ahem," said Kapust, who by now had a pretty good idea as to the reason for the colonel's visit, "if you could kindly sit and explain what this might be about, I would be happy to—"

"You know why I'm here, you bloody mongrel!" the colonel shouted. "Your so-called medic Nightingale witch just decommissioned one of my troops. Not going to happen!"

"Who?" said Kapust, still attempting to understand the irregularity about his opponent, who seemed to be somehow . . . larger? . . . than usual.

"I demand that Pre-Private Aubergine be medically cleared immediately!" the colonel said, menacingly leaning on the desk, which groaned under his weight. His eyes were frighteningly red, his pupils huge.

It occurred to Kapust that the single-minded Nightingale had probably chosen this Aubergine person merely for being the first in alphabetical order. He barely managed to avoid a smile. "So he's not a trooper, really," he said, "just a draftee, a Pre-Private. What do you care? Most of them get killed or decommissioned even before seeing combat."

"Lies! Absolute lies!" the colonel cried, dangerously wobbling in his place. "And at times of war, too! How are we supposed to fight the bloody insects if the bloody Navy takes all our bloody soldiers?"

"It's just one draftee—"

"You think the insects are just going to kill themselves?" the colonel said, his trembling body emitting strange creaking noises.

Suddenly, Kapust understood: Colonel Havock was wearing, under his clothes, his light combat armour suit, boots included. This made him about twice as wide and a head and a half taller than his natural, rather modest dimensions. The armour suit was turned off, of course. The thing was dangerous and utterly forbidden to operate anywhere outside combat practice or, well, actual combat. Therefore, Kapust noticed, the dear Colonel was bravely fighting for balance on the small carpet, the cabin's sole attempt at luxury. Before he knew it, he smiled.

"Is this a laughing matter to you?" the colonel yelled. "You think you can mess with the Mobile Infantry and get away with it?"

"Look here, Havock," said Kapust, now relaxed after solving the mystery to his satisfaction. "Just sit down, and we can talk about it. I assume wearing this suit," he pointed at the colonel's chest, "isn't the easiest of exercises, so if you could just—"

"Still laughing, eh? You think that a political officer can laugh in the face of the Mobile Infantry, eh?" said Colonel Havock and thumped his own chest. Something underneath his uniform emitted a blip.

"Absolutely not," Kapust said hurriedly, above the ominous sound of servo motors and mechanical relays waking up and getting ready for action. "I have the utmost respect toward—"

"I'll teach you respect!" the colonel shouted and reached out with his left hand. This appendage, mightily augmented by the recklessly operational armour suit, easily lifted the desk off the floor, despite the former being firmly screwed into the latter.

"Havock, for crying out loud!" said Kapust. "Stop this nonsense imme—"

"Respect, I'll teach you!" screamed Havock. Still holding the desk in his left paw, he reached for Kapust with his right, grabbed him by the collar, and promptly lifted him up. Considering the commander's girth, this was a rather impressive feat, even for a mechanized armour suit.

"Repeat after me," the colonel said, "*nothing* overrides the Mobile Infantry!"

"Gnhh!" gargled Kapust. His real-fabric shirt, a political

officer's unique privilege, was vastly more durable than the common paper uniform, to its wearer's clear disadvantage. But now it started tearing up under the strain.

"Again!" said Colonel Havock.

It was this precise moment that Ensign Berserker chose to reappear in Commander Kapust's cabin, having performed the task with which he was entrusted in a most complete and regulation-abiding manner. His determination to demonstrate his obedience and performance was so great that he completely ignored the state of the cabin and its occupants. As the situation lacked any equivalents in naval or Infantry regulations, the ensign considered it to be merely one of those weird and unexplainable things that happened to people other than himself.

"Sir!" he said loudly above the din, "I am hereby honoured to report that lunch this shift will consist, per officer above the rank of Lieutenant, of one hundred and fifty grams of meat paste, two eggbits, medium size, one pack of preserved salad, one bar of chocolate, and also black coffee, no quantity given."

Both Commander Kapust and Colonel Havock turned to him, though the former did so merely with his eyes, now dangerously bulging, his feet still off the floor, his breath short and wheezing. For a long moment, no one spoke, and the only sound in the cabin was the slow unravelling of Kapust's shirt. The ensign took this to be a good sign.

"Eating will commence at oh-five-hundred hours," he continued, "which leaves us, uh, five minutes to get into full regalia, as per—"

Colonel Havock threw the desk at him.

This would have been the grandiose and glorious end of

the gallant Ensign Berserker were it not for the fact that Havock's previous actions had set loose the table, which happened to be the one thing that held the carpet in place. Thus, the latter quickly slid from under the colonel's feet, the desk missed its target by a hairsbreadth and smashed into the doorframe instead, and the two officers crashed into a messy heap on the floor.

For some time, Commander Kapust lay quietly under the fallen Havock. The colonel, having failed to wear the combat helmet usually attached to the armour suit, had banged his head on the floor. Now he lay where he had fallen, his eyes closed, mumbling softly.

"The place for you, the place for me," the colonel whispered, "must be the Mobile Infantry."

Eventually, Commander Kapust managed to push his head out into the open air. He glanced up with some effort, only to see the frozen figure of Ensign Berserker, still at attention, staring at him and shaking only slightly.

"Sir," said the ensign after a long moment of mutual gazing, "I am hereby honoured to report that lunch-time is—"

"Be quiet," Kapust panted, "and call the bloody medics."

"Sir," the ensign said, "what should I—"

But the commander had already sunk into blissful, hushed darkness.

HE WAS JUST ABOUT to give the first speech in his new capacity as minister of the interior and head of the House of Lords when, against the background noise of a million loyal citizens cheering in the square facing the main balcony of the royal palace, his repentant up-until-recently-ex wife entered the room, winked at him, and said, rather loudly and inappropriately, "Kapust!"

"Lord Kapust, my dear," he answered sweetly, winking back at her, "or just my lord."

"Kapust!" she repeated and slapped him in the face, and when he opened his eyes, she was promptly replaced by the irksome Lieutenant Commander Doctor Nightingale.

"I say!" he croaked, trying and failing to stand up, "this is rather unacceptable!"

"This one's awake," said Nightingale, turning away from him. "How's the other one?"

"Not yet, ma'am," said a young, shaky voice, whose owner was beyond the limited range of Kapust's vision.

"Slap him," the lieutenant commander said. "Enjoy this one-time opportunity to hit an outranking officer."

"But, ma'am—" the young voice said.

"This is an outrage!" said Kapust. "What is the meaning of this?"

"Be quiet," said the nefarious Nightingale, stepped away from him, and did something that sounded just like a large side of beef being flattened with a pastry board.

Someone emitted a terrible cough, gargled a bit, then declared, loud and clear and with Colonel Havock's voice, "Squad will advance, about turn!"

"Shut up," Nightingale said. "Now listen to me, you two."

From the assumed location of Colonel Havock, a growl was building itself up to a roar but was promptly cut short by another slap from the incredibly disobedient Nightingale.

"Colonel Havock," she said. "Unauthorized operation of

combat armour suit inside a naval vessel, assault of a fellow officer, general misconduct and," she paused, pretending to read something from one of the monitors, "self-injection of at least two ampules of unidentified yet highly illegal amphetamines."

"Such behaviour, especially for a senior officer," Kapust said, as always quick on the uptake with regard to the humiliation of a colleague. "Unheard of!"

"As for you, Commander Kapust," Nightingale said. "Ignorance of regulations, failure to abide by military dress and cabin sanitary codes, general misconduct, and," she was clearly enjoying this, "about half a bottle of unauthorized Bohemia IV brandy."

"For shame," said the voice of Colonel Havock, now noticeably calmer, the bastard. "A political officer, drunk like a pig!"

"Now," said the insolent Nightingale, "I'm going to leave you two here to rest a bit and consider your options."

"You will absolutely not—"

"I'll kill you and leave your carcass—"

"You two will be absolutely nice and quiet, else I go straight to the captain."

Oh, no, thought Kapust miserably. *Not the captain. Not her. Not after the thing on Puddabest Station.*

"Come, Grippe," Nightingale said, and both she and her sidekick departed.

For some time, the only noise in the cabin was Colonel Havock's furious breathing.

"Well, Havock," said Kapust eventually, "seeing that we're stuck in this thing together, and despite my own personal feelings regarding what has just, ahem, transpired, I would like to suggest that—"

"Captain or no captain, you're not taking my soldiers, you Navy trash," growled Havock.

"That is very understandable," lied Kapust. "But what if I was to suggest that, instead of the one you lost, I give you one of mine?"

"One of your worthless weaklings for one of my troopers?"

"Come on, Havock. He is not a trooper yet. He was just drafted."

"Absolutely out of the question."

"Ahem," said Kapust, who was, after all, much better trained than his opponent in the art of negotiation, "what if I give you two?"

"Two?" Havock said. While Kapust could not see his face, he was absolutely sure of the greedy expression with which it was now decorated. "Two, you say."

And thus was Fux assigned to the Mobile Infantry.

4

FUX IS DRILLED

Education is free. Freedom of education shall be enjoyed under the conditions fixed by law and under the supreme control of the state.

MY CAPITAL STRUGGLE: AN AUTOBIOGRAPHICAL GUIDANCE BY ADOLPHUS MARKS, FIRST GRAND COUNCILLOR OF THE EMPIRE

"TO THINK that this had to happen to me!" said Sergeant Zimmer, drill instructor of the First Platoon of the First Company of the First Battalion of the 91st Regiment of the Mobile Infantry. Admittedly, following recent cosmo-political events, no second platoon, company, or battalion was in existence anymore, and rumour had it that the 91st regiment was somewhat optimistically enumerated.

"You apes," the sergeant continued. He was standing on a circular platform at the bottom of the parade grounds, a fancy and traditional name for the drilling compartment. This was a flattened sphere big enough to contain a mature sperm whale, were any such beasts still in existence. The other thing it shared with the extinct animal was the colour of its insides, a rather disgusting mix of emergency-red and dark purple, simulating hard visibility conditions. The decoration didn't help either: obscure bits of grey-green training equipment hanging from nets on the concave walls. All this made the parade grounds, the UPS *Spitz*'s largest undivided space, also its ugliest.

The sergeant held his baton threateningly and showed every sign of toughness and uncompromising self-control. His gaze, under his bushy eyebrows, was fierce, his back was almost painfully erect, and his mouth, when he was not talking, was as clenched as one could make it without dislocating one's jaw. But all this was merely a front. In fact, he was bored.

Facing him on the platform were sixteen draftees, including two unfamiliar faces: one replacing the recently rejected Pre-Private Aubergine and one additional soldier whom Colonel Havock got from somewhere but smugly refused to discuss. They were consistently failing to stand in three straight rows, in part due to their lack of discipline and in part because sixteen does not divide well into three. The remainder of said division, a stocky idiot insolently wearing a blue cap and a naval one-time uniform instead of an Infantry weekly one, was idly walking back and forth between the rows.

"You there, you baboon!" the sergeant shouted. "Stop walking! Stand in your place!"

"Yes, sir, absolutely, sir!" the draftee said with a strange accent and promptly stood to sloppy attention, positioned somewhat in front of the second row but rather behind the first.

"One step forward! Align with the first row!"

"Yes, sir!" the draftee said. "Which of the two, sir?"

"What?"

"I dutifully request to be instructed, sir, which of the two? One step forward or align with the first row?"

"Are you being clever with me, you miserable excuse for a soldier?"

"No, sir, not clever, sir," said the draftee.

"Exactly," the sergeant said. "And always remember— you are all idiots until I say otherwise, which in your case I fear may never be the case, you undignified herd of—"

"In fact, sir," said the draftee loudly, "I am *confirmed* to be an idiot, sir. Second-class, sir."

Sergeant Zimmer had already trained thirty-seven Mobile Infantry platoons over too many years to recall and thus considered himself immune to infancy, lunacy, and general idiocy on the part of his designated flock. Still, he was taken by surprise. Two surprises, in fact: the incredible infantility of the draftee and the fact that he, Zimmer, was actually enjoying this.

"Well, in my book, you're a first-class idiot," he said aloud. "Come here."

"Yes, sir, thank you, sir," said the draftee, strolling unhurriedly toward his superior. "I am deeply honoured to be upgraded to first-class, sir, though, to be exact—"

"Be quiet, you cow, you dog, you beast of the field! Come here, I said!"

The insulting draftee soon arrived at his destination and stood at attention. "Again, I am honoured, sir, as in our town, cows and dogs are valuable animals, not to be trifled with, sir. I used to be an expert in acquiring purebred dogs—"

"Shut up!" the sergeant roared.

The draftee nodded obediently.

"That's better," Sergeant Zimmer said. "What is your name?"

The soldier-to-be, smiling amicably, stood in his place and refrained from answering.

"What is your *name*, soldier?"

The idiot silently raised one hand and pointed a finger at his own mouth.

"What's wrong with you, you pig, you snake?"

"His name is Fux, sir, and you told him to be quiet, sir," said one of the other draftees somewhere in the second row.

"You!" said the sergeant and turned to the unlucky speaker, relief in his voice and murder in his eyes. "Did I ask you to speak?"

"Sir," said the sergeant's new victim, who was a thin, bespectacled man of at least fifty years of age, "I was just—"

"Don't you 'sir' me, you elephant, and don't you 'just' me!" the sergeant shouted gleefully. "And what's that stupid thing on your nose? Take it off right now!"

"My glasses," the victim said. "I can't see anything without them."

"I've never heard of such stupidity before," the sergeant said.

"Sir," said another soldier, "he comes from a primitive planet on which there's no—"

"The Mobile Infantry doesn't care where you come from, you camel! The Mobile Infantry doesn't care who you are! The Mobile Infantry doesn't care where, why, or who! Once in the Mobile Infantry, always in the Mobile Infantry! Now take this bloody thing off you and go!"

The older man hesitantly took off his eyewear. "Sir," he said.

"On your feet! Run!"

"Sir?"

"Around the group! Run! Run, you monkey!"

The speaker, lacking the stamina and determination necessary for such a feat, attempted it anyway. It wasn't satisfying to watch.

"As for *you*," the sergeant said, turning back toward the main attraction, "stop this nonsense, talk when you're talked to and not otherwise—"

"Yes, sir!" said Fux.

"Do not interrupt me, you she-goat!"

"Yes, sir!"

"Now," the sergeant added, ignoring his growing conviction that nothing would come out of this irksome draftee except for maybe a headache, yet still determined to achieve some degree of jolliness from the situation, "drop and give me twenty!"

"Immediately, sir!" said Fux and promptly started rummaging in his pockets.

"What are you doing?"

"I'm looking for a twenty, sir," Fux said and fished something out of his pocket, a parcel of some sort.

"What?"

"A twenty, sir, as per your request," the idiot said and opened the parcel, which turned out to be an oversized leather wallet. "Here," he added, taking some papers out of it, "one, two, three—"

"Are you *bribing* me, you buffalo?"

"What's going on here?" said a new, awfully familiar voice behind the sergeant's back.

"Sir!" Sergeant Zimmer said, feeling his stomach sinking to his knees. "This soldier here—"

"Here's your twenty, as requested, sir!" said the soldier in question, pushing a bunch of dirty papers into Zimmer's hand before he could retreat.

"What is the meaning of this, Sergeant?" said Colonel Havock, for he was, indeed, the owner of the aforementioned voice, awful familiarity and all. Despite wearing specially issued platform army boots, he was at least a head shorter than the sergeant. This, however, detracted nothing from his aura of terror.

"The soldier, sir," the sergeant stuttered, "he, that is, I humbly—"

"He asked me for a twenty," the heinous Fux added helpfully.

"I said *drop* and give—"

"Enough!" the colonel said. "All of you, back to the barracks, on the double!"

"But, sir!" the sergeant cried. The soldiers, suddenly obedient in the extreme, were running around him back to safety. Even that horrible Fux was wisely slouching away. "It was him!" added Zimmer, pointing at the retreating Fux. "It was he who did it, sir!"

But the colonel would not hear of it. "Sergeant," he said with an evil smile, "you and I are going to have a *talk*."

Sergeant Zimmer opened his mouth to explain that this was nothing more than a monstrously peculiar coincidence, that he would not have dreamed of taking money from a soldier, or from anyone, for that matter, and that he had no idea that pieces of paper could serve as currency, or perhaps he had heard about it once, maybe his grandfather mentioned something of that sort, when he, the sergeant, was merely a toddler and yet to develop any military ambition, but even then, it was nothing more than a rumour, and honestly, sir, what use is this paper money thing upon an imperial light frigate such as the *UPS Spitz*, or upon any other military vessel, or any vessel at all, or . . .

"Silence!" the colonel roared before Zimmer had a chance to utter even a single syllable of this perfectly logical, if somewhat sentimental, explanation. "You're lucky that I do not behead you right here on the spot. Taking payment from soldiers and in front of the whole platoon, too. You scum."

The sergeant somehow managed to gather his scattered thoughts into a single, piercing sentiment. "I asked him to drop and give me twenty!" he wailed.

"*And* raising your voice at a commanding officer, I see!" said Havock, who, in full accordance with current military textbooks, would not let go of a victim until death or total political submission and re-orientation.

In less than ten minutes, poor Sergeant Zimmer was court-martialed and found guilty of numerous charges, ranging from insubordination at the battlefront to improper dress code. He was sentenced to one shift of recalibration in the correctional closet and two additional years of Army service.

The former, it was generally agreed, was much worse than the latter.

And thus did Fux first gain the attention of his fellow soldiers.

5

FUX IS DISCIPLINED

Our heroic forefathers have perfected and implemented a just and moral social order. This did not come easily: they had to quench the old Turk and Brit empires, take control of the wild natives of North and South Columbia, and merge the biggest nations of the other continents into one coherent political entity. After this, they turned their gaze outwards. The external colonies of Luna, Mars, Titan, and Neptune fought bitterly for their inferior, feeble-minded "independence" but eventually gave up to join our universal wave of progress.

All this was achieved in slightly less than two centuries, which is, of course, no less than astonishing.

Unfortunately, the good work was far from complete. There still remained, all across the galaxy, the renegade, criminal, dangerous infestations of old Europe, ancient Chinippon, and primal Africa. They did not merely exist—they were thriving.

And so, the United Planets Fleet was built, the mighty UPS Ermordung and its frightful sisters, the UPS Scharf, UPS Schmal, UPS Schlaue, UPS Platzen, and, in time, many more. In their bellies, those invincible machines of war carried the mightiest warriors ever to have existed in the entire history of the universe: the Mobile Infantry.

STARSHIP TROOPERS, AN OFFICIAL HISTORY OF
THE IMPERIAL ARMED FORCES

DUE TO A SERIOUS lack of fitting personnel, or any personnel whatsoever, the first platoon and the first company commanders, replacing Lieutenant Robert (RIP) and Captain Anson (RIP), were, in fact, a single person. This fine specimen was a second lieutenant whose mother, in a rather brave subversive act, tried to name after a certain historical figure (RIP) of whom no one would speak. As the birth registration system blatantly refused to process that name, the ideologically stubborn mother decided to shorten it, letter by letter, in the hope of eventually fooling the system into acceptance. In this, she eventually succeeded, registering the baby as "Win."

Eventually, however, this brilliant move did not go unnoticed and resulted in the offspring's compulsory drafting into the Mobile Infantry at the ripe age of twelve. He was assigned to a special program meant to turn exceptionally intelligent children into brilliant Army strategists. This would have been an absolutely outstanding endeavour were it not for the fact that any truly gifted children were way too smart to let themselves into it.

Since the program had to report success at all costs, its headmaster was determined to prove the greatness of his flock of underachievers by any means necessary. The result was batch after batch of young officers utterly resilient in the belief of their own genius and of being better and smarter than their peers, not to mention the enemy. This did not contribute, to say the least, to their life expectancy. Second Lieutenant Win was, in fact, unique among his former class-mates for the single reason that he was not yet RIP.

His only true gift, at least to the knowledge of his subor-dinates, was a rather mean left kick. This means of discipli-nary action he applied at least once a shift to the unfortunate among them, which, on the final count, included everyone. This depended slightly upon the time of hift and mostly upon his mood, determined by the usually poor state of his ongoing courtship of whatever female officer he fancied at the moment.

Nobody called him Win. They called him "The Big W" or just "The Big." He thought that the adjective referred to his physical power and the letter referred to his name. In this, he was sadly mistaken.

This outstanding young officer got his first clue of Fux's existence by way of an unusual noise that penetrated the thin metal wrapping of his tiny sleeping capsule and woke him up. Waking up was not included in the rather short list of his favourite activities, which consisted mostly of strate-gizing future combats and conquests of both planets and female fellow officers, and then failing and ending alone with a drink. Those occupations were the reason, not only for his recent slumber (RIP) but also for a rather fetching purple bruise on his right cheek, courtesy of a handsome navigation officer. He was not, therefore, a happy man.

"Sergeant Zimmer," he groaned. There was no reply, in part due to the second lieutenant being sealed inside his capsule and in part due to the sergeant being nearby only in the broadest meaning of the term.

The capsule's metal ceiling, a few inches above his head, had a dreadful green hue to it, and the smell inside was as foul as one could achieve without being dead for a month. So far, nothing unusual. Without leaving his bunk, the brave young officer reached out for the hatch and, after a short struggle, managed to open it. A gust of fresh air entered the capsule and, with it, the source of the commotion, which seemed to be an ongoing burst of laughter. This was rather unusual, but before he could properly reflect on the rarity of this phenomenon, it was abruptly replaced by a disgusted cry.

"What in the name of all that's holy—?" someone shouted but was cut short by the sound of a slap in the face.

Then a sort-of-whispering voice said loudly, "It's just The Big W, Private. You'll get used to it."

"Zimmer!" shouted the subject of this unflattering statement and kicked the wall separating his cabin from the adjacent one, which usually served as the sergeant's dwelling. This produced neither a proper noise nor the presence of the desired noncom.

"Sir," declared the same loud voice, which, Second Lieutenant Big vaguely remembered, belonged to a corporal whose name he forgot and whose face he regretted recalling. "Sergeant Zimmer is indisposed at the moment, sir!" This caused some more laughter in a manner totally unbefitting a military organization of any kind.

"Indisposed?" said the young officer, who was not entirely sure what the word meant, both in general and as applied to sergeants of the Mobile Infantry in particular.

"Sir," the corporal said. In Big's defence, it should be said that she was a new transfer from another unit, and so his failure to recall her name or anything else about her was almost justified. "We were given to understand that Sergeant Zimmer was court-martialed and is now in the brig, sir." This was accompanied by a series of sniggers of various degrees of loudness and insolence.

Even in his current weakened state of mind, Second Lieutenant Big quickly went through a familiar logical chain. First, he knew, there existed only one person who could and would put Sergeant Zimmer in the brig; second, this wasn't surprising in the least; third, it was only a matter of time before said person got bored with his current victim and came down to the barracks to look for more entertainment; and fourth, and most importantly, said entertainment was most likely a certain young First Platoon and Company commander, and being in Colonel Havock's sights, figuratively or literally, could very well end with one becoming a RIP.

This line of reasoning crashed through the second lieutenant's mind with all the speed and grace of the UPS *Scharf* (RIP), achieving in less than a second an effect surpassing that of ten cups of coffee and one really good kick in the head.

"Atten-*shun!*" he shouted and immediately grabbed his own head in pain, thus luckily missing the first responses.

Those went along the lines of "What did he say?" and "Who's that?" and "Careful, he likes kicking," and, for some reason, "Can I have your canteen, honourable Corporal?" in a rather suspicious accent.

The second lieutenant recovered just in time to hear a unique and bizarre monologue carried on by the same strange voice. "Sir," it stated, "I am humbled and gratified, sir, by this rare honour of being noticed by one of our empire's fine officers, sir, and hereby declare myself ready to do as you bid, come water or fire, sir, in peace and war alike, sir. We shall keep fighting till our last breath, sir!"

A moment or two passed in absolute silence. Eventually, someone said, "He's got to be kid—" only to be cut off by the familiar combination of a slap in the face and the corporal's voice saying, "Shut up."

Second Lieutenant Big painfully crawled out of his capsule and into the barracks' main area. He tried, against all odds and in defiance of past experience and, in particular, the intentions of the original designers of the UPS Spitz, to do so in an elegant and dignified way. He failed. During this complex operation, he heard the reluctant shuffling of feet and at least one hushed voice whispering something about a canteen and the urgent need to be quiet.

By the time he collected himself from the floor and managed to stand again, albeit shakily, the forty or so soldiers and draftees comprising the First Platoon were already standing in three rows. This was obviously the work of Corporal Whoever, who was standing at the front, tall and wide of shoulders, her hair cut so close to her skull that its colour was anyone's guess, and her face carefully devoid of expression.

The grunts, standing in the narrow free space left between rows upon rows of dull-grey cylindrical acceleration beds, all looked the same: tired and slightly resigned and making a point of looking straight ahead and absolutely not at their commanding officer. All, that is, except for one fat oaf of a man who stood out, insolently wearing a blue cap and a red nose, and a suspiciously innocent smile. As if that wasn't enough, the man looked the second lieutenant straight in the eye, stuck his left hand deep into his pants in a rather obscene manner, and moved his right hand in a way that might have been considered a salute were it given by a five-year-old.

"You, fool!" croaked the young officer, pointing at him. "You listen to me now, you dumb—"

"Yes, sir!" the man said.

"What?"

"Yes, sir, I will listen to you, sir!"

The second lieutenant noticed some strangeness in the way this idiot spoke, which did not improve his mood. "Be quiet," he said. "You don't know me yet, but soon you *will* know me. And when you know me, you will . . . drop that smile off your face!"

"Yes, sir!" the man said, his expression unchanged.

"I said, drop that smile off your face, you fool, or I will drop it for you!"

"I am not smiling, sir," said the oaf, beaming.

The second lieutenant answered this with a smile of his own. Up until now, he had been somewhat confused as to what course of action to take, but this kind of behaviour was something he was well-equipped, by both training and nature, to handle. Without bothering to answer, he ran straight at the offending soldier, jumped off the ground, and delivered a mighty kick straight at what he had once heard referred to as a man's nether region.

It was, everyone agreed afterward, an awesome example of what one could achieve by preparation, rigorous training, sheer determination in the face of an enemy, and a regulation metal water canteen, Mark II. The only one who failed to see the incident this way was the young second lieutenant, initially due to being indisposed, the meaning of which word he had plenty of time to learn during his time at the infirmary, and later due to the matter of his pride, which, like his foot, suffered a multiple fracture.

And thus did Fux, even before receiving the rank of private, become a hero to some of his fellow troopers.

6

FUX IS EQUIPPED

The introduction of the combat armour suit, as a part of the new United Planets Fleet order of battle, was nothing less than a revolution. Even the earliest models of this portable self-powered human-machine hybrid were hugely influential during the first conquering stage. They enjoyed a clear advantage in mobility, protection, and firepower over any enemy. Today, the new and improved model is an assault platform capable of supersonic speed in any atmosphere, carrying a huge array of ammunition: small-calibre bullets, smart projectiles, photon and electron pulses, and even nuclear and chemical devices.

The radical effect of this manifested in several ways. First, it doubled the single soldier's capacity for destruction. Second, it became a major deterrent and a source of discouragement for our enemies, though it is notable that none of the renegade planets showed the presence of mind to surrender without a fight. But *third, and most importantly, the presence of the combat armour suit redoubled the need for tight political control over the fighting forces. Even a single rogue fighter equipped with a suit could cause immeasurable damage. The development of high-accuracy Behavioural Controllers soon followed . . .*

LIFE-LINE, A MEDICAL OFFICER'S HANDBOOK

THE QUARTERMASTER SERGEANT of the First Platoon, Company et cetera, was a private named Bolon. He was short, fat, and of a jolly disposition. His domain was the huge armoury, in which, between piles of everything from kitchen utensils to spare escape pods, rows upon rows of packed Mobile Infantry combat armour suits stood in menacing silence.

Menacing to the uninitiated, that is; not to Private Bolon, who was, in fact, rather fond of them. He was also fond of many other things: of mostly being left to his own devices in his own small roofless office inside the hall; of the majority of his guests, who were of the lower ranks; and of the fact that the closest Infantry institution was the regimental kitchen, with whose personnel he maintained a warm and mutually lucrative relationship. This was of the utmost importance to him since the one thing that Private Bolon absolutely could not do without was a regular diet of at least two meals per shift.

So far, of all the people aboard the *UPS Spitz,* he was arguably the most satisfied.

Therefore, he wasn't at all disappointed at the appearance of a stocky, sloppily dressed soldier sporting a rather un-soldierly blue cap. Any quartermaster worth his title is accustomed to weird personnel issued by the Army and also to weird issues of Army personnel.

"Hello!" he said pleasantly. "I'm Private Bolon, and I'm the sergeant around here, yes? And who might you be?"

"Sir, I'm Fux, Pre-Private," his guest said. "It is a very nice place that you have got here, Sergeant Private, sir."

"I like that." The quartermaster smiled. "it shows good taste. But you can call me Bolon, yes? Now, what did they send you here for?"

"The corporal told me to give this to you, sir," said Fux, taking a metal object out of the pocket of his pants, which were too large by at least two measures, and handing it to Bolon. The quartermaster took it and examined it closely. It was an unbelievably bent and twisted regulation metal water canteen, Mark II.

"Sir, I was also asked to tell you that it was damaged in the course of action," added Fux.

"Of course," said Bolon, wondering what particular action could have caused this particular damage to this particular item, but not too much since it was almost lunchtime. "I will log it as such and supply you with a replacement, yes? Anything else?"

"Well, sir, the corporal told me that I should be assigned a combat suit for initial practice."

"I see," said Bolon. "Well, we shall do so in the most efficient manner possible." His smile became even more pronounced. "Please step right in here," he added, pointing to a small door on the other side of his office.

Fux raised an eyebrow.

"It's the measurement booth," said Bolon.

"Yes, sir, immediately, sir," said Fux and promptly walked to the door.

"Just Bolon, please, yes?" said the quartermaster. He followed Fux into the booth and locked the door behind them.

A small red light turned on, revealing several humanoid contraptions. "One of the great things about this place," said Bolon, "is the fact that it is completely impenetrable to the political controller."

"I'm sure I am not familiar with any person of that name, sir."

"Did you take the pill they gave you?" said Bolon.

"Yes, sir," said Fux. "They were very nice about it, too. They let me sleep in a very comfortable chair that can also become a bed. I was very much gratified."

"Right. That's the analysis pill, then. It reports to the machine in the infirmary, the controller."

"Yes, I saw it there, sir. I think they had some difficulties at the time."

"I'm glad to hear it," said Bolon, who, not really minding being a "sir," decided against insisting on the usage of his name. "However, controller malfunctions cannot be trusted to continue. Whenever you talk, whatever you do, you must assume it is recorded and sent to the machine. If not by you, then by everyone who sees or hears you. Understood?"

"Yes, sir."

"Good. Now, the machine cannot hear or see us while we're here, inside the measuring booth, but it will do so when we get back outside, so you are not to repeat anything we say here out there, yes?"

"Yes," said Fux. "Thanks, Bolon, that is very good to know."

"Ah, I see what you're doing here," said Bolon with a smile. "Don't worry. You can call me Bolon outside, as well. Everybody does."

He then proceeded to give a very quick and highly illegal description of the order of battle of the 91st Regiment, with particular stress on its inventory of mechanized armour suits and their combat readiness, or, rather, lack thereof. As a matter of fact, only two suits were anywhere near operational order. One belonged to Colonel Havock and the other to the entire First Company, traditionally used by whoever was registered as commanding it at the moment. The rest were either grossly malfunctioning or merely metal hulks, their power units removed and relocated to serve as replacements for other suits, now lost in combat or in the haze of time. The only operational parts, without exception, were the comm units, by order of the political division. Other than that, the suits were useless.

"So, to summarize, our order of battle could, in fact, be called a *dis*-order of battle," concluded Bolon, who had invented this sophisticated pun all by himself and was shamelessly proud of it.

Fux, seemingly unsure as to what an order of battle might be, eventually laughed appropriately.

"Of course, our inventory registers all the armour suits as pristine and combat-ready," Bolon said. "Things would go very bad for us otherwise, yes?"

"This reminds me of a funny thing that happened back in the day in my hometown of Praha," said Fux. "There was this dog breeder I knew who purchased from me two second-hand mutts, good as new, looking just like real purebred Alsatians. He insisted on having their certificates of authenticity, lineage, and all, even though you really couldn't tell the difference. Really, they were two very nice puppies, house-trained and everything, and capable of running for two months straight on battery power. And so, I had to make those certificates myself and put some real work into inventing the proper lineage and everything, and a week later, he tried submitting them to this purebred dog show in Olom, and, to make a long story short, the police arrived at my place and arrested my housekeeper."

"Your housekeeper?" said Bolon, whose long history of dealing with all sorts of misfits featured nothing even remotely like this particular, unique breed of soldier. He, therefore, quickly became, to his enjoyment, fascinated.

"She wanted a raise, so I appointed her the bursar of Fux Canine, Highest Quality Dog Breeding, Training and Purveying, You Ask We Find, No Returns Whatsoever, Limited. And when the police arrived, she was the only one there, as, at the time, I happened to be on vacation."

"A rather sudden vacation, I'm sure," said Bolon.

"Coincidentally, it was."

"Not bad," said Bolon. "I would love to hear more, but this will have to wait for another time. We cannot stay here for too long, or they'll begin to suspect foul play."

This was absolutely true. The other absolutely true thing was the imminent arrival of lunch which, regardless of any feelings of comradery or friendship or even intoxicated love Bolon might feel toward another human being, he was still totally unwilling to share.

Bolon lifted a long metal pole off the floor and used it to prod one of the packed suits away from the wall.

"This is a combat armour suit," he said. "A *perfect* suit." The packed suit hit the floor, which shuddered. A few metal scraps tore loose from it and buried themselves in the walls. "It's vitally important to *keep* it perfect," Bolon added. "At *all* times. Yes?"

"Do not worry," said Fux, and lifted the suit off the floor. "This is like second nature to me."

"I believe you," Bolon said.

Fux bent over to collect some of the debris that flew off the suit, but Bolon waved him away. "Don't worry about it," he said and noisily opened the door. "It's perfect. Just make sure never to let down your guard out there."

Fux clanked his way outside, leaving a trail of small metal objects in his wake. The door closed noisily behind him. Inside, Bolon was smiling. This was a person after his own heart.

And thus was Fux equipped with a perfectly maintained nonoperational armour suit, a new water canteen, Mark II, some reasonably good advice, and, against all odds, a true friend.

7

FUX IS CONSIDERED

Always remember that recalibration, while naturally performed for the good of society, mostly concerns itself with the good of the individual. For without perfectly balanced individuals, no perfect society can exist. As nature is never perfect, nor does it create perfection, politically or otherwise; it must be assisted. Ideological perfection must be synthetically created and maintained.

Human history saw numerous attempts at achieving this, all of which failed miserably. In contrast, our own modern society employs advanced technology: any deviation from the required norm is safely and easily fixed by Recalibration. As opposed to more extreme methods (see Chapter XII: Recycling), here, the patient's behavioural pattern is only slightly adjusted, using nerve manipulation techniques in a familiar Pavlovian pattern. Be assured that the process, despite its appearance and according to

advanced and scientifically proven political studies, is
absolutely painless and, with the exception of the occa-
sional slight confusion and marginal memory loss,
leaves no mark on the psyche . . .

I SHALL FEAR NO EVIL, A POLITICAL OFFICER'S
HANDBOOK

WHILE FUX WAS SLOWLY BEING ABSORBED into the
Mobile Infantry and, therefore, strictly confined to its quarters, he was also strongly present in the minds of certain
naval officers. Their conversation was, politically speaking,
out of bounds, and thus, they had to resort to some rather
lame substitutes.

"The reason I came here," said Lieutenant Lipton, trying
in vain to position himself comfortably against one of the
medichairs, "is that, after further consideration, I think we
should re-examine the storage conditions of our supply of
cheese and other dairy products."

Lieutenant Commander Doctor Nightingale sighed, but
quietly. She didn't want any of her patients to get even a
whiff of the conversation, especially not the young fool
named Aubergine, who had been recently dismissed from
the 91st Regiment on suspicious medical grounds. Like
Lipton, she knew that cheese and dairy products were
amongst the main exports of Bohemia IV, that Bohemian
Brie was a famously sought-after delicacy, and that this fact
alone had caused the planet to be invaded, conquered, and
occupied by foreign forces every decade or so, ending only
when Bohemia willingly joined the United Planets. This,

she remembered, was done in a most harmonious way, involving no more than three divisions of the armed occupation police force, right after the Bohemian capital peacefully and publicly avoided global redecoration by means of imperial nuclear asteroids. In any case, as both officers were acutely aware, the UPS *Spitz*, despite decades of constant reports to the contrary, had never harboured even the tiniest bit of Bohemian Brie, nor any other cheese, nor any foodstuffs even remotely related to actual dairy.

"To my knowledge, in my capacity as chief medical officer on board this ship," said Nightingale carefully, "all Navy regulations regarding storage of said ingredients were met and doubly verified."

"That is absolutely correct," said Lipton. He was doing a passable job of ignoring the main controller, a hastily assembled unit yet to function as per spec but already doing a passable job of lurking menacingly on the back wall, hissing to itself. "However," the lieutenant continued, "it seems that some new circumstances have presented themselves, and so the matter needs to be re-examined."

"How so?" Nightingale asked. Noticing the hidden urgency in the lieutenant's manners, it had occurred to her that a possible reason for his visit could be, alas, romantic. This would not be his first such entanglement, either.

"It seems that our newest provisions of cheese and dairy products, being Bohemian and thus substandard as compared to regular Army supplies,"—Lipton did not even blink while uttering this atrocious lie—"do not do well when stored in a Navy Refrigeration Unit Mark VIII, despite the unit in question, number thirty-seven, functioning extraordinarily well as per spec."

Nightingale, who had logged many hours of such conversations, knew as well as Lipton that the only Mark VIII fridge on board had been disconnected long ago after repeated demonstrations of the tendency of its elaborate and unnecessary electrical design to become a fire hazard. Said design, however, made its insides a radiation-isolated space. A safe place. And Lipton would not dare to try any of his unnecessary romantics inside a Mark VIII.

Nor is he the kind of person to resort to such cheap trickery, Nightingale thought. *He's almost decent, for a male.* "Thank you for bringing this to my attention, Lieutenant," she said aloud, rising to her feet. "We shall examine the unit and apply immediate corrective action. Come with me."

Lipton stood up and saluted. "Yes, Lieutenant Commander," he said, about-turned, and walked out.

Nightingale quickly followed. In the corridor, under an ever wakeful cam, both officers pompously marched toward the nearest elevator, their manner totally and deliberately satisfying to all the local political logging equipment.

THE INSIDES of Navy Refrigeration Unit Mark VIII Number 37 were as true to its name as its number. That is to say, it was warm and damp and currently employed by some industrious kitchen personnel as an onboard greenhouse for some highly popular plants and their derivatives. It smelled accordingly.

"Sorry about that," said Lipton.

"So?" said Nightingale, who, in the course of her medical career, had smelled worse things, although not too many and not by much. *I was right*, she added to herself. *Not even the craziest, most deranged male would try any romantics in this kind of . . . atmosphere.*

"So, this won't hold," said Lipton. "Sooner or later, they're going to send Fux back to us."

"Havock giving up on a soldier? I don't think so."

"Have you talked recently with anyone in the 91st?"

"I try not to," said Nightingale. "One of them is in the infirmary now, but we had to sedate him."

"That would be Second Lieutenant Big W," said Lipton, "and it's a direct result of Fux's involvement."

"Nice name," said Nightingale. "Does the W stand for what I think it stands for?"

"Yes," said Lipton.

"Ah."

"Also, Sergeant Zimmer is now in the correctional closet."

"Zimmer? The drill instructor? How?"

"I would very much like to know," said Lipton. "But he is currently being recalibrated, so your guess is as good as mine. All I know is that it happened immediately after Fux was transferred to his platoon. Add that to the previous incidents—"

"A pattern emerges," said Nightingale.

"Yes," said Lipton. "And it won't be long before Havock sees it, too."

Both officers spent an uncomfortable moment contemplating a Colonel Havock conclusion, inevitably to be followed by a Colonel Havock solution, typically in the form of a full-blown Colonel Havock explosion.

"Crap," said Nightingale.

"Yes."

"When is our next combat round?" asked Nightingale. At this stage of the war, the Mobile Infantry was notorious for its survival rates, or lack thereof.

"Knowing the captain, I'd say as soon as possible, but probably still at least a week from now. But also, you know—"

Nightingale nodded. Common as it was in this everlasting war, sending people to their deaths was something that both officers, along with a surprising number of their colleagues below a certain rank, found abhorrent. "Sorry."

"Also," said Lipton, "judging by his achievements so far, I would be quite surprised if anything actually happened to him. To anyone around him, sure, but Fux himself . . . I think he's a survivor."

Both officers spent a moment in deep thought.

"This kind of thing is why I refuse to have anyone directly under my command, you know?" said Lipton. "No orderly, no midshipmen. The political risk isn't worth the perks."

"Spoken like a true officer," said Nightingale.

Lipton had no ready answer.

"Well," said Nightingale after a moment of uncomfortable silence, "perhaps it can't be avoided, but it might be evaded."

"I thought of asking for a transfer," said Lipton. "But it'll take time and also probably get me killed."

"Don't be so bloody literal, Lipton, that's one. Also, there are other ways, that's two. Also, for instance, well, there's the poo. That's three." POO, an acronym prohibited by regulations and thus vastly popular in any unmonitored conversation, stood for Political Officer. On board the *UPS Spitz*, there was only one person known by that nickname.

"I suspect Commander Kapust will not fall for the same trick twice," said Lipton.

"Doesn't have to be the same trick," said Nightingale. "He can be fooled."

"Fool-poo? Poo-proof?" said Lipton and promptly got a scolding look for this uncalled-for pun.

"You will work on that angle, then," said Nightingale. "I will try another."

"It being?"

"I've no idea."

"Great."

"Don't worry," said Nightingale, "I'll think of something."

IN THE CORRIDOR leading to the political division office, Lieutenant Lipton passed by a vaguely recognizable figure. "Corporal," he said after examining the person's insignia, "do I know you?"

"No, sir," the corporal said. He had a rather ludicrous moustache, which Lipton found to be eerie. "I don't think I've had the honour of meeting sir, sir."

"Your name?"

"Corporal Kraut, sir."

"Kraut?"

"Yes, sir," the corporal said, his moustache quivering in a nonexistent wind. "Kraut is my name, sir."

"I could've sworn I've seen you somewhere, Kraut."

"No, sir. I'd've remembered meeting sir, sir."

"Never mind," said Lipton. "Carry on, Corporal."

"Yes, sir."

"SIR," said Lieutenant Lipton, standing at attention in front of Commander Kapust's restored desk, which showed no sign of the recent trauma it had received except for being boldly askew. "I would like to suggest a correctional course of action in regard to our handling of Pre-Private Fux, sir."

Commander Kapust, who just came back from lunch—the timing of Lipton's visit was deliberate—twisted his mouth. He, too, showed no sign of recent trauma due to the combination of an exceedingly high collar and a pair of dark glasses. "What could you possibly want, Lieutenant?"

"I would like to suggest that, in consideration of recent events, you ask Colonel Havock to return Pre-Private Fux to us."

Kapust lifted his head and spent a long moment staring at the ceiling, unintentionally revealing the red marks on his neck that his collar was meant to cover.

"What makes you think," he said eventually, "that, in consideration of, ahem, of recent events, I would be willing to have any contact whatsoever with Colonel Havock?"

"I would like to suggest that not asking for Fux's return to us may result in failure to avoid an unfortunate series of events culminating with him not being un-prevented from serving in the Mobile Infantry, and thus possibly becoming unnecessarily un-disqualified from serving in other units on board this vessel."

It took Kapust half a minute to calculate the actual meaning of this artful tangle of negatives. It was a common way of conveying inconveniently true information without getting recalibrated for one's trouble.

"I see," he said eventually.

"I am sure that Colonel Havock will be quite receptive to a request from a distinguished officer such as yourself," said Lipton, lying in every possible way. Kapust, recognizing this, wisely decided to ignore the insult and concentrate on the important fact: that asking Havock for Fux would ensure the latter staying under the former's command no matter what, and thus in the Mobile Infantry, and thus not in the Navy, which would serve both Lipton's and Kapust's interests.

"Assuming that I agree to this, ahem, this course of action," said Kapust with caution, "how would you suggest we go about this?"

"Sir, I am merely a junior officer and am not worthy of venturing into the strategies of my superiors and betters."

But of course, thought Kapust. *He won't have anything of that sort on record. The bastard.*

"Ahem," he said. "I'll think of something."

NOT LONG AFTERWARD, Commander Kapust received another unexpected visit, this time from Lieutenant Commander Doctor Nightingale. Their conversation wasn't long and, due to some strangely local and absolutely random equipment malfunction, wasn't logged.

And thus did Fux, not entirely to his own benefit, get himself even more tangled with the political division.

8

FUX IS ASSIMILATED

Conquering the renegade colonies was a complicated, costly task, yet in hindsight, it was relatively easy. Bayern III was the first to surrender, Molvadia II, Franca VII, and Volscia V soon followed. Even the stubborn peoples of Bohemia IV, after mere decades of futile resistance, failed to stop the advancing imperial forces. But it was during that time that a vastly fiercer threat appeared: the insects. An alien race of mighty shape-shifting fighters, it had first made itself known by obliterating several far-reaching outposts along the Nietzsche-Marx arm of our galaxy. The United Planets fleet, in response, left with only a few rebel human worlds to conquer, reassigned its major vessels to fend off the alien intruders.

And so, the true war had begun.

STARSHIP TROOPERS, AN OFFICIAL HISTORY OF
THE IMPERIAL ARMED FORCES

THE UNSUSPECTING SUBJECT of senior staff scrutiny spent the same shift serving his superiors in a strikingly superb and straightforward style, sticking to the strategy suggested by his current counsel, a certain sagely Sergeant Private supervising stores and supplies. In this, he was no different than most soldiers in the platoon, the company, and the universe.

Dragging the heavy armour suit behind him in a most undignified manner, he returned to the parade grounds and presented himself to the senior officer available. This was the very corporal who helped him survive a certain attack by a certain second lieutenant. Her name, which eluded the mind of that fine young and currently hospitalized officer, was Clementine. She had only recently transferred to the 91st Regiment, which, she felt, was a bit of bad luck, though not as bad as what had happened to her previous outfit.

"At ease, Private," she said. "I can see that you have been properly equipped. Good, good."

"Yes, sir," said Fux. "Not a Private yet, sir, currently Pre-Private, sir."

"Ma'am," said Corporal Clementine. "And don't worry about it. Now, I suggest you cover the armour suit that you were given and—"

"The armour suit is in perfectly good condition, sir ma'am," said Fux.

"Just ma'am," Corporal Clementine said patiently. "And you are correct, Private: here at the Mobile Infantry, we take pride in the high quality of our equipment, and our maintenance is performed accordingly." She remembered recent combats in which this lie cost dearly in human life, but the Army issued excellent sedatives, and a few weeks had already passed since her last breakdown.

"Now, in the back pocket of the suit's spine, you'll find a fitting suit cover," she added. "The suit is to be stored inside it at all times while not in training or combat."

"Yes, ma'am," said Fux, then dragged the suit forward with some effort, found said spine pocket, and discovered with no great surprise that, except for one battered screwdriver and some old wires, it was empty. He lifted his gaze and looked around, saw no nearby cameras. He then put back the pocket cover, turned toward the corporal again, hesitated, and eventually added, "Like this, ma'am?"

The corporal nodded. "Very good," she said. "Now, go to the barracks and stay there. We're supposed to have an armoured drill at some point, so get some rest before that."

That command was easy and desirable enough to obey. It was later agreed that Fux managed to follow it with almost no mishaps whatsoever.

IN THE BARRACKS, Fux's sisters- and brothers-in-arms were engaged in a deep philosophical argument concerning the tactics, strategies, and general state of affairs of the currently ongoing war. While this subject was a political minefield to any officer, the powers that be realized that, to the grunts, no punishment was worse than being sent to the battlefield. Clearly, any Infantry person put in detention was actually being rewarded. Therefore, as long as the common soldiers refrained from discussing outright mutiny, a word that officially didn't exist, their barracks banter was ignored.

Originally, there wasn't supposed to be that much of it. The barracks were fitted with various harmless ways for its occupants to pass the time: educational informatica, ideological presentations, morale-enhancing games, and uplifting music. All of these were designed by Terra-actual Political HQ, also known as PoliDiv Central, to achieve maximum ideological awareness and correctness and therefore were incredibly boring. Which is why, over numerous years and battles, they were repeatedly sabotaged and gradually destroyed by their frustrated target audience.

The only remnant of those worthy efforts aboard the *UPS Spitz* was a single morale unit stuck at the back of the barracks. By now, it was well into its third consecutive shuffled loop of jolly old war hymns, some of which it sang with its own shaky voice, others recordings by the Imperial Naval Choir, the only military unit to remain intact despite the war. On one of the barrack's partitions, a political informatica was taking place, featuring a speech by the Navy's top commander, the notorious High Admiral Frosch. The morale unit was, mercifully, louder.

The combined noise had no effect whatsoever on the ongoing discussion, which had just covered a rumoured recent engagement with the enemy. The skirmish was celebrated by top command as yet another glorious victory but strangely lacked returning eyewitnesses. Having dealt with that, the soldiers in the barracks now gleefully turned the conversation toward the glorious future.

"I heard that next time we're going to nuke the planet before dropping us in," said a curly redheaded youth. His uniform was at least twice his size and therefore tied with bits of cardboard and the occasional improvised cloth clip.

"They're *insects*, Johnny," said a slightly older draftee, who still seemed to be barely out of her teens. Her long black hair was gathered in a thin khaki rubber band. "They don't care about radiation."

"Arise, ye prisoners of oppression," the morale unit sang, "Arise, ye wretched of the earth!"

"You don't know that, Daisy!" said the smitten youth.

"You don't know that I don't know that!" said Daisy. "You don't know better than me, anyway."

"For justice thunders in our leader," the morale unit continued, "a better world's in birth!"

"You're both wrong," said a yet older, bespectacled person, who happened to be the very one punished by Zimmer just before, cosmic and military justice and all, the sergeant was punished himself.

"I bet *you* have a better explanation," said Daisy.

"Mister Roseneck *always* has a better explanation," said Johnny.

"Indeed I do," said the flanked Mister Roseneck, who, despite being a draftee, had a definite look of a Mister about him, and who seemed to be used to this kind of thing.

The morale unit, ignored, refused to give up. "No more fake propaganda binds us," it sang, "arise to fight, no more in thrall. The planets rise on new foundations; praise our leader, do we all!"

To make sure the message was clear, this part was repeated several times. Some soldiers joined it, perhaps a bit more gleefully than its creators intended. The only one who was completely impervious to it was Mister Roseneck, who never let anything stand in the way of one of his Better Explanations.

"The insects, you see, are merely a metaphor," he said, "which our superiors, not to mention the state itself, use in order to dehumanize the actual, oppressed peoples, the natives of many peaceful planets, against whom this unjust war has been raging for—"

"That's totally stupid," said Johnny. Some of the other draftees mumbled in disagreement, but Johnny didn't seem to notice. "You think that mere people could actually survive in face-to-face combat with the Mobile Infantry?"

"Not to mention our losses?" said Daisy. This got a murmur of approval from some of the other youngsters among the draftees and looks of discomfort from the older ones.

This statement was stressed by the morale unit, which by now reached the chorus. ""Tis the final conflict; let's each stand till our last breath. For our pure empire, we shall fight unto the very death!"

By now, most of the soldiers were at least nodding to the catchy tune. But not Mister Roseneck.

"You two are young and underestimate the human spirit," he said levelly. "Perhaps when you are slightly older, having gained some more experience and—"

"You're old, and you underestimate the power of the Mobile Infantry," said Johnny.

"I've been here longer than you," said Mister Roseneck, who had indeed spent three consecutive cycles as a draftee yet still managed to avoid becoming a fully-fledged private. "I think I can safely say I've a better estimation of the power of the Mobile Infantry." His tone of voice clearly implied, *or lack thereof.*

The song, perhaps mercifully, ended. The morale unit turned quiet, having either run out of songs or, as was more common, suffered a communication malfunction. This had the unfortunate effect of unmasking the ongoing televised speech of High Admiral Frosch.

One of the soldiers turned to the morale unit in an attempt to restart the loop.

"Leave it alone," said another one. "Give it a minute; it'll be fine. Don't worry about it." This was accompanied by a tap on the shoulder to indicate that something more interesting was about to take place.

"So, you don't appreciate the power of the Mobile Infantry?" said Johnny.

"So, maybe we should give him a demonstration of the power of the Mobile Infantry, Johnny," said Daisy.

"You will find, soon enough, that there are no superpowerful insects in existence," said the unperturbed Mister Roseneck. "The power of the Mobile Infantry, my foot. My explanation is still the better one."

"Shut up, old man," said young Johnny heatedly, rising from his bunk, "or I'll give you a better explanation!"

"I also have a better explanation," said a loud and clear unexpected voice. Everyone turned toward it. It was Fux, sitting on his bunk, which now featured one strangely dismantled armour suit and lots of unidentified electronic and mechanical parts.

Everyone started speaking at once.

"Hey, Fux!" said Johnny, his recent rival forgotten.

"How's The Big W?" said Daisy, who enjoyed the young

officer's humiliation even more than most of the others due to some unwanted attention he had occasionally bestowed upon her.

"I would be happy to discuss any other possible explanations falling within the limits and dictation of simple logic and human nature," said Mister Roseneck, whom they all suspected of being originally a schoolteacher.

"What's your explanation, then?" said Johnny, but without much enmity. He was rather envious of the whole water canteen episode and wished that it was he, instead of Fux, who had managed to hospitalize Second Lieutenant Big and so win the respect of his comrades and, in particular, of Daisy.

"This reminds me of a story," said Fux. "Back in my hometown, two streets down from my apartment, there used to live this fishmaker, whose name was—"

"What's a fishmaker?" said Daisy.

"Have you ever wondered where fish come from?" said Fux.

"No," said Daisy, who, like most of her contemporaries, was born on a planet similar to old Terra in many ways, including being long devoid of any natural marine life. "I saw some in an informatica once."

"Aren't they supposed to come from the water?" asked Johnny, who shared Daisy's planet of origin, but whose father, a citizen of no meagre means, had a small aquarium occupied by a few synthetic sardines.

"And who puts them in there?" said Fux.

"The fishmaker?"

"The fishmaker."

"Fux," said Mister Roseneck, "what is this blabbering?

What fairy tales are you selling to these two innocent children?"

"Who are you calling children?" said Johnny.

"Or innocent?" said Daisy.

"This fishmaker, then," said Fux, undeterred, "whose name was Ryba, was a bit of what you might call an artist. Or, at least, he had some artistic aspirations. He was this quiet, lonely lad, mostly keeping to himself. No one thought that he would amount to anything. So, one day I go down to have a few beers in Kalicha. Good old Kalicha, that's a bar in Vordl Street. They also have a very good lunch if you can afford it, or, if you are after some strudel, best strudel you have ever tasted, as God be my witness."

This last utterance promptly achieved what Johnny and Daisy had failed to do since arriving at the Mobile Infantry: it made Mister Roseneck jump off his bunk, along with most of the rest of the assembled troops. The agitated old man then confronted Fux, his face as white as an empty political assessment form. "Shhhh!" he hissed. "Be quiet!"

"Sure, not to worry," Fux answered and lowered his voice to a loud whisper by way of complying. "Absolutely the best strudel you have ever tasted, swear to God!"

Some of the more veteran troopers emitted various gasps and choking sounds. "Don't mention that name!" creaked Mister Roseneck. "Do you want to get us all recalibrated?"

"What name?" said Fux.

"You know who," said Mister Roseneck and rolled his eyes heavenward by way of explanation.

"Oh," said Fux and nodded. "You mean the captain?"

This immediately caused a phenomenon that had never occurred in all the history of the UPS *Spitz*: the entire population of the barracks stopped breathing at the same time. For a long moment, there was no indication that any of the soldiers had any plans of ever breathing again. Mister Roseneck went even further by losing his balance and quietly falling into an awkward sitting position. This was followed by an absolute silence.

"So," said Fux, who took this as a sign of a good captive audience, "I get into Kalicha, and what do I see? First, sitting on the bar, there is this very striking woman whom I have never met before. Very beautiful. Very posh. And beside her, hugging her shoulder, who if not Ryba the fishmaker!"

"Fishmaker," mumbled Mister Roseneck from his sitting position on the floor, still in a state of shock.

"Indeed," said Fux, encouraged by this apparent attentiveness. "And that is not all of it, because soon Borek and Bolek, two of the regulars, also brothers, come over. And they tell me that this amazing woman is none other than Countess Syrkasa." Here Fux paused for effect so as to let this amazing fact sink in, which, judging by the still-stricken expressions of most of his audience, indeed seemed to be the case.

"Yes, the very Syrkasa of Syrkasa Cheese," he added gracefully.

On the floor, Mister Roseneck emitted a strange gurgling sound, followed by a wet cough. After a moment or two of such dangerous activities, he seemed to compose himself, at least partially, and sank into a relative calm, interrupted only by the occasional pant. Johnny and Daisy just stared at the two older men, eyes big and mouths shut.

"You are probably asking yourself, just as I did, what was such a respectable woman doing in such a bar as the Kalicha, of all places?" said Fux. "The beer and food are good, yes, but even I have to admit that it is not so clean, and sometimes it can smell like a dog shop. At least before you have had your fourth beer. And sometimes even after that. I am telling you, it was embarrassing, the countess sitting right in front of me and the place stinking to high heaven."

This last word caused Mister Roseneck, still on the floor, to slowly crawl toward his bunk. His mouth was very deliberately shut, a thin, angry red line in his narrow face, which was very deliberately turned away from Fux.

"And also, what is a royal such as Countess Syrkasa doing with a miserable potato such as Ryba the fishmaker?"

No one dared answer that loaded question. Everyone was too gripped by a mortal fear of imminent death over the mentioning of heaven, God, and, much worse, the captain.

Young Johnny seemed to be the first to recover, if only partially.

"What," he said. "What . . .?"

"That is just the question we all asked," agreed Fux. "And then Borek says, maybe Ryba kidnapped her, but she does not look very kidnapped to me. Believe me, I should know, because once we kidnapped one of Mister Sloblich's cows, and in the end it did not go so well, and there was a lot of—"

"But what . . .?" said Johnny, still failing to form the exact question on his mind.

"But never mind the cow now. Maybe I will tell you that story some other time," Fux said. "Anyway, so Bolek agrees with me that it does not look like a kidnapping. And then he suggests that the countess may have decided to spend some time with the common people, as royals occasionally do, no one knows why, though it may be for some kind of bet. And then I say, no bet in the world would make me sit and hug someone like Ryba the fishmaker. And then Ryba himself turns to us all and says, 'Hello everyone, I would like to introduce you to the countess Vilhelmina Syrkasa, my future wife."

Mister Roseneck, who by now was already in his bunk, face down and buried in his blanket, managed a stifled cry, followed by some incoherent mumblings.

"All this time, the countess does not even glance in our direction. Her hands are on Ryba, her eyes are on Ryba. That is true love if I have ever seen one," said Fux, perhaps a bit wistfully. "Especially considering the smell," he added. "We all agreed that it was quite amazing to see. Even little Kundera, the kid regular, who always plays it tough, agrees with tears in his eyes, even though with him you can never know because he is most famously a member of the secret police."

Young Johnny finally found the right words. "Why are you telling us all this?" he said.

"Shhh!" said Daisy. "I want to know how it ends."

"But—"

"Quiet!"

"I will tell you how it ends," said Fux. "A few days later, it is all over the news: Ryba the fishmaker arrested by the royal guard while attempting to enter the royal Syrkasa castle accompanied by an illegal copy of Countess Syrkasa made out of spare fish parts." He smiled triumphantly at his audience.

"And?" asked Johnny.

"And that is it," said Fux.

"But what about the insects?"

"What insects?"

"What do you mean, what insects?" cried Johnny. "What have we been talking about all this time? What's this story of yours all about?"

"As I have mentioned, it is about Ryba the fishmaker," said Fux.

"Are you insane?" asked Johnny.

At the sound of this, Mister Roseneck finally lifted off his bunk. "Insane!" he declared. "That's the explanation! He's completely off his rocker! Deranged! Mad as a teapot!"

"Just an idiot, sir," said Fux humbly. "Second-class."

"No, wait, I'd like to clarify this," said Johnny. "You promised us a better explanation. How is this story a better explanation?"

"Excuse me?" said Fux.

"Indeed," joined in Mister Roseneck, "I would also like to know how this ludicrous, infantile, fabricated, false, and utterly useless story can be in any way a better explanation of the real identity of the insects, our so-called enemies, than the one that I have provided."

"Or mine," said Johnny.

For a moment, Fux seemed to be deep in thought. "I see," he said eventually. "It is not."

"What?" shouted Johnny.

"I told you so!" said Mister Roseneck triumphantly.

"Then why did you tell it?" said Daisy, who was somewhat less invested than the others in the question of the true identity of the enemy.

"Well," said Fux, "I just thought that it was a very good story."

After the briefest of moments it took for this

extraordinary explanation to sink in, everyone in the barracks started shouting at once. This, however, was cut short by a loud metallic crash from the direction of the entrance hatch, followed by a cry of "Attention!"

Everyone turned toward the door to find Corporal Clementine standing there, a baton in her hand.

"Shut up, get your gear, and be at the parade grounds in two minutes," she said. "It's training time!"

Everyone started shuffling toward the hatch.

"Not you, Fux," the corporal added. "You go in the shower first."

And thus was Fux saved from being lynched.

9

FUX IS TRAINED

Those who have no understanding of the political world around them have no right to criticize or complain. It therefore follows that, in order to run an efficient government, only those in charge should be in possession of all the relevant facts.

MY CAPITAL STRUGGLE: AN AUTOBIOGRAPHICAL GUIDANCE BY ADOLPHUS MARKS, FIRST GRAND COUNCILLOR OF THE EMPIRE

"TO THINK that this had to happen to me!" said Sergeant Zimmer, drill instructor of the First Platoon of the First Company of the First Battalion of the 91st Regiment of the Mobile Infantry. He had just returned from recalibration in the correctional closet. This last experience had left his military instincts mostly intact and his short-term memory somewhat stirred and his vocabulary slightly disturbed.

"You carps!" the sergeant continued. He held his baton threateningly and showed every sign of toughness and uncompromising self-control. His gaze, under his bushy eyebrows, was fierce, his back was almost painfully erect, and his mouth, when he was not talking, was as clenched as one could make it without dislocating one's jaw. But all this was merely a front. In fact, Zimmer, facing the trainees, had only the faintest of recollections as to who they were and was struggling to remember what it was that he was supposed to do with them.

Even in this hazy state of mind, he noticed among them a stocky idiot insolently wearing a blue cap over a suspiciously new set of Mobile Infantry uniforms, standing at attention in the front row and smiling for no apparent reason. He had a vague notion that something was off about this person but could not fathom what it might be.

"You!" he shouted at the apparition by way of flexing his drilling muscles. "You blowfish, is this how a soldier is to stand while being observed by his seniors?"

"Not yet a soldier, sir!" the trainee said.

"Do not answer me, you salmon, you sea cow!" roared Sergeant Zimmer, feeling better and better with every utterance yet suspecting foul play. Some of the trainees moved uncomfortably in their places. They, too, seemed to notice that something was off.

"While you may not yet be a private," the sergeant added, "you're a soldier from the moment I set eyes on you, even if you do not deserve that honourable title, you cod!"

"Welcome back, sir," said a tall woman standing nearby.

He found her familiar in a way devoid of any context. Luckily, she was wearing her stripes.

"Thank you, Corporal," he said, blessing the Army for this easy method of identification, so useful when you failed to reckon someone's name or any other characteristic for that matter.

"You're most welcome, sir," she answered. "I took the liberty, in your absence, of putting the trainees through basic procedures and procuring. They are now fully equipped with armour suits, all tested and ready for training, sir."

The familiarity of this collection of lies, which had been told by and to Zimmer and every other soldier countless times in the past few decades, brought immediate relief to the drill instructor's mind. It cleared some of the murkiness of his memory, to the point of understanding, albeit partially, his role in this whole drilling affair.

"Very well, Corporal, thank you," he said wholeheartedly, a rare thing in itself. "Let us, then, proceed with," he added, then discovered mid-sentence that he was still devoid of any knowledge regarding what should be done now and had to hastily correct his course. "Proceed, then. You, Corporal, will proceed, yes, proceed according to all regulations and specifications, under my supervision."

"Yes, sir," the corporal said, showing no sign of surprise or resignation.

"This is a test, of course," added Sergeant Zimmer so as to avoid losing face.

"Of course it is, sir. Thank you for the opportunity, sir."

"Carry on, Corporal."

"Yes, sir," the corporal said and turned toward the expectant draftees. "Platoon—at ease!" she shouted. All members of the platoon immediately complied, except for the stocky idiot with the blue cap, who kept at attention or as close to it as he was able, which wasn't much. Sergeant Zimmer was about to trample this traitorous tuna like a ton of tilefish, but the corporal was quicker.

"Fux," she said, "run to the barracks and fetch your armour suit. Go!"

"Yes, ma'am!" said this Fux person and promptly started walking leisurely toward that destination.

Sergeant Zimmer could not contain himself. "Stop trotting, you trout!" he shouted. "Run! Run!"

"Yes, sir!" said Fux and did nothing of the sort. Some of the other yet-to-be soldiers were gazing quite boldly at the sergeant, whispering among themselves.

"Sir," the corporal said, "with all due respect, sir, Pre-Private Fux is somewhat feeble of mind, a condition quite common among the inhabitants of Bohemia IV, caused, I hear, by their humble roots and inferior moral spine, sir."

"That is no excuse, you mackerel!"

"That's it!" said one of the soldiers, an untidy, curly redheaded youth, hardly more than a boy. He was trying to whisper, but it came out quite loudly. "I found it!"

"What?" said a dark-haired young woman by his side, obviously the only intended recipient of this message.

"What?" the corporal said. Sergeant Zimmer just stared in confusion.

The curly-haired youth, excited, did not stop to consider the sudden, rather dangerous accretion of his audience. "It's fish!" he declared. "He's started cursing with fish!"

"What?" Zimmer said.

"Quiet!" the corporal said.

"I will *not* be quiet!" the sergeant roared. "What is the meaning of this disgraceful behaviour, you albacores?"

"You're right!" the black-haired soldier said to her companion. "So he does!"

"That's quite understandable," said another draftee, a thin, bespectacled man of at least fifty years of age. "He went through a light recalibration, you see, and this also manifested in his vocabulary, which has drifted from the common derogatory usage of animal kinds into creatures of the sea."

"Don't you 'derogatory' me, you sea elephant, and don't you 'creature' me!" shouted the sergeant gleefully. "On your feet! Run!"

"Sir?"

"Around the group! Run! Run, you guppy!"

The speaker, lacking the stamina and determination necessary for such a feat, attempted it anyway. It wasn't satisfying to watch. What's more, all this felt rather too familiar to Sergeant Zimmer, who was now engrossed in a strong sense of deja vu. So powerful was this feeling that all thoughts of insubordinate soldiers flew away and abandoned his clean slate of a mind.

This continued for an indeterminable amount of time. At some point, he detected a murmur from the corporal's direction, wondering aloud what was taking so long for one man to bring one suit and whether someone else should be sent to the barracks, followed by some other whispers he could not bring himself to be interested in. This light confusion was, all things considered, the sergeant's happiest experience since returning from the correctional closet.

Eventually, a loud assortment of metallic noises returned Sergeant Zimmer's attention, at least partially, to the present.

It was that Fux person, who dropped a sloppily packed armour suit on the floor beside the corporal. This was accompanied by a whisper that the sergeant couldn't decipher but was probably some kind of insolence.

"Very well," the corporal said. "Gather around, everyone. I'm going to demonstrate the basic handling of a mechanized combat armour suit, Mark XXII. This will include putting it on and taking it off, haptic controls, augmented walking, running, and lifting, and reading your head display."

Sergeant Zimmer's memory refreshed with each word. He remembered that there hadn't been an operational armour suit for any trainee for the past decade or so. He remembered the complex linguistic manoeuvres performed by every drill instructor with every new batch of trainees in order to both clarify the situation to them and simultaneously convince the political apparatus that all was going well.

"Therefore," the corporal continued, "I need a volunteer."

The stocky idiot with the blue cap immediately raised his hand.

"Very well, Fux, come here," the corporal said.

There followed the usual sequence of events, in which a fresh draftee was put into an armour suit by a drilling instructor. The process was by far less dangerous than in the past since no matter what the unskilled soldier did, the suit would not respond. This, despite the presence of the all-powerful chest hair-trigger designed to invoke the suit's lightning-quick initiation and full combat preparedness in less than a second. The stocky Fux person did involuntarily touch that trigger several times, but to no effect whatsoever, which wasn't at all surprising.

"It is important to keep steady in a suit at all times," the corporal said, and Sergeant Zimmer smiled. A functioning suit stabilized itself automatically. This part of the practice was only included to avoid injuries in non-functioning suits, the only kind ever to be worn by these poor soldiers. "Keep your legs slightly apart," the corporal continued, "and try to balance using your hands, but make no sudden movements."

"Yes, ma'am," said Fux. He seemed to be surprisingly steady in the suit.

"Now comes the interesting part," the corporal said and looked quite forcefully at each and every member of her flock to make sure they understood that there was more than one level to said interest. "I will count down from three, Fux, and when I get to zero, you will turn on the suit, as I've just explained."

"Yes, ma'am!"

This, the sergeant remembered, was the point in which most past draftees failed, expecting the suit to employ some power or to do anything at all, and thus wrongly compensating, and thus falling on their faces.

The corporal, clearly aware of this, stood by Fux, ready to catch him. "Three, two, one, zero!"

"Yes, ma'am," Fux said and clenched his right fist. A slowly rising hum came from within the suit, soon accompanied by a series of clicks. It took Sergeant Zimmer a moment to recognize the ominous sound of servo motors and mechanical relays waking up and getting ready for action. His jaw dropped.

Beside Fux, the corporal hastily retreated. She opened her mouth to say something, probably along the lines of, "Turn off that suit right now, you idiot!" but thought better of it. Zimmer fully agreed: such a command would be quite difficult to justify later when the political logs were analyzed. What reason would one have for turning off a fully functional suit?

"Good, good," said the corporal shakily, having got hold of herself. "Now, we shall proceed and practice basic augmented walking." She was eyeing Fux rather pointedly, hinting at the hair-trigger chest switch and, through that, at turning the thing off.

"Yes, ma'am," said Fux obediently and lifted his right foot. The suit emitted a corresponding whine.

Fux carefully started lowering his foot. The suit's whine slightly increased. Fux's foot shot down blindingly fast and hit the floor much like, the sergeant thought later, the famous *UPS Scharf* (RIP) smacking into the second moon of Polkskvich III (RIP) at a quarter of lightspeed.

The suit jumped mightily in the air. Were that event to happen anywhere else on board the *UPS Spitz*, it would have been the end of Fux, or the vessel, or probably both. The parade grounds compartment was the only space fortified enough to tolerate such forces, and even that just barely. As it happened, Fux's head, wrapped in a combat helmet, hit the ceiling at a mere ninety kilometres per hour, leaving almost no dent at all.

This bold manoeuvre may have caused a slight movement of Fux's right hand, so delicate that the only clue of its occurrence was the suit's powerful right arm shooting up and striking the metal above his head. This caused the suit to promptly shoot down diagonally and, as it happened, straight at the compartment's main pressure seal. On the one hand, this was perfectly safe, as the seal was designed to withstand a decent amount of abuse. On the other hand, the seal enjoyed a maintenance quality similar to that of the common combat armour suit.

This philosophically fascinating examination of nature vs. nurture was, interestingly, averted at the last moment as the combat armour suit emitted an involuntary burst of its one-time emergency jet. Thus the contraption hastily propelled itself back toward the ceiling, with which it collided at a surprisingly gentle angle.

Face and chest turned upwards, leaving a trail of smoke behind it, the suit now gave the impression of a huge and distorted cockroach running in circles in a desperate attempt to break out of a glass bottle. This, luckily for all involved, only lasted for the short time it took the emergency jet to fully consume its rather modest propellant supply. Suit and occupant drifted back down in a relaxed and calm manner, which gave everyone on the floor ample time to break out of their shock, awe, and, in at least one case, reverie, and scatter in all directions: everyone but the corporal and Sergeant Zimmer, the former being made of sterner material and the latter still under the soothing influence of a light recalibration.

The idiot's combat boots finally touched the floor, not far from his original point of ascent, now marked by a noticeable bend in the metal surface.

For some time, the only sound in the huge chamber was that of broken metal parts falling from the ceiling. Eventually, the corporal said, very deliberately, "Get out of that bloody suit, Fux." Her glare could have burned planetary objects just like the unlucky UPS Scharf did.

The idiot, however, failed to respond. He was slumped

within the suit, head down, fat chin touching his barrel chest, and seemed to be either unconscious or, may they all be so lucky, dead.

"Wake up and get out of there!" shouted the corporal, who seemed not to believe in luck.

"I don't think he can hear you," Sergeant Zimmer said. "The acceleration probably pumped the blood out of his head."

The corporal's answering silent gaze implied that it might as well be herself taking all the blood out of someone's head. It was not clear, though, whose head this was going to be. Sergeant Zimmer took one step back, just in case.

The rest of the scattered trainees hesitantly returned to their places. They were clearly impressed by this display of superior Mobile Infantry technology. They were also taking small items out of their pockets and quietly exchanging them.

"Attention!" the corporal said. "I will now demonstrate the taking off and dismantling of a fully operational mechanized combat armour suit, Mark XXII." Her voice was almost steady. She slowly and carefully approached the suit and warily pressed the chest hair-trigger switch.

Nothing happened except for Fux emitting a rather loud snore.

This, for some reason, caused quite a stir among the other trainees. Some of them clapped one another on their backs, yet others sulked, and at least one elderly person could not contain himself and uttered a cry of disappointment.

The corporal turned toward them. "I was under the

impression that we have already discussed the usage of statistics-related incentives among military personnel!"

Of course, thought Zimmer. *I, too, would have bet good money that the fat bastard is dead.* He smiled. *Also, how quickly has Corporal whatshername adjusted her dialect to her new commanding status.* He felt vaguely proud. Then he remembered his place and position and quickly set his expression to the regular Army growl expected of his kind. He was almost certain that no one had noticed the lapse.

The trainees quickly shoved the remaining objects, whatever symbols of monetization that came to hand, into their pockets. The old bespectacled one seemed rather sore about losing the bet.

The armour suit creaked ominously, then turned quiet, except for the low whining of a lonely servo motor. Inside it, the idiot coughed, gargled a bit, and opened his eyes.

"Honourable ma'am sir," he said, "I dutifully report that the combat suit, which I received in perfect working condition, was further maintained by myself and is now in an even better perfect working condition." He beamed and added, as an afterthought, "Ma'am."

"What have you done to the suit, Fux?" said the corporal, who knew, same as Zimmer, that by now there was no point in worrying about the political logs of one's speech, since some more urgent explanations would be required in regard to the recent unwanted modifications to the regiment's order of battle.

"Back home, I used to fix dogs," the fool said without any relevance or provocation.

"I don't care what you used to do back home or anywhere. What is the meaning of this?"

"Dogs," said Fux, "are not so different from combat suits."

"What?!"

"You just have to ensure that the relays aren't stuck, there is no leakage, and the power units are charged."

"I—"

"And sometimes, if you have several good dogs, but your customer wants an even better dog, you just mix and fix. For instance, you take the crankshaft off one dog and the gearbox off another and—"

"Are you telling me that you bloody *fixed* a mechanized combat armour suit?"

Fux smiled. "No, ma'am. It was in perfect working condition."

For a moment, the corporal merely fumed. Then her face lit up as if she'd just had an epiphany. She turned toward Sergeant Zimmer.

"Sir," she said, "I would like to report the successful conclusion of secret armour suit test number one, as requested by yourself."

"What?" said Zimmer.

"I congratulate you for your daring innovation, sir, especially since it has been such a short time since your recalibration, sir."

"But," Zimmer said and discovered that this, for the moment, had exhausted his vocabulary.

"Pre-Private Fux," the corporal said, "I am hereby recommending that you promptly receive the rank of Private, all honours included."

"I," Zimmer said.

"Yes, ma'am!" Fux said, and clenched his right fist. The suit quieted down and sagged.

The corporal turned toward the sergeant. "Sir," she said, "I hereby volunteer to accompany the soldier to the regimental headquarters and take care of this myself."

"Well," Zimmer said.

"I am honoured to have earned your," Fux said, and, suit and all, noisily fell forward and smashed into the floor, face down.

And thus did Fux improve the order of battle of the mighty Mobile Infantry, albeit against the latter's wishes.

10

FUX IS PROMOTED

All for one and one for all!

A FAMOUS QUOTE FROM A COMMON FOLK TALE
ON FRANCA VII, USED AS THE SLOGAN OF ITS
UNDERGROUND FORCES BEFORE THEIR
INEVITABLE ANNIHILATION BY THE HEROIC
IMPERIAL OCCUPATION FLEET

THE PROPOSED promotion of Fux from Pre-Private to Private did not go unnoticed in certain circles outside the realm of the Mobile Infantry. Such matters, like many others that had no relevance to it, were supervised by the political division. All requests to that esteemed unit were received by its secretarial personnel before being forwarded to the proper top-ranking officers. Thus, considering the limited number of secretarial—or any—personnel whatsoever, nothing could have prevented this particular message from

falling straight into the expectant hands of the current occupant of the political headquarters office, Ensign Berserker.

The ensign, contrary to common belief, did not hate the
soon-to-be private. Fux was not even included in Berserker's
top-twenty traitors list, which the ensign updated zealously
within his encrypted draftpad on a bi-hourly basis. Said list
consisted of everyone who had ever made fun of the ensign
in the officer's mess, of various sergeants of varying levels of
political ignorance and/or offensiveness, and, occasionally, of
a female person.

The first place in the list, which the young ensign was
rightly too afraid to commit even to an encrypted form and
thus kept in his head, was unwaveringly occupied by
Commander Kapust. The only high-ranking officer omitted
entirely from the list, in any form, was Colonel Havock, of
whom the young ensign was too scared to even think.

And so, on the personal level, Berserker cared for "that
Fux person" as much as for any other plain, uneducated,
evil-spirited, and probably traitorous soldier on board. The
ideological level, however, was another matter. People like
Fux, who came from outside the core of the empire and
spoke differently, were obviously not as well-bred and loyal
as, for instance, certain young ensigns. Their very existence
annoyed Berserker to no end. This merely added to his
current state of mind, which, due to some recent occurrences
involving his direct commander and another officer of whom
he was too scared to even think, was rather fragile. He
accepted, as a universal truth, everything he had ever read or
watched as part of his political indoctrination—or, as some
would call it, his childhood. He also accepted the universal
truth concerning the poor behaviour and lack of moral fibre

of each and every officer on board the *UPS Spitz* and, in particular, of his direct supervisor. As hard as he tried, he could not find a way for those two universal truths to exist in the same universe.

Therefore, upon reading the short message FROM MIFHQ TO POLIDIVHQ REQUEST APPROVE PRPVT FUX JOSEPH PROMOTE TO PVT FUX JOSEPH URGENT CONFIRM TNX, the ensign's doubts, fears, and annoyance turned into sheer fury.

Enraged, he started composing a reply on his draftpad:

FROM POLIHQ TO MIFHQ 1 USE POLIHQ NOT POLIDIVHQ 2 USE SHRTCTS W/O EXCESSV SPELLNG 3 NO NEED FR DEGENERT POLITENSS-MARKRS SCH AS "TNX" 4 FUX IS TRAITR SO ARRST & RECYCL URGENT URGENT CONFRM RECYCL URGENT TNX.

Having completed this poetic text to his satisfaction, he slammed the draftpad onto his desk, inhaled deeply, exhaled, lifted the draftpad again, read his creation, and promptly— also shamefully—erased the last word. Leaving this embar- rassing error behind, he re-read his literary masterpiece and decided that Item 1 was implied by Item 2 and, therefore, could be removed. This left him with a deeply satisfying piece of prose that, in order to completely avoid any TNX- related embarrassment, he quickly improved by removing Item 3. Following these changes, Item 2 revealed itself to be vastly less important than Item 4, to the point of detracting, and so had to be erased.

The remaining precise, strongly worded, and brilliant item was now single, thereby making the enumeration obso- lete. The thrice-repeated urgency, while reflecting the true,

honest feelings of a patriot, now seemed to be slightly excessive. A few more such logical-yet-painful trimmings occurred
in quick succession. The immortal composition eventually
transmitted was rather shorter than first intended:

FROM POLIHQ TO MIFHQ RE PRPVT FUX
JOSEPH REQST DENIED.

This will show them, thought the ensign, now pacified, if
still slightly out of breath following the excitement and
mental effort entailed by this exercise. *Where is our honour?
What happened to our national pride? Giving a proper rank,
a rank equal to that of our own people, to a foreigner who is
also a pervert, who cannot even speak properly? Preposterous!
Unheard of!*

The door opened with a hiss and a whine, revealing a
rather red-faced Commander Kapust. "Preposterous!" the
superior officer shouted and angrily approached the ensign.
"Unheard of!"

"Yes, sir!" the ensign answered, momentarily wondering
whether Kapust was somehow reading his mind. "The insolence! The gall!"

"The gall indeed!" Kapust said. "Since when do ensigns
take it upon themselves to make decisions in the name of
their betters?"

"What?" said Berserker, unsure as to whom, exactly, was
referred to in this surprising turn of dialogue.

"Or, for that matter, any decisions whatsoever, you
miserable excuse for a person?"

Ensign Berserker's face turned as white as a recalibration
sheet. "Well," he attempted, trying in vain to retreat deeper
into his chair, "in good faith—"

"*Faith?*" roared Kapust.

"Intentions! Good intentions, sir! A literary expression, and mere slip of the tongue, which I most humbly regret and apologize for, in the hope that you would find such a minor hitch understandable, considering the given circumstances, in someone as humble as—"

"Be quiet!"

"But I don't understand—"

"Indeed, you do *not* understand! Understanding, as you repeatedly demonstrate, is not your strong suit! Which is why, when receiving any request involving any kind of decision whatsoever, you are to forward it to your superior officer, who, just to ensure this is absolutely clear and understood, in case you have forgotten, is *me!*"

"But ranks approvals are a routine matter, and you've specifically told me not to bother you with such trifles because, as you said, 'It's a bloody headache, and they'll all be dead soon anyway—'"

Kapust's face achieved the impossible by darkening even more, the red tint replaced by an interesting shade of purple. "I have *never* told you *any* such thing!" he roared, unintentionally glancing at the local logcam. "There is *no* matter related to the political division that is not important enough for my *undivided* attention!"

"Yes, sir!" replied the ensign, who knew a logcam-intended performance when he saw one.

"Now, Ensign, why did you deny the Mobile Infantry request for promoting Pre-Private Fux?"

"Sir, this Fux person is clearly dangerous! Ideologically and socially! He is a menace! Even his very name—"

"Shut up! And stand up when talking to me!"

For a moment, Ensign Berserker's pedantic mind was

torn over the question of whether to stand up or not since shutting up seemed to contradict the need to do so. Then he got a hold of himself and clumsily rose from his office chair.

"Now, listen carefully," Kapust said. "You are going to do exactly as I say, without any extra interpretation, extra volunteering, extra information, or extra anything. The slightest deviation from my specific and exact orders will cause your immediate transfer from this unit. Am I being clear?"

Ensign Berserker, who knew that there was only one possible destination for said transfer, nodded vigorously.

"I cannot hear you, Ensign!"

"Yes, sir!"

"Now," Kapust said, "I am going to get out of here. In two minutes' time, you will send a message to Mobile Infantry headquarters, a correction to your last communication—"

"But, sir," the ensign said, "That's impossible! I cannot belie my own . . . that would be completely . . . I would . . ."

"Are you arguing with me, Ensign?"

"No, sir!" cried Berserker, who was mentally unable to handle contradictions, especially in regard to his own opinions and actions. "It's just that I *did* say that the request is rejected, and so—"

"In two minutes," Kapust said, "you will—am I being clear?—you will *absolutely* send a correction to your last communication. Yes? Yes."

"But—"

But Kapust had already stepped out. The door slid shut behind him.

He never said ahem, *not even once,* Ensign Berserker thought. His mind stuck to this observation like a man in a faulty spacesuit to a lifeline. He had never used a spacesuit, nor had he ever ventured outside of a ship into actual space. But if Kapust was angry enough to completely forget his usual pompous *ahem*, Ensign Berserker's first meeting with space might be devoid of a suit.

The door creaked. Berserker lifted his head and saw it slowly opening, revealing a vaguely familiar figure. "What?" he said.

"Hello, sir," said the guest, who bore shiny new corporal's insignia and an absolutely inappropriate moustache. "I was sent here by Commander Kapust to make sure that his orders were carried out."

"Well!" said Berserker, and then, in a desperate attempt to change the subject, "Do I know you, Corporal . . .?"

"Name's Kraut, sir, Corporal Kraut," the corporal said through his moustache. "And I don't think so, sir. I'd've remembered meeting sir, sir."

"THEY'RE GOING to send a correction to their last communication," said Corporal Clementine, who knew that the other option would be a month-long committee investigating the officially-impossible discrepancy between the perfectly harmonious Navy and Infantry.

"I do not want to cause any trouble, Honourable Corporal ma'am," said Fux.

"You have a strange way of not causing trouble, Fux."

"I hope to—" began Fux, but the corporal hushed him with a wave of her hand.

The oversized communication terminal of the Mobile

Infantry headquarters emitted some indecisive noises. The official reason for its existence was its highly encrypted fortification against enemy tampering. The actual reason was to make it easier for the political division to log all high-level communications. This made it dangerous to use but also a pretty easy way of embarrassing anyone careless enough to miscommunicate.

"I guess something caused trouble somewhere," the corporal mused, "only this time, it isn't your fault. I wonder what Commander Kapust is up to?"

"I have not had the honour of meeting the esteemed commander," said Fux, "but I am sure he is a fine officer."

"Yes, of course," the corporal said. She had already met Kapust once and was unimpressed by his conduct, manners, intelligence, or any other quality except, maybe, for his appetite. His little helper was no great bargain either. Ensign Whatsisname was just so bloody . . .

Ah, she thought. *The ensign. That explains it.*

"While I am fully dedicated to fighting our enemies to the death," said Fux by way of passing the time, "I must admit that I do not insist on any honours, ranks, and the such, as I am perfectly happy to be—"

The terminal chirped. Corporal Clementine turned and put her hand on its touchpad. The terminal coughed, shot a laser into her eye, mumbled something, and then sang: "FROM POLIHQ TO MIFHQ RE PRPVT FUX JOSEPH CORRCTN REQST APPROVD REPT APPROVD."

"See?" Corporal Clementine said.

"I humbly," said Fux, but the terminal continued.

"FROM POLIHQ TO MIFHQ RE PRPVT FUX

REASN FR CORRECTN LOCL MLFNCTN IN POLIHQ COM."

"Of course," said Clementine. "There has to be a reason for every—"

"FROM POLIHQ TO MIFHQ RE COM MLFNCTN DUE TO NATURL EXTRNL FACTRS UNRELTD TO POLIDIV CMD & PERSNL."

"What?" said Clementine.

"I heartily agree," said Fux. "It cannot be a human error because—"

"FROM POLIHQ TO MIFHQ RE EXTRNL FACTRS CLARIFCTN MST BE UNPREVNTBL ACT OF HIGHR PWR."

"Oh, my," said Clementine. "Now there's going to be *real* trouble."

"I completely and utterly—"

Clementine raised her hand. "Shhh," she said. "I want to listen to this."

IT TOOK three Navy chiefs half an hour to break into the political headquarters office. Berserker dedicated this time to eliminating any chance of his political promotion, or even survival, by means of increasingly inappropriate communications to MIFHQ, and then to any other HQ he could think of. It took another ten minutes to subdue the raving ensign and tie him to a stretcher. "A higher power does not exist!" he shouted. "The only higher power is the power of the state, which has nothing to do with the political division!"

"What is he talking about?" said one of the chiefs, who should have known better.

"Gag him," said Commander Kapust, who had delayed his arrival for as long as possible, and whose face was now yellow with a drop of disgust and an ocean of fear.

"The power of the state, manifested in our leader, being the embodiment of the supreme force of nature and beyond it!" the ensign cried as one of the chiefs ran outside to grab some gagging material from the brig.

"Shut his mouth!" Kapust said to the remaining chiefs. The one who had miscalculated his speech before now made the mistake of obeying that order, only to emit a cry and promptly remove his hand.

"What now?" said Kapust.

"He bit me!" the chief said, caressing his wounded hand.

"The leader, therefore, by way of being the manifestation of everything powerful and good and honourable and awesome in our universe," the ensign announced, dangerously twisting on the stretcher, "can truly be called God!"

"You!" Kapust shouted at the remaining chief, "take your shirt off!"

"Sir?"

"And therefore comes the perfect union between the state, all us loyal citizens, and God Almighty!"

"Take your bloody shirt off right now!"

"Yes, sir," said the chief and started doing so.

"God is good! God is right! In God we trust!" shouted the ensign. "In God we trust!"

"Come on," said Kapust.

"I'm trying, sir," said the chief, fighting to obey the

command in the cramped quarters without getting anywhere near the wriggling Ensign's teeth.

"Try faster!"

"In God we trust!" roared Ensign Berserker. "In God we trust!" He managed to repeat this hearsay a few more times before Kapust stuffed the chief's paper uniform shirt into his mouth.

IT WAS ONLY after the successful restraining of the raving Ensign that Kapust and the chiefs noticed the other occupant of the office, a vaguely familiar Corporal sitting placidly in the farthest corner.

"You!" said Kapust. "Corporal . . .?"

"Corporal Kraut, sir."

"I told you specifically to make sure that he obeys my orders, Kraut!"

"Yes, sir!"

"Do you call *this* obeying my orders, Kraut?"

"Sir, sir did not tell me what sir's orders were, sir."

The chiefs were too busy dragging the restrained Ensign Berserker out of the cabin to wonder about the abrupt and speedy exit of Commander Kapust.

"FROM POLIHQ TO MIFHQ RE PRPVT FUX JOSEPH DSMSS PREV COM PRMTN REQST APPROVD."

"Pity," said Corporal Clementine. "I hoped he'd have more to say." She smiled, then added, "Poor bastard."

"I would assume you do not mean the honourable person of—" said Fux, but she cut him off.

"Enough," she said. "Congratulations, Private Fux."

"Yes, Ma'am Corporal Sir."

On the wall, there now appeared a new all-hands informatica, this time regarding the recycling of a certain Corporal Kraut due to gross negligence.

"Another poor bastard," said Clementine after the dreadful display was replaced by the only slightly less dreadful visage of Commander Kapust. "This just shows you how careful you need to be, Fux."

"Yes, Ma'am Corporal."

"Just ma'am would be enough since you're already a private," said Clementine. "Now, let's get you some insignia."

And thus was Fux, against all odds, promoted.

11

FUX IS ENCOURAGED

It's never the soldiers' business to decide when or where or how or why they fight.

STARSHIP TROOPERS, AN OFFICIAL HISTORY OF
THE IMPERIAL ARMED FORCES

AS IF SOME higher power had decided that the Mobile Infantry has had enough excitement for the time being, the First Platoon and Company and so forth commenced enjoying a blissful period of calm.

Sergeant Zimmer slowly recuperated, albeit in a placid and oceanographic manner. Initially, he attempted to decipher the bizarre incident in the parade grounds, but soon reached the logical conclusion that this better be left in the capable hands of Corporal Clementine.

The latter, left to her own devices, spent the majority of that time ensuring the safety of her flock by removing the power connectors from all the company's armor suits. The recent incident redoubled her conviction that the suits should retain a level of perfection entirely in the realm of political theory.

No higher officer or power bothered interfering with the troops in any way. Fighting among them went no further than the occasional barbed insult. The most newsworthy incident in the barracks was a card game in which Mister Roseneck beat his youthful rivals to the tune of four kilograms of canned meat, twelve hundred potatoes and one bar of chocolate, all of which were also entirely in the realm of political theory.

To everyone's amazement, Fux displayed almost exemplary behavior. He was relatively quiet and unobstructedly polite. His sins went no further than idle tampering with the now utterly inactive suits, and a tendency for lengthy yarns and improbable anecdotes. Those paled in comparison to his previous feats, to the point of being tolerable. From time to time, after combat suit practice or weapons practice or just before a meal, he would disappear for an hour or two. This worried Corporal Clementine until she learned that he was simply visiting his new friend, the quartermaster. Sergeant Private Bolon seemed to like Fux so much that he started visiting the barracks as well, which unexpectedly cheered the other soldiers, as the quartermaster made a habit of bringing small parcels of food he liberated from the regimental kitchen.

Officially, this was absolutely impossible, as no such foods existed anywhere within the complex supply management and monitoring system. However, since their nutritomat machine went out of commission some years before, the kitchen personnel had to learn to actually cook. This involved digestible ingredients, as opposed to pre-packed tasteless nutrients destined for the machine. This, in turn, gave rise to some commercial entrepreneurship, in the form of Quartermaster Bolon, who knew a good deal when he smelled one.

Soon enough everyone got used to the sight of Fux and Bolon occupying the bunks furthest away from the door, eating and sharing whatever substitute foodstuffs the regimental chef dubbed "lunch" that shift, and telling long tales of impressive business opportunities, incredible strokes of luck and implausible pets.

A few shifts passed by peacefully. Then a zero-grav period was announced. The UPS Spitz required this in order to shut its engine, jump through an FTL hoop, turn around and start breaking instead of accelerating. This caused some hilarity in the barracks, proceeded to upset several stomachs among the young and inexperienced, and ended up not detracting much from the overall tranquility. There was some excitement in regards to the exact time of the FTL jump, it being the first of its kind for the new recruits, but soon it was discovered that A. FTL did not stand for Faster Than Light, but rather for Freight Transfer Link, and B. the jump had already occurred while they were asleep. Mister Rosenek remarked that despite the disappointing initials it *was* in fact faster than light, but was hushed by his mildly frustrated comrades. Then he moved on to point that the turning around and the FTL jump mark half the time it will take them to get to their destination, which couldn't be a Good Thing, but this promising line of discussion was prematurely terminated by the arrival of

Quartermaster Bolon with a pack of fake sweet chestnuts, and there was much rejoicing. Subsequent shifts found the troops increasingly enjoying their fabricated armor suits maneuvers, pretend heavy weaponry fire and make-believe maintenance. Real arms were absolutely forbidden on board the UPS Spitz, as on any other United Planets ship. Anything to do with weaponry was, if one were to limit oneself to the kindest possible words, badly simulated. This was, as Daisy and Johnny kept telling anyone who was interested in hearing, plus everyone else, even better than the sweet chestnuts.

The first sign that this idyllic state of affairs was less permanent than one would have hoped for was the eventual return of Second Lieutenant Big W from his recent vacation in the infirmary. Initially this passed quietly, as the young officer entered the barracks at some indeterminable time during a platoon weapon-simulation exercise-simulation. He was discovered by his subordinates only upon their return, sleeping in his capsule, which hatch he did not bother to shut. He woke up in the middle of one of Quartermaster Bolon's funny stories about an R&R gone wrong on Franca VII, crawled quietly out of his capsule, and seemed to enjoy the brief commotion this had caused in the barracks. After the initial shouts of "officer on deck" and "attention" subsided, and the troops were standing in a sort of orderly fashion, he took his time looking at each and every face. This gave everyone enough time to compose themselves and take a better look at their commander, and especially the purple biocast covering his left foot.

Then the young officer's searing gaze finally reached Fux.

"You!" Big hissed.

Oh no, thought Corporal Clementine.

"Yes, sir!" said Fux. "Welcome back, sir!"

Big seemed to be taken aback by this cordial greeting. Then his eyes narrowed.

"What are those things I see on your uniform?" he asked. "Stolen insignia?"

"Those are mine, sir. I am most happy and gratified to dutifully report that in your absence I was promoted to a full soldier and private also, sir!"

"Are you playing me for a fool, you idiot? You don't know me yet, but let me tell you—"

"Sir," said Corporal Clementine, "it was under extraordinary circumstances."

"*You* will speak only when *spoken* to, Corporal."

"Yes, sir," said Clementine. The young officer turned his gaze back to Fux too fast to notice her smile.

"I said you don't know me yet, but you are going to," said Big, now eyeing the whole platoon so as to make it clear that no one will be spared from this educational rant. "You lot are going to know me so well, that I will be not only here, but in your heads, every waking hour, and in your dreams too. You are going to know me so well that you will bow in fear even thinking about me. You are going to wish that you didn't know me, but after knowing me, there's no going back to not knowing me. You will know me starting now and until the end of your natural lives."

That speech, thought Clementine, *is stolen. I wonder where he took it from.*

"Sir," said Fux, "I am sure I speak for everyone here in saying that we feel honored and gratified to know you, sir, and also we are going to do whatever is in our power to get to know you even better, sir."

This was met with a chorus of muted chuckles.

"Don't get cheeky with me, soldier! You think you know me, but you don't really know me!"

"Yes, sir," said Fux, smiling. "I am eager to know you, sir."

"When you do get to know me, you'll regret wishing to know me!"

"I will always be honored to have known you, sir."

"You think you're smart, but when you really get to know me you will—"

I wonder, thought Clementine, *whether this is going to end anytime soon.*

"—Believe me, those who knew me are not around anymore to tell you about knowing me—"

Indeed, thought Clementine, *though of course he won't mention the exact reasons and circumstances.*

"—I've commanded soldiers ten times tougher than you bunch of wimps, and they shook in fear every night in their bunks after getting to know me—"

Clementine was fighting to stop herself from laughing. In this she got unexpected help from the local morale unit, which chose that moment to embark upon a popular Army song.

"Oh I come from planet Terra with a big gun on my knee," it croaked, " and I'm going to destroy the empire's evil enemy—"

"Turn that thing off!" Big shouted.

"This might not be advisable, sir," said Clementine, "considering the—"

"Shut up, you, you... before you get to know me!"

"Oh Johanna, do not cry for me!" wailed the morale unit, "For I'll soon die for our leader with a big gun on my knee!"

"If that thing doesn't shut up within one second, each and every one of you will get to know me in a way they don't really want to get to know me!"

This might have gone on for much longer, were it not for a sudden interruption by a new and incredibly loud metallic voice that filled the barracks and marked, alas, the true end of the miraculous period of calm:

"BATTLE STATIONS, BATTLE STATIONS!"

CONTRARY TO THE desires and wishes of many among its personnel, the UPS Spitz was not entirely unfit for its purpose. Anything which had to do with its propulsion, life support, docking and troop delivery systems was in fact in excellent shape, as the captain made it clear that the slightest deviation from this state of affairs would have serious consequences. She emphasized this point in a most gentle and civilized manner by maintaining an ongoing and constantly updated exhibition in the main corridor of the naval quarters: a collection of dog tags of crew members and officers she executed with her own hands for this very reason. And so the food wasn't great and the air smelled funny and the cabins were tiny and true comfort was hardly achievable, despite Quartermaster Bolon's consider-able efforts. But the main goal was maintained: deliver the troops alive and mostly well to places in which they will enjoy those two rather temporary conditions no more.

Thus, every piece of equipment which could be used to maintain the ship was salvaged from equipment less relevant to this specific purpose. Such as, to Colonel Havock's continued impotent rage, the Mobile Infantry's combat armor suits.

The maintain-at-all-costs list featured just one item type related to the Mobile Infantry: the transport pods. Each of those, visible behind the huge transparent doors separating it from the breathable space of the pod bay, closely resembled a giant banana forcibly bloated into a roughly spherical shape. Unfortunately, the soldiers of the First Platoon and Company et cetera weren't given any time to contemplate the historical and culinary significance of those similarities. Instead, bathed in the red emergency light, they were busy fighting their way into their useless combat armor suits in front of the pod's looming hatch. All of them showed clear signs of mortal fear: the less experienced were contemplating their impending heroical doom in the line of duty, while the veterans were dreading the more immediate calamity of being personally briefed by Colonel Havock. What little free time remained before this dreadful event was spent on dispensing the armor suits power packs and weapon components to everyone, as per regulations. While most of these were somewhere between mildly inoperative and completely fake, Corporal Clementine took no chances, and accompanied their distribution with a stern warning to keep them inactive.

"One shot or even a single movement in an operative armor suit inside the pod," said Corporal Clementine by way of introduction, "and everyone on board is dead. Either exposed to outer space or burned on atmospheric entry. I don't know about you but I, if you don't mind, would prefer to die on a planet and not above it."

"I prefer not to die," said Mister Roseneck, spectacularly failing to comply with both modern political theory and political-division practicality.

"That is definitely possible," the corporal said, and added, "theoretically speaking. Especially if you keep the damned thing off."

Mister Roseneck did not reply. After a moment he lowered his head.

He's learning, the corporal thought, but quickly realized her mistake as an increasing rumbling noise heralded the arrival of an active armor suit wrapped around, alas, Second Lieutenant Big W.

"Attention!" the corporal shouted. Around her, the platoon clunkily came into some sort of, for lack of a better word, order.

"Listen up!" Big said. "Today we fight!" He hesitated, glanced down at something he was holding, then raised his head again. Corporal Clementine sadly recalled her recent battle experiences, prior to her joining the UPS Spitz and the 91st regiment. She was with the 73rd then, on board the UPS Stecken. Neither existed anymore.

"We shall fight!" Big announced. "We shall fight in . . . in a... France? ... on the seas and oceans, we shall fight with growing confidence and growing, er, strength in the air?" Another hesitation, another glance at the thing in his hand. "We shall defend our . . . Island?.. Whatever... whatever the cost may be!"

None of the assembled soldiers interrupted this unique oration. They were all gazing interestedly at the young officer, who, having overcome all those unexplainable terms contained in the text he was visibly reading from his pad, commenced to utter the rest with confidence and aplomb.

"We shall fight on the beaches!" he declared. "We shall fight on the landing grounds! We shall fight in the fields and in the streets, we shall fight in the hills; we shall never—"

But they never found out what they shall never, for upon uttering that very word, The Big W magically left the safe confines of the floor and drifted upwards in a rather undignified manner. This soon revealed, behind him, the suit-clad, heavily armed, absolutely enraged Colonel Havock.

"What the Space do you think you're doing, you mongrel?" the colonel shouted.

"Sir, a speech before the battle, sir! It's a strategically-sound system of—"

"Who gave you permission?"

"Sir, I took the initiative, sir!"

"And who," said Havock, casually shaking the young officer up and down, "allowed you to do *that?*"

"Sir!" whined Big, who currently seemed undeserving of his nickname, feet dangling uselessly in the air. "It is the military spirit, sir, guts and glory and fame and—"

But Big's other ingredients of the military spirit would forever remain a mystery, as Colonel Havock, after what he considered to be a lengthy and careful consideration, cut short the aspiring speaker by throwing him down at the floor. The noise was abysmal.

"Stay there," the colonel said, "and shut up. When the troops need a speech, I'll give them one."

This was answered by a loud cough emitted from above.

"Hear hear!" said a metallic voice, though different than

the one which previously called for battle stations. "A word to our brave soldiers, courtesy of the political division!"

Colonel Havock promptly lost all interest in the young fallen officer and raised his head toward the hidden speakers in the ceiling.

"Bastard!" he shouted.

"In a free republic," the voice intoned, "the ideal citizen must be one willing and able to take arms for the defense of the flag, exactly as the ideal citizen must be the father of many healthy children."

Corporal Clementine found this to be a welcome break from her bleak memories of being chopped by enemy artillery along with all her previous comrades.

"Well," she said, "I don't think that I'm going to be a father anytime soon." This earned her a curious look or two from the assembled soldiers, but luckily not from Colonel Havock, whose furious stare was fixed at the ceiling.

"A race must be strong and vigorous," the voice continued, to Havock's obvious rage. "It must be a race of good fighters and good breeders—"

"Hey!" said one of the soldiers. It was, Clementine noticed, young Daisy. The corporal turned her head toward the draftee and tried to convey without speaking the need to Shut the Space Up.

"—else its wisdom will come to naught and its virtue be ineffective," the voice droned, "and no sweetness and delicacy, no love for and appreciation of beauty in art or literature," and Colonel Havock's suit barked and emitted a round of small caliber projectiles that hit the ceiling. There was an awful noise of some membrane tearing up and the speech subsided into a series of mostly unintelligible mumbling, something about "great virile virtues", perhaps, and then mere static.

"Now," said Colonel Havock, enjoying the undivided attention of everyone inside the transport pod loading deck. "Here's what you need to know: we land near the enemy stronghold, the bloody insects are down there, and we're going to eradicate them. That's it. Corporal, take them in."

"Yes, sir," said Clementine. She turned toward the great transparent doors and the pods behind them, and noticed the soldier standing by them. *Oh no,* she thought. *Well, nothing to do about it now.*

"Open the pod bay doors please, Fux."

"Yes, ma'am," said Fux promptly, raising a shred of hope in Clementine's mind. But not a long-lived one, since this obedient utterance was followed by no visible action.

"Fux! Open the pod bay doors!"

"I dutifully report," Fux said, "that I am giving it my best effort, yet admittedly am somewhat short of knowledge as to how exactly to face this demanding task, which, as your honourable ma'am would agree, is very important, even urgent in nature, and therefore—"

"Shut up!" said Havock. "What insolence is this? Corporal, open the door and make sure this soldier goes in last!"

"But, sir!" said Clementine, who knew that the last to get into the pod is the first to come out, usually under hostile conditions, and should, therefore, be one of the more experienced soldiers.

"Quiet, Corporal!"

"Sir, yes, sir," said Clementine. As Sergeant Zimmer was not approved for combat, she was currently the company's highest-ranking fighting noncom. She approached the pod bay door, glancing at Fux with a mix of rage and pity.

The doors opened with a nasty hiss. "That's better," Havock said behind Clementine's back. She could hear the fierce joy in his voice. "See you, whoever remains of you, on the other side!"

And thus was Fux set to be cannon fodder.

PART TWO
THE TROUBLESOME TROOPER

12

FUX IS MOBILIZED

The very first prerequisite for success lies in the steady and constant application of force. This persistence, however, can always and only arise from a definite spiritual conviction. Any violence not springing from a firm, spiritual base will be wavering and uncertain.

MY CAPITAL STRUGGLE: AN AUTOBIOGRAPHICAL GUIDANCE BY ADOLPHUS MARKS, FIRST GRAND COUNCILLOR OF THE EMPIRE

HIGH COMMAND WAS famous for treating almost any information as confidential. This included the very basics, such as the general progress of the war and any description of the enemy beyond the word *Insects*. It also went down to particulars, such as the destination of a given fighting company or even whether it was a planet or a moon. And so, each target was always referred to as Planetary Body X, though the political division made it clear that it shouldn't be referred to at all.

The journey to Planetary Body X was as uneventful as one could expect from being stuffed inside a lump consisting of a few tons of rubberized metal hurled at ludicrous speeds toward another lump consisting of a few sextillion tons of whatever. First, there was the mighty launch, which would have caused some damage were it not for the soldiers being encased in flexible wrapping, much like Quartermaster Bolon's sweet chestnuts. Then there was a quiet period of drifting in space, having nothing to do but look at each other in the dim red light of the windowless cabin. This was used by some of the younger soldiers for voicing last thoughts and regrets, a sure way of sparking an all-platoon panic attack, which Corporal Clementine was determined to stop. But before she could come up with a proper retort, a disgusting noise cut through the talking and silenced it. Soon, this was accompanied by the rather distinct smell of half-digested chestnuts. Private Fux, against all regulations, acceptable manners, and common sense, had burped.

"I'm going to kill you!" shouted Mister Roseneck, ending a brief period of uncomprehending silence. "I'm going to cut you to pieces and bury you in the ground! I'm going to sterilize your corpse with bleach, you . . . you . . ." but here he had to stop since everyone else in the pod was laughing.

Corporal Clemente felt nothing but gratitude: partially for the brilliant, albeit disgusting, boost to morale, but mostly for the fact that Second Lieutenant Big, who was not equipped to see the humour of the situation or any humour of any situation, was safely stuffed away in the officer's nook.

Soon, the smell subsided as the pod circulated more and more oxygen into its life systems in preparation for combat.

"Listen," Corporal Clementine said. "Don't try to be heroes down there. First thing is to take cover, see what's going on, get our bearings. If anyone wants to die, there's plenty of time for it later. If you don't know what to do, follow me."

"I don't want to die," said one of the younger soldiers, probably Johnny, in a clear and brave breach of standing Infantry regulations.

"I'll never see my children again," said a feminine voice. "I can feel it."

"Aren't you a bit too young to have children? Especially more than one?"

"We just married. We planned on having twins just before—"

"Well," said someone else, "*I* was planning on marrying my love, but then her husband—"

Let them vent, Corporal Clementine thought. *It's good for them.*

"I left Duke Franz behind," said an older voice. "What will he do without me?"

"I didn't know you were of royal blood."

"What?"

"Dukes and barons and the such. Did you also leave a countess behind?"

"Or did you sneak behind a duchess?"

"Oh, no, Duke is—"

"Maybe both the duke *and* the duchess snuck behind him."

"The more, the merrier!"

For now, thought Corporal Clementine sadly.

"A true royal soldier we have here!"

"I salute you, my king!"

"Salute!" shouted some of the soldiers together, laughing.

"I won't argue with you," the new royalty said meekly, "but Duke is my dog."

Now even Corporal Clementine laughed.

"I left a queen behind me," said someone else. "You may not know it to look at her, but just try to disobey her commands!"

"I left a good man behind me," said someone at the back sadly. This caused a pause in the hilarity. Clementine could see that some of the soldiers were now quietly pondering their fates. *Soon they'll find out.*

"I left my housekeeper behind," said a new voice from the front. Fux, of course. "And a dog too. A dog or two." He seemed lost in thought, perhaps a happy recollection of the past. "I wonder," he added eventually, "whether she managed to sell the Alsatian mini poodle substitute."

"You mean your good old lady?" said someone.

"She is rather old, I'll give you that," said Fux, "though I cannot honestly say that she is particularly good."

"Not an uncommon state of mind among husbands, that."

"She recently raised my rent, which was totally unprovoked," said Fux. "It was I, after all, who released her from police custody."

"Weren't you the one who caused that, though?" said

Johnny, who loved Fux's story about the fake dogs and his timely escape, as told on various occasions by both its protagonist and the delighted Quartermaster Bolon.

"That is no reason to be unreasonable about it," said Fux and sighed. "Oh, what can you do? The past is the past. Though I do hope she did manage to sell those mutts."

"No wife, then?" said someone. "Children?"

"Just mutts," Fux said.

Corporal Clementine thought, for just a fleeting moment, that there was something odd about his smile. But then, an overhead light started pulsating, each time flooding the cabin with a murky green swamp-like ambience.

"Enough," the corporal said. "We need to get ready. Remember what I told you. Don't be heroes out there."

"What about the suits, ma'am?" asked someone from the back rows.

"They're useless for attacking, but they can give you good cover. Try not to lose them."

"They're perfectly maintained, ma'am," said Fux.

"This pod is insulated," Clementine said. "The suits' com signal can't get out. Our voices aren't recorded. So you don't have to continue with this."

"I humbly agree, though I am not sure what you mean by that," said Fux, "as it is above the level of understanding of a simple soldier such as myself, not to mention being an idiot, ma'am, second-class."

"Fux!"

"However, ma'am, I would like to dutifully report that, in fact—"

The pod started shaking, then lurched violently as it

entered the atmosphere, hinting that Planetary Body X was actually a full-fledged planet.

"Fux, what have you done?"

But speech became impossible, with or without coms. By now, the corporal knew, the yellow heat shield was fiercely burning outside, inflicting a terrible noise upon the insides. There was no point thinking about its possible failure—the end would be quicker than an eyeblink. The cabin's atmosphere quickly approximated a tropical kind of weather, and Clementine could feel sweat slowly rolling down the back of her head.

Above the din, she heard the hollering of a claxon. The proximity alert. *One, two*—she shouted, "Hold tight!"—*three*, and the pod slammed mightily into something as the heat shield exploded. Someone cried in pain, and a second detonation blew out the second layer of protection, a thin sphere made of whatever composite materials were in fashion two decades ago. The cabin started rotating rapidly as another series of explosions burst high-pressure gas into the compartmentalized space between the outer walls and the insides of the sphere. This was done in a most asymmetric and stomach-disruptive manner.

Clementine heard once that, originally, the pods contained stabilizers to tame this wild behaviour, but she'd never seen any evidence of that. The cabin rolled crazily on every possible axis and maybe several impossible ones. Something horribly wet flew past the corporal's face and smacked straight into the chest of a nearby young soldier, whose following scream was loud enough to be heard above the overall mayhem.

Of course, she thought. *There always has to be at least one puker.*

The claxon started again. There was no point in shouting or in anything else. "One!" it bellowed. "Two! Three!"

Impact.

Darkness, the screaming of metal and people, air hissing, something liquid. Hopefully not blood. A loud *pop* and then, perhaps unfortunately, light. A cold feeling on her face. Wind. The hatch had opened. A second hiss, this time from the melting flexible wrapping that held everyone in place and was now rapidly becoming a puddle on the floor. More wind.

Something's off about the wind.

"Everybody out!" the corporal shouted. Someone, in obedience, blocked the light coming from the hatch. This was followed by nothing in particular.

"Out, I said!"

"Ma'am," said someone who was, despite the general mess, definitely Fux, "I am trying most urgently to do so. However, at this time, I find myself to be somewhat unfit in size, especially due to wearing the suit, to pass through the—"

"I don't care what or how, get out *right now!*"

Something was definitely wrong with the wind.

A metallic scream announced the prompt obedience of Private Fux. Light suddenly flooded the cabin as the hatch was transformed from a narrow elliptical shape into a rough, big, jagged circle. Now she could see Fux clearly, standing at the entrance and holding a lump of torn metal with his suit's arm. "Ma'am," he said, "I dutifully report that—"

"*Out!*"

Fux dropped out of the hatch. Other soldiers followed. The wind grew stronger. It was awful. Someone must have made a horrible mistake.

"Outoutout!" Clementine shouted. "And take cover!"

Soon it was her turn to go. She jumped smoothly onto the wet ground. The sky was an uninviting grey, the ground was an unappetizing brown, and the air was cold and absolutely, grossly intolerable. Positively poisonous.

There was no point in holding her breath or defending herself in any other way. The armour suits were equipped, as detailed at length in their maintenance manual, with limited-time oxygen supply bottles. The captain happily confiscated those whenever possible, which was always. The Mobile Infantry was never supposed to be deployed into alien atmospheres. The captain was harsh, yes, and to a certain degree even evil, for sure, but mass murder of the troops was supposed to be beyond even her.

This, thought Clementine, *is the end.*

It was then that she noticed the cows.

"This is not so different than some of the farms back home," said Fux after some time. "Which reminds me of a—"

"Is there any place in the universe that does not remind you of your bloody miserable planet?" said Mister Roseneck from the back.

"I would not know, sir," said Fux. "This is my first time anywhere else. Barring the locker room and the barracks and the infirmary and the parade grounds and the armoury and the company kitchen and—"

"Fux," said Clementine, "enough."

"—and the honourable political office and the communication room and the pod, of course."

"Fux!"

"Yes, venerable ma'am. I hope I have not forgotten anything."

Corporal Clementine sighed. Something, she thought, was definitely off about the cows.

And thus did Fux embark upon his first visit to a foreign planet.

13

FUX IS ENGAGED

Forever young, I want to be forever young . . .

A FAMOUS FOLK BALLAD ON BAYERN III,
COMMON IN PROTESTS DURING THE INITIAL
STAGE OF THE IMPERIAL OCCUPATION

IT DID NOT TAKE LONG for the First Platoon of the First et cetera to discover, upon landing on the Now Positively Planet of X, that they had arrived, despite the political division's explicit prohibition in regards to that name, at hell.

The transport pod, now looking to anyone with a sufficient historical background like a giant deflated soccer ball, sat proudly on top of a brown hill. It was surrounded by brown fields, brown slopes, brown meadows, and lots of additional brown, dreary geography. It was also surrounded by cows.

The closest ones, which weren't too close, were peacefully lying on their sides. Some of them were shaking their heads as if getting rid of bothersome flies. Others wagged their tails against the ground. Farther away, cows were attempting to stand up with various degrees of success. Even farther, yet more cows were slowly walking about, somewhat drunkenly. As Clementine watched, one of them gently fell to the ground and lay there to rest, its legs still dreamily moving. Another rose up in its stead, took a few steps, and promptly emitted a very familiar yet extremely unwelcome sound. Another cow followed suit and another. And the wind, the terrible wind . . .

Other than that and the occasional soldier emerging from the hatch, everything was quiet. There was no sign of the giant armoured mechanisms Corporal Clementine was used to—if one can ever get used to—fighting. There were no structures, no weapons, no enemies. Unless that is—unless one took into account the cows.

"Follow me, single file," Clementine said. "Let's get out of this spacehole!" She started marching. Behind her, there were various complaints, grunts, and sighs as many members of the Infantry became, grudgingly, mobile.

"Shut up and move!" she said. The groans subsided to a degree. The company, reluctantly, obeyed.

"Most venerable ma'am Corporal," said Fux behind her back, "shouldn't we wait for the honorable officers?"

"You can wait for them if you want to, Fux," Clementine said, but without malice, as she didn't mind at all being called venerable. "I, however, am going to put as much distance as possible between myself and this stink."

"Stink, ma'am?"

"The bloody cows," the corporal said, but slightly distractedly. Something was still not right.

"Lovely creatures, ma'am. Back in my hometown of Praha, there was this herd of cattle that—"

"Fux," she said. Something was wrong, but the stench made it hard to think. They had to get away from it.

"Yeah, silence the idiot," said someone else behind her, in all probability Mister Roseneck.

"No, *you* be quiet." This, clearly, was Daisy.

"—used to graze in one of the nearby villages, by the Vlt."

"Vlt?" said Johnny.

"That is our river. We are very proud of it. It flows from the north and passes by most of the nearby villages and then through the middle of Praha. Maybe a bit to the right. It is very convenient. Also very famous."

"Not on board this ship, it isn't," grunted Mister Roseneck.

"Well, now it sort of is," said Johnny.

"We're not on board the ship anymore," said someone.

"Be quiet and let him continue!" said Daisy.

"And so those cows," said Fux, showing no concern for being interrupted, "they had an owner, and that owner was one Kuche Sloblich. Sloblich would always forget to collect his cows after a day in the pasture. That is, they were in the pasture, and he was in the barn, hiding from his wife. And so, by evening, Sloblich was always sort of forgetful—well, maybe not really forgetful, more sort of totally drunk."

"No, *you* be quiet," said Mister Roseneck.

"And so his cows, with no one to guide them, would go down to the river bank, where the grass was thick. And then they would follow the river downhill, that is south, or maybe south by southwest—"

"No, *you* be quiet! You tell him, Corporal!"

"—and after some time, arrive at the Svatt bridge. And this, the bridge, where the cows arrived, was not far from Kalicha. And I already told you that the three of us, Borek and Bolek and I, used to sit in Kalicha maybe seven, eight times a week, that is for lunch, of course, not counting the evenings—"

"As if I didn't have enough cows in my life at the moment," muttered Clementine, and walked even faster. By now, she wasn't sure whether she was trying to get away from the cows or from her own troops. Behind her back, Fux's story steadily continued, regardless of the circumstances and also of its growingly divided audience.

"And Borek says, 'What is this God-awful smell?' and I say, 'What smell?' and Bolek says, 'You have got to be kidding, for it is—'"

"Again with the blasphemy!" shouted Mister Roseneck, who evidently was still traumatized by some of Fux's previous unholy utterances in the barracks. "Be quiet!"

"Here we go again," said someone.

"Don't worry about the blasphemy, Roseneck," Corporal Clementine said.

"But the political division—"

"Is yet to arrive on this planet. Pipe down."

"And Bolek says, 'How can you not smell it, even in the deepest and awfullest of the seventeen sections of hell there could be no stink like that of those infernal creatures—'"

"Hell! Inferno! Blasphemy again!"

The corporal sighed. *Let them play*, she thought. *It's*

*probably the last time they can do so, either on this planet or
in their lives.*

Mister Roseneck was now in full swing. "Wait till the
officers hear of this!" he shouted.

"Which reminds me," said Daisy. "Where *are* the
officers?"

"Be blessed that they're not here yet," the corporal
said.

This bold declaration was immediately stressed by a
remote-yet-loud popping sound, not unlike that of the cork
flying out of a bottle of horribly shaken cheap bubbly wine,
fifty millilitres per soldier per imperial holiday. Clementine
turned around just in time to see a speck rise from the
deflated pod, rapidly grow into a flying yellow coffin, and
rush right over the retreating platoon and straight into a
nearby hill. It hit the ground with a wet *splat*. For a moment,
its four sides seemed undecided as to whether they should
disintegrate or just fall to the ground. Soon enough they
settled for both. By doing this they revealed the coffin's
insides.

"Ladies and gentlemen of the First Company," the
corporal said, "I hereby present to you, as requested, your
officers. Forward march, on the double!"

IT DIDN'T TAKE them long to arrive at the landing site of
their superiors. One of those excellent leaders, clad in his
heavy armour suit and custom-made high-heeled combat
boots, was planted in the ground like a carbon-fibre tree,
emptily gazing at the horizon. The other, perfectly suited

and helmeted as per regulations, was lying face down in the mud. Both were motionless.

"Don't touch them," said Clementine. "It's just the deceleration." As an afterthought, she added, "They'll be fine." She did her best to conceal her hopes to the contrary.

Mister Roseneck approached the standing, silent figure. "Colonel Havock, sir," he said. "I'd like to register a complaint."

"For the love of Space, shut up, Roseneck!" said Clementine.

"And so," said Fux helpfully, "after lunch, Borek and Bolek and I decide to go down to the river to see what it is all about."

"Is this still about the cows?" asked Daisy.

"A pervert, sir!" said Mister Roseneck. The colonel, however, failed to show any sign of recognition or of anything whatsoever.

"Roseneck, shut up this instant!"

"I've had enough!" said the querulous old man.

"You will have enough when the colonel wakes up and shoots you, you idiot!"

"That, honourable ma'am," said Fux, "would be me. Second-class."

By now, the corporal wasn't sure who was the bigger idiot, nor did she intend to find out.

"We're going to wait here until they wake up, which shouldn't take long," she said. "Meanwhile, no shouting. We don't know where the enemy is, and this, trust me, isn't the way you want to find out."

Mister Roseneck didn't answer, though his gaze was too defiant for the corporal's taste.

"So we walk, and we take quite a long time to get to the river," said Fux, "what with having drunk our share of beer and maybe one or two shots of something stronger. But eventually, after a few false tries and almost being caught by the municipal police, the three of us find Kuche Sloblich's cows."

"Were they as smelly as the ones we see here?" asked Daisy.

"I do not smell anything here or there," said Fux. "But Borek and Bolek suddenly act very strangely. Borek, especially, is shouting like a crow and would not be quiet. And he says, 'What in the name of God and His angels and the devil and his demons and the Holy Spirit and its little holy spirits is this hellish stink?'"

"Colonel, sir, he's doing it again!" shouted Mister Roseneck, stepped toward the officer, and grabbed his shoulders.

"Back off this instant, Roseneck!" said Clementine, but too late. The colonel emitted a mighty yawn, blinked a few times, and cleared his throat.

"Sir!" said the encouraged Mister Roseneck, "I would like to bring to your attention the promiscuous behaviour of Private Fux here, sir!"

"What?" Colonel Havock said and then noticed the hands of the unlucky Mister Roseneck, which were still grabbing his shoulders. "What is this supposed to mean, soldier?"

"Sir, that's exactly what I was asking, sir! He was blabbering off about God and the devil, sir! And not being punished for it!"

"God and the devil?"

"And angels and demons and the Holy Spirit, sir!"

"How dare you!" shouted Colonel Havock.

"Exactly!"

"Blasphemy!" the colonel roared. "For this, I will execute you right here on the spot!"

"Sir!" shouted Clementine, but the colonel had already pushed Mister Roseneck away and was now messing with his armour suit. A series of hums and clicks hinted at the operation of something nasty inside.

"Sir!" shouted Mister Roseneck, who only now figured out the identity of the soon-to-be executed. "Not me, sir! Him!"

"I was just telling them about Kuche Sloblich's cows, sir," said Fux helpfully.

"See?" said Mister Roseneck. "He keeps doing it!"

"I shall not suffer such behaviour in the Mobile Infantry!" roared the colonel and aimed his right hand straight at poor Mister Roseneck.

"Wait!" the corporal shouted.

Something clicked into action inside Colonel Havock's armoured right fist. Then the world exploded.

AS EXPLOSIONS GO, this one was rather wet. Or maybe just damp. This did not take anything from its force, which promptly smacked Corporal Clementine into the stinking brown mud.

Poor Mister Roseneck, she thought. *A fool, for sure, but even fools do not deserve this kind of death.*

Carefully, she raised her head. Around her, the rest of the platoon was also lying down. In fact, no one was up. Not even Colonel Havock.

He must have set his launcher to full power, she thought.

Roseneck probably got disintegrated on the spot. Oh, my. What a way to go.

There was another explosion. Bits of mud flew in the air, somewhere to her left, near the top of the hill.

Why is he shooting again? she thought. *This really is too much. He has already proved his point.*

Something slammed into the ground somewhere to her right, not far from the fallen shape of Second Lieutenant Big, who, conveniently, was yet to show any signs of life. The ground emitted a fountain of mud. Curiously enough, it did so in silence. Well, maybe not complete silence. Some hint of sound was still noticeable above the ringing in her ears.

Interesting. Ringing. Am I deaf? Why would a launcher affect my hearing? It's bloody magnetic; it shouldn't . . .

Behind her, something was happening. Bits of mud flew up in the air and landed on her head.

For crying out loud, she thought, *this is way too much, even for bloody Havock.*

Someone was waving at her. It was, how curious, none other than Mister Roseneck. *But how . . .*

"Take cover!" she heard a faraway cry. The voice was familiar. Mister Roseneck was still waving at her. "Take bloody cover, everyone!" the voice repeated. She was only mildly surprised to discover that it was her own. "We're under attack!"

And thus was Fux initiated into the art of war.

14

FUX IS LAUNCHED

The insects *can appear in many forms, but they're all highly contagious. Our combat armour suits are, therefore, perfectly sealed against their toxic agents. Still, in the rare and improbable case of suspected infection, and for the sake of their comrades and the common good, the soldiers in question are hereby ordered to be left behind.*

DOUBLE STAR, A MOBILE INFANTRY OFFICER'S HANDBOOK

IT WAS THEN that Corporal Clementine discovered what was out of place. The stench of the mud, the reek of the cows, the foulness of the air were wrong. In addition to their offensive animal aroma, they smelled heavily of gasoline.

But before she managed to draw any conclusions from it,

this anomaly was overshadowed by another: all around her, the cows were slowly leaving the ground and gently floating in the air.

Everyone tried to speak at once, momentarily over-loading the coms. Then a sharp voice cut through the noise, marking an officer's channel override.

"It's a trap!" Colonel Havock shouted. "Bloody insects! Attack!"

"Sir, wait!" said Clementine. "We don't know—"

But the colonel had already embarked upon a mighty armour-suit-powered leap and quickly became a tiny dot in the sky. At the top of his flying arc, he started shooting. Corporal Clementine couldn't hear the near-silent launcher at this range, but thin lines of tracer particles connected the tiny form of the colonel to the more substantial forms of the floating cows. The latter, unhurriedly and politely, started to explode.

Some of the soldiers cheered. This was cut short by a few more of the by-now-familiar wet explosions nearby.

"Look!" said someone and pointed at the floating cows. One of them got hit by a launcher slug. It exploded nicely but, in doing so, emitted a few brown projectiles, which flew from the position recently occupied by a cow to the position currently occupied by some of the company's slower soldiers. There was a momentary cloud of brown mud and maybe some other brown things. Then it subsided into nothing but a puddle.

"Take cover!" the corporal shouted and started running around the hill toward its protected side. "Follow me!"

She noticed that the floating cows were getting closer.

Behind her, the remaining soldiers were slowly obeying. All of them, that is, but the defiant form of Private Fux, who was fumbling within his suit.

"Bloody Space!" the corporal shouted, stopped, turned around, and started running in the opposite direction. "Get on with it!" she shouted at the surprised soldiers and pointed at the hill. "Go over there and hide. Run! Run!"

She glanced backward, saw that most of the troops were running in the right direction, and turned back toward Fux. As she got closer, she could see that, inside his helmet, he was smiling.

"Fux!" she shouted. "What are you doing?"

To her right, not too far, something crashed. From the corner of her eye, she saw it was merely the ungraceful return of Colonel Havock to the ground, if not, alas, to his senses. He, too, was focusing on Fux.

"Stop right there, soldier!" the colonel shouted through the com.

For once, he's right, Clementine thought. *Maybe he* has *returned to his senses.*

Fux waved at them happily, lowered his hand, and raised his head.

"Fux, no!" Clementine said. Beside her, Havock was shouting something too, but she couldn't—well, wouldn't—get the exact wording over the sound of her own voice and the constant ringing in her ears.

"Whatever it is that you're doing," she shouted, "just—"

An awful metallic crash cut her off. Fux's armour suit shot up diagonally, flew madly, and smacked head-first straight into the nearest floating cow.

"Fux!"

But he was gone. Only the cow remained.

It took Corporal Clementine a moment or two to realize that this, in itself, was another anomaly. The cow did not explode, nor did it blast, evaporate, or disintegrate. Most importantly, it did not emit any projectiles. It was merely floating, gradually sinking toward the ground. Of Fux, there was no sign.

She took one hasty glance at the retreating troops, who were already safe around the far side of the hill, then ran in the other direction. Colonel Havock jumped again. By the time she reached it, the cow had landed. So did the colonel, too close for comfort.

"You idiot," she muttered, unsure whether it was directed at Fux, at the colonel, or at herself. Her hearing was getting better. Above the dim din of the battlefield, she now noticed a sharp, high note. It reminded her of something, but she couldn't fathom what. The cow, she saw, though still in one piece, was slowly decreasing in size. The sharp, high note was not so high anymore, its pitch gradually lowering. Almost like the sound of the red balloon she received for her fifth birthday, a sound that was accompanied . . .

The cow, she realized, wasn't shrinking. It was *deflating*. Its hide, white with large patches of black and some suspicious stains of brown, gradually lost its round shape. From inside it, something heavy fell to the ground with a thud. Then another one. The cow's head sank into the collapsing mass, and soon another thud followed. The thing now resembled a circular tent, almost like the one that used to appear in Clementine's hometown every summer along with the circus that owned it, except for being somewhat shorter and less colourful and lacking any clowns whatsoever. Another noticeable difference was the central pole, which now, the hide having lost the last remains of its former roundness, took a very familiar shape.

Corporal Clementine opened her mouth. Hesitated. Closed it. Opened it again. "Fux?"

The central pole, still covered in cowhide, lifted its hand merrily. "Yes, ma'am," a muffled voice said.

Well, the corporal thought, amazed. *Maybe not a* total *lack of clowns, after all.*

She smiled, but this was not to last.

"What is the meaning of this?" said Colonel Havock and took a step toward the former cow.

"Sir!" Clementine said hurriedly, "it's Private Fux, sir! He—"

"Not for long, he isn't!" said Havock. "Not after I finish with him! I'll show him what happens when you disobey a direct—"

"Sir!" the corporal shouted. "He was . . . he was acting under my orders, sir!"

Behind them, something hit the damp ground. A small jet of mud erupted from the top of the hill behind which the troops were hiding. The colonel turned his head toward it.

"Eh?" he said.

"He was, he was," the corporal continued, desperately stalling for time. "He, yes, my direct orders, sir. Yes. We . . . we found a way to incapacitate the cows, sir!"

"I can take care of those cows myself, Corporal!" the colonel said, turning to the corporal again. "I do not need any volunteers to do it for me!"

"Sir, this was done while you were still . . . still incapacitated, sir!"

"I was *never!*" the colonel shouted. "Incapacitated? Me? Who dares say that I was? Do you imply that I was? You shall be punished with the most—"

"I'm sorry, sir, I misspoke. I meant that you were too quick for us, and therefore, having failed to follow your example, we had to find our own way, sir."

Colonel Havock sniffed, then shook his head.

"Well," he said. Behind them, another cow-generated projectile hit the base of the hill.

The nearby ex-cow tore apart. Something emerged from the resulting hole. It was Fux's head, still smiling.

"The honourable corporal ma'am is absolutely right," the head said. "We only aim to follow the heroic example of our commanders, sir!"

That piece of flattery was shameless enough to give pause even to Colonel Havock.

"Oh?" he said. The ground shook again, a bit closer this time.

"Sir," said Clementine, "this being a minefield with no actual enemy presence, I suggest we relocate ourselves to a better tactical position." She pointed toward the hill behind them. She was smart enough not to use the word "retreat" anywhere near a senior officer of any kind.

"Retreat?" said the senior officer of this particular kind. "Not on my watch, Corporal! We shall fight until the enemy is gone. We shall exterminate it!"

The shadow of a cow, floating high above them, gently covered the sun. It was accompanied by a slight whirring sound. The cow emitted a momentary flash of light, quickly followed by another explosion, this time too close. A fine spray of mud showered over the three of them. Fux took this opportunity to step out of the thing previously known as a cow. His smile never wavered.

Cut down by cows, thought Clementine miserably. *That's what the official casualty notice will say if I don't fix this right now.*

"Sir," she said, "I suggest that we need to confront the real enemy, as opposed to these cows, which are clearly, sir, a decoy."

For a terrible moment, Colonel Havock just stared at her, saying nothing.

Do something, she thought, *or else the only thing that will remain of us is a note in the regiment's histories.* She wondered who was in charge of that. *They'll probably find it funny, us dying by cows. They'll call it the Battle of the Cattle.*

"There may be something in what you say," said Colonel Havock eventually. He stood up even straighter than usual.

"Attention, First Company, position change!" he shouted into the com, then briefly glanced at his suit's instrumentation. "Go north-northwest of your position one click, move!"

"Sir, yes, sir!" said a new voice in the com and groaned. It took Clementine a moment to identify it as belonging to Second Lieutenant Big. She turned toward the foot of the hill, which was now occupied by the fallen form of the young officer sitting idly in the mud.

"All sergeants, apply a new strategy: group your men and go north-northwest on the double!" Big added. This vigorous and brave command he followed with no movement whatsoever.

All the sergeants of the First Company obeyed as one, which was, in fact, the case, the one sergeant in question being Corporal Clementine. "You heard the officers," she said.

The cow overhead was really close now. From the corner of her eye, she saw Colonel Havock raising his right arm toward it. "Sir, no!" she shouted, but Fux was quicker. Before the colonel's arm finished its arc, Fux shot up and, again, straight into the cow.

Is he really such an idiot? Clementine thought. *Or a madman? Or is it a death wish?*

"I like this man!" said Colonel Havock. This was, as far as Clementine could remember, a first.

"Corporal," said someone over the com, "we would like to obey, but we're not sure where's north-northwest." The hill hid the soldiers from her view, but it wasn't hard imagining their disarray and fear.

"Incompetence!" said Colonel Havock. "I will have your hides for this, soldiers!"

"Strategically speaking," said Big's voice, "it might be preferable to—"

"Run straight away from that hill," Clementine said. "Move!"

She turned and started running in the same direction, which for her meant toward the hill and the serene form of Second Lieutenant Big. Behind her, Havock took a suit-powered jump and so arrived at his placid second in command slightly before her. By the time she arrived, the colonel was raising the combat spirits of the second lieutenant in the only way he knew how, which consisted of grabbing the latter's suit and shaking it like a ragdoll.

"Sir," Clementine said, "it's no use; it's probably deceleration sickness."

Havock dropped his toy and turned toward her. "Are you attempting to override my authority, *Corporal?*" he said.

"No, sir," she said. "I'm trying to—"

Both jumped as a cow fell from the sky right beside them. This one made a dreadful farting sound as something tore its hide quickly from inside. A metal-clad arm appeared, followed by Fux's head.

Clementine turned back to the crumpled Big. "He needs help," she said. "We need the medkit."

"The medkit is for officers only," said Havock.

"He *is* an officer, sir."

"Second lieutenants barely deserve the title," said Havock. "It's a disgrace that they share a mess and kitchen with their betters."

"Sir, it's either that or we have to carry him."

"Carry him, then," said Havock. "The medkit is invoked only by those of a higher rank." He pointed at his own shoulders, which were decorated with golden lion heads embedded in golden fig leaves.

This drew Fux's attention. He quickly stepped out of the cow and approached the colonel. "Very nice, sir," he said. "Impressive."

"As it should be, soldier," smiled Havock.

Fux stepped closer to him to better examine the lovely insignia. "Very good," he said. "I am sure I could get a great price for them at the Praha Princely Pawnshop."

"What?"

In the sky above, more cows were lazily gliding toward them.

"Come on, we must be going!" said Clementine. "Sir, I beg you, invoke the medkit!"

"Do not take that tone with me, Corporal!" said Havock. "The medkit will come for these ranks," he pointed at his own shoulders, "and for these ranks alone!"

"That problem has an easy solution, sir!" said Fux, and before Havock could react, reached out with both hands and tore the insignia out of the colonel's shoulders. Havock tried to grab him, but Fux's suit seemed to be vastly more powerful than it had a right to be, and the colonel's hands slid off it helplessly.

This action was so far off any experience Clementine had had in her military career, not to mention her life, that for a few long seconds, she remained dumbstruck. The same, she noticed, was true of Colonel Havock. This was time enough for Fux to attach the stolen insignia to Big's shoulders. Clementine felt as if she was dreaming.

"Squeeze the lion's heads," she said weakly. "This will call the medkit."

"Yes, ma'am," said Fux. Something clicked. Somewhere behind them, something—not a cow projectile, for a change —exploded.

"I . . . I!" said Colonel Havock. "You . . . you!"

The cows above were approaching. There were at least ten of them.

"Good job, Fux," said Clementine. He nodded and smiled.

"You . . . you will not get away from me, you degenerate!" shouted Colonel Havock, finally finding his voice. "And as for *you*, Corporal," he said and was promptly smashed down from behind by a barely subsonic flying medkit. The following gust of wind gently but forcefully pushed Clementine and Fux into the mud.

Good thing that he was wearing his helmet, thought Clementine in a haze, painfully rising from the muck. *Well, maybe not exactly good in the usual sense of the term, but . . .*

"Venerable Ma'am Corporal," said Fux, who managed to stand as well. "I dutifully report that we have two officers down, which, as far as someone such as myself is capable of understanding military rules, leaves you in command."

"Yes."

"This reminds me of something that happened back in—"

"My first command, then," said Clementine, "is for you to save your stories for later, after we're off this planet."

"All of them, ma'am?"

"All of them, Fux."

"Yes, ma'am."

"Good."

"Even though this reminds me of—"

"Fux!"

"Gnhhh," said a new voice and added, "Aw." This was Second Lieutenant Big's first contribution to the conversation. Evidently, the medkit, having effectively decommissioned one officer, somehow managed to recommission the other.

"Fux," she said, "take the insignia from Big and put it on Havock again."

"Ma'am?"

"Just do it before either of them fully wakes up."

"Yes, ma'am."

"Strategically speaking," Big said, but then his voice dwindled into an incoherent mumble.

"Company One," Clementine said into the com, "prepare for evac."

The com emitted some static noise in return.

"We need to go over the hill and get them," Clementine told Fux. "You carry Big, I'll carry Havock. If a cow gets too close, drop everything and do that thing that you do."

They walked in relative silence. From time to time, she groaned with the effort of carrying the limp Havock, suit and all.

"You may want to activate your suit, ma'am," said Fux eventually.

"*Now* you're telling me?"

"I thought I mentioned before that the suits are perfectly m . . ."

"Just remember, Fux, when we get back on the ship, all of this had never happened."

"The suits were always perfectly maintained, ma'am."

"Right."

BEHIND THE HILL, the remains of the First Company were waiting. That is to say, some remaining soldiers and some remains of soldiers. It wasn't a happy sight.

All this, Clementine thought, *without ever meeting the actual enemy. Again.*

"Gather here, defensive formation," she said without much conviction. She dropped Havock to the ground, contrary to all her instincts and convictions, as gently as she possibly could. She then turned to his insignia, pushed her finger into a crevice in the hollow metal, found the secret *request evac* switch inside, and pressed it firmly. There was a tiny, reassuring beep.

"Stay where you are," she said. "We're going out. Don't do anything stupid."

"Stupid, ma'am?"

"Just don't do anything at all."

Maybe she shouldn't have been surprised by how perfectly her soldiers obeyed this particular order.

THE JOURNEY back was relatively quiet. The escape pod's cabin was too empty for anyone's comfort. The only one who seemed to keep his good spirits was Fux, who considered this a good opportunity to finish his cow story. It was almost short, but not really. It ended with the cows being found and returned to their intoxicated owner. There followed a lengthy and incoherent explanation of the build and workings of such creatures, including interesting findings as to the typical smell they emit when constructed from relatively cheap spare parts. That, at least, was the conclusion reached by Bolek and Borek since even while telling their side of the story, Fux himself kept denying the existence of any olfactory phenomenon whatsoever. Corporal Clementine wished she'd had that smelly information prior to the battle. It would have greatly helped. It would have saved lives.

As if to answer her thoughts, Fux, who on this return trip was stowed right by Clementine, turned to the corporal and whispered in her ear a detailed and highly illegal specification of the proper perfect maintenance of certain Mobile Infantry armour suits, and in particular how it could be achieved without arousing anyone's suspicion.

"Thanks, but please don't do anything like that again without telling me," she whispered back. "And never talk about it."

"If I cannot talk about it, venerable ma'am," said Fux, "how can I tell you when I'm about to do it?"

"Exactly."

CONTRARY TO ALL Infantry and naval regulations, rumours of the Battle of the Cattle spread like wildfire on board the UPS *Spitz*. Those included ludicrous tales of flesh-eating monsters, insect-like aliens, a long-lost colony whose cannibal inhabitants attempted to consume every human in sight, and a herd of floating projectile-shooting farm animals.

Another rumour dealt with Colonel Havock, who supposedly regained consciousness while still in the escape pod officer's nook and got out of his grav-couch in order to better deliver his wrath upon the head of a younger officer who also happened to be there. It would have gone badly for poor Big were it not for a small matter of timing, as in the timing of the pod's big braking engine. Thus, a powerful six-grav thrust smashed both officers together and eventually made a very interesting case for both the pod maintenance team and the infirmary personnel.

The political division vehemently denied all this and forcefully forbade such dangerous talk among the crew on pain of recalibration. Our brave soldiers, it declared, fought the enemy face to face and, as always, won the day.

And thus did Fux become a heroic fighter for the cause of the United Planets.

15

FUX IS STYLED

Every soldier is remembered. Every soldier has a name. Which, in times of need, every soldier will gladly give up.

STANDING ORDERS, POLIDIV CENTRAL

SERGEANT ZIMMER HAD BEEN TAKEN off the fighting personnel roster long ago for a non-political reason: he was the sole remaining Mobile Infantry drilling instructor in the local galactic quadrant. This instruction, issued by powers far superior to anyone on board the *UPS Spitz*, infuriated Colonel Havock to no end. The commander of the 91st Regiment did not believe in the concept of non-fighting personnel. He also thought that the sergeant was a miserable slob who should have had it coming. Havock expressed his displeasure by forcing upon the sergeant the second-hardest post-combat task of welcoming back those who *did* make it to the fighting personnel roster. Or at least the ones who remained, relatively, in one piece.

"Welcome back, heroes of the empire!" Sergeant Zimmer said aloud so as to ensure proper reception of his speech by all possible listening devices.

Facing him stood the entire remaining First Company in various stages of exhaustion. This consisted of Corporal Clementine, a rather solemn Mister Roseneck, four or five young draftees whose names the sergeant never managed to remember, and, alas, that unbearable Fux person. The rest of the platoon was, in the language encouraged by the political division, temporarily absent.

The sergeant had a prepared speech that he hoped, in vain, was not too embarrassing. "Today," he said, "we celebrate the glorious return of our heroes of the battle of—"

Belatedly he remembered that no one bothered to tell him anything about the battle.

"The battle of the planet of—"

Fux raised his hand as if in a classroom. "The cows," he said.

"The cattle," said Corporal Clementine absentmindedly.

"The battle of . . . the cattle," the sergeant said. This did not sound right.

"Less like a battle and more like a massacre," Mister Roseneck mumbled grumpily.

"What's that, soldier?" the sergeant said and, for the first time since the ceremony started, smiled. Disciplinary issues were much easier to deal with than speeches for dubious victories. "Attention, you mollusc!" he added.

The newly titled sea creature, formerly known as a hero of the empire, previously identified as Mister Roseneck, was unprepared for the rapidity and extremity of those name changes. Moreover, he was still shaken by recent events and thus had completely forgotten some previous occurrences involving himself and the sergeant. Therefore, he failed to answer the question and instead spent a long moment gazing at the sergeant, mouth open.

"Are you also deaf now, you sea cucumber? I said, 'What's that, soldier?' *What did you just say?*"

This unexpectedly resulted in the old man gaining back some of his previous spirit of defiance. "I said that this wasn't a battle," he said aloud, "but rather—"

"No battle gives you the right to raise your voice at your superiors, you manatee!" the sergeant shouted.

"I said it wasn't a battle, sir; it was a massacre, sir!"

"It doesn't matter, you eel! It can be a battle, it can be a massacre, *nothing* gives you the right to raise your voice at your superiors!"

"But, sir, we just returned from—"

"Don't you 'sir' me, you leviathan, and don't you 'just' me!" the sergeant shouted gleefully. "On your feet! Run!"

"Sir?"

"Around the group! Run! Run, you mullet!"

To Mister Roseneck's credit, it would be said that he clearly made an effort. He managed two steps, then fell to the floor and sat there.

"What is the meaning of this?" the sergeant shouted.

"Sir," said Corporal Clementine, "we've been through a lot."

"Quiet!"

To his surprise, no one disobeyed.

"That's better," he said. "Now, where were we? Oh, yes.

Today we celebrate the glorious return of our," and this was as far as he got before being cut off by an awful metallic voice coming from above.

"Hear, hear!" the voice declared. "A word to our brave soldiers, courtesy of the political division!"

"Oh, come *on!*" the sergeant blurted, then regained his self-control and closed his mouth. He waved toward the soldiers, silently mouthing the words *sit down*, then sat. The soldiers followed suit.

"This is a solemn but a glorious hour," said the voice from above, which sounded quite a lot like a certain political officer of the sergeant's acquaintance. "I am informed that, yet again, the forces of evil have surrendered to our glorious Army. The flags of freedom fly over all the liberated United Planets."

"Flags?" said one of the soldiers, that Fux person. "I do not remember us having any flags."

"The flags, just like our armour suits," Corporal Clementine answered quickly, "are *perfectly maintained.*"

"Of course, venerable ma'am!" Fux said and winked.

"Shhhh!" said Mister Roseneck.

"*You* shhh!" said one of the young soldiers.

"For this victory," the metallic voice continued, "we join in offering our thanks to our leadership, which has guided and sustained us through the dark days of adversity."

"Hear, hear!" said Fux.

"Yes," said Sergeant Zimmer after a short pause, in which he considered the odds against his being recalibrated following today's events and found them meagre. "Hear, hear!"

The speech from above continued for some time. The

sergeant did not dare interrupt it. Not even when, one by one, the exhausted remaining soldiers of the first company fell asleep in their places.

SHORTLY AFTERWARD, Sergeant Zimmer and Corporal Clementine were summoned to Colonel Havock's cabin for the truly hardest post-combat task. The colonel would have been delighted to inflict it upon the sergeant's head, but this stood contrary to a) Mobile Infantry HQ Standing Orders and b) the colonel's desire to leave no authority whatsoever for anyone other than himself.

The task was given the deliberately vague title Tactical Reassignment Review. Past such *reviews* had had a great impact on the future of the fighting unit and required attendance of all officers and noncoms. Considering this, The Big stood out in his absence.

"Sergeant, Corporal," Havock said, "I've selected the soldiers designated for temporary absentee duty."

Both noncoms nodded. The colonel brought up two mugshots on his desk projection: a frowning Mister Roseneck and a smiling Fux.

"Sir," the corporal said, "may I ask *why* these particular two?"

"They were selected by the political controller," Havock said.

"Isn't this somewhat . . . irregular?" Clementine said. "I mean, the designation of a male—"

"A very proper and correct decision, Corporal," the colonel said. "Also, a perfectly fitting disciplinary action." He pointedly looked at the corporal. "Or perhaps you would like to discuss your concerns with the POO?"

Clementine, determined to avoid ever meeting the chief political officer, had no ready answer for that. The colonel turned his gaze to the sergeant, who had yet to move or utter a word or even breathe. Zimmer, clearly still under the influence of his recent interactions with the colonel, mutely nodded.

"Excellent," said Havock. "We are in complete agreement."

"Sir, with all due respect, I suspect that in this case, the decision, I mean the selection, may have some . . . repercussions."

"Explain yourself, Corporal."

"Sir, it may . . . backfire."

"Are you suggesting, Corporal, that we should avoid proper tactical decisions, not to mention *political* ones," the colonel sneered at the hated word, "due to the feelings and opinions of the simple soldiery?"

"Sir, I'm merely suggesting that there may be better candidates for temporary absentee duty—"

"It is decided, then."

". . . and therefore, in the interest of both morale and the proper order of battle of our battalion, you are hereby returned from temporary absence."

Fux and Mister Roseneck, facing the colonel's desk, looked at each other.

There's no way they'll understand, thought Sergeant

Zimmer, who was standing to the colonel's left, with Corporal Clementine to the right. *Even with the young and susceptible soldiers, it takes effort, and* these *old shrimps . . .*

"I do not remember being absent, honourable sir," said Fux, "but I might be mistaken."

"You two have been absent since I said so," said Havock in what he probably considered to be a soothing manner.

He's getting even for what happened down there, thought Zimmer, who had already heard from the corporal, by way of hints and signs, about the true events of the so-called battle. *Oh, my.*

"We are, of course, happy to comply, sir," said Mister Roseneck. The corporal's tale included Roseneck's near-death-by-friendly-fire experience. The mister's current behaviour showed that he had gained a slightly better grasp of the temperament and mindset of his top commanding officer.

"Good, good," said Havock. "I, therefore, welcome you back into active duty, Private Johnny, R," he pointed at Fux, then turned toward Mister Roseneck, "and Private Daisy, F."

Kids, Sergeant Zimmer thought. *They all die so fast, only to be replaced by other kids. Well, fine, by the elderly and the fools in this particular case, but still . . .*

Fux raised his hand.

Here it comes, the sergeant thought.

"Sir," said Fux, "I would like to point out that Daisy and Johnny are—"

"Heroic names, soldiers," Corporal Clementine said quickly. "Famous names. Names well appreciated by all members of the Mobile Infantry."

"Hear, hear!" said Fux.

That was easy, though Zimmer.

"Therefore, you two will promptly return to your platoon, fully aware of the proud heritage of your very names," the colonel said, now stressing his words with nods toward the dimwitted soldiery, "Johnny F and Daisy R. Do you understand?"

Mister Roseneck seemed to be deep in thought, and Fux was staring at the colonel in an odd way. Did he notice that, along with his name and sex change, he had been promoted to private?

"Well? Answer me!"

Mister Roseneck, aka Daisy, slowly nodded. He seemed confused.

"Sir," said the newly minted Johnny, "I would like to humbly suggest that your honourable offer may put too great a trust in this worthless soldier, sir. I am merely a Fux, sir, and also an idiot, second-class, sir, as confirmed by proper authorities of the city of Praha in the country of—"

"Sergeant! Corporal!" said Havock. "Private Johnny has temporarily lost his marbles, no doubt due to the pressures of combat from which he just returned. Make sure to—"

"I also take issue with this," a new voice declared, and it took the sergeant a moment to realize that it was the up-until-recently subdued, up-until-recently Mister, up-until-recently Roseneck.

Colonel Havock tried to say something, but Daisy née Mister Roseneck wouldn't stop, quickly rising to the level of hysteria.

"I find it insulting to the utmost degree that it is I, the older and senior and infinitely more reliable soldier, sir, not to mention loyal, sir, got the name of the *girl*, sir!"

"Soldier—"

"While this Fux person, who is clearly a treacherous bastard, got an honourable manly name! This is utterly unfair and shows disrespect toward—"

"Are you sure you want to say that a girl is less heroic than a boy, Mister?" said Corporal Clementine.

"It is heroic in a girly way and not in a manly way, which is—"

The colonel rose from his seat to his full unimpressive height. "Be quiet!"

"I completely agree, honourable sir!" said Fux. "He is the senior soldier, and definitely the more reliable. He should get the boy's name, and I should remain as I am, sir. Because I, being an idiot, do not know how to be anyone else, sir."

There's no chance the POO isn't listening on this, thought Sergeant Zimmer. *We are all going to be wiped out.*

"Sergeant, Corporal, restrain the soldiers!"

The two noncoms quickly exchanged glances. Sergeant Zimmer turned toward D Roseneck and Corporal Clementine toward J Fux.

"I will not be a girl, sir!" shouted Daisy Roseneck vehemently as Zimmer caught both her-or-his hands and sharply pulled him-or-her forward and downwards.

"I am also not a girl," said Fux, "but I do not mind being a girl as long as I get to be a Fux."

"Shut up, Fux!" said Clementine, advancing toward him.

"I thank you, honourable ma'am, for keeping with my proper name at this time of—"

"I mean Daisy. I mean Johnny! Quiet!"

Havock climbed up and stood on his desk, holding a gun.

"I will not have this kind of disobedience in the Mobile Infantry!" he shouted. "You are hereby sentenced to—"

An incredibly loud siren broke out. Instinctively, everyone in the room, even the raging Havock, put their hands on their ears. This didn't help much. Everyone sank to their knees. This went on for much longer than necessary.

Eventually, the cabin turned quiet, except for everyone's strenuous breathing.

"I hope that by now I have your attention," said a familiar voice originating in the same hidden speakers that delivered the siren.

I knew it, the sergeant thought. *He* was *listening the entire time.*

Colonel Havock was the first to regain his composure. "Kapust!" he shouted.

"Shut up," said the remote Kapust, clearly enjoying himself, "by order of the captain!"

The room turned awfully quiet awfully quickly.

"That's better," said Kapust. "Colonel Havock, report to POLIDIV at once."

"I'll kill that bastard," mumbled Havock.

"Did you say anything, Colonel?"

"No," the colonel said.

Even he wouldn't dare to mess with the captain, the sergeant thought.

"Are you sure you didn't say anything?"

"I'm sure!" the colonel said. "Don't overdo it, Kapust!"

"I remind you that I'm speaking in the name of—"

"Well, maybe the captain will be interested in what *I* have to say about a certain POO—"

"Just get here, Havock."

Havock grunted, climbed off the desk, pushed Daisy née Roseneck out of his way, and stepped out.

Sergeant Zimmer and Corporal Clementine turned toward each other.

"Well," the sergeant said eventually, "as you were, soldiers. At ease. Get out of here."

And thus was Fux renamed, more or less, or perhaps not at all.

16

FUX IS RESTED

You fight for peace. Your glorious achievements will soon bring it upon us all. It will come any day now. However, we must be vigilant. We must be prepared even for the remote and unlikely possibility that the fight will last forever.

ENDING THE FOREVER WAR, POLIDIV CENTRAL
SPECIAL GUIDANCE, YEAR OF OUR PEACE 317

THE SOMEWHAT-RENAMED soldiers returned to the barracks, where they joined the rest of the remaining troops, with the notable exception of Corporal Clementine and the notable addition of Sergeant Private Bolon. The quartermaster had brought along some wondrous and amazing gifts: a whole side of cured so-called meat, three loaves of bread extract, five red sausages, and a small jar that soon proved to contain real mustard. He was now guarding those treasures against the combined efforts of the rest of the first company.

"At last!" he said upon the couple's entrance and pushed away a young soldier who probably had a name, although no one remembered it.

"How kind of you, Sergeant Private Bolon, sir!" said Fux.

"It is merely my duty," said Bolon. "We are, after all, celebrating the success of our returning heroes, yes?"

He started slicing the bread. The young anonymous soldier tried to grab the loaf from under him. Bolon slapped his hand good-naturedly but with considerable force. The soldier cried and retreated, holding his dislocated wrist.

"I call these 'Victory Sandwiches,'" Bolon said, handing one of his culinary creations to the wounded soldier. The youngster, after some hesitation, grabbed it and quickly retreated to his own hammock, as far from Bolon as possible. He kept eyeing the rest of the food greedily.

"Huh. 'Victory,'" said the old private still known to everyone as Mister Roseneck.

"Glorious victory," Bolon said. He smiled, but sadly. He finished making another sandwich and held it out for the grumpy old soldier to take. "Neither the first nor the last," he added, "on the United Planets' triumphant road to obliterating the treacherous enemy."

"Huh. 'Enemy,'" the old newly private said, nevertheless taking the offered food. Some of the others nodded.

"Stop this foolishness, Roseneck," said Bolon.

"Remember how I told you that the enemy was a metaphorical one so as to obscure the real identity of the oppressed people against which we—"

"No," Bolon said and meaningfully rolled his eyes

upward. "Nor do I wish to."

"Well, almost everyone present at the time is no longer with us," said the former Roseneck.

"Soldier!"

"I was here," said Fux. "I remember your better explanation quite well."

"Oh, right," said Roseneck. "*You.*"

"Though I, too, had a better explanation," said Fux.

"I wish I could forget," said Roseneck. "But now it is clearer than ever that I was right. What we have been through proves my point. The cows—"

"The Buoyant Bovine," remarked the hurt young soldier from his corner.

"Fine," said Roseneck. "But before that, there was the battle with those swine—"

"The Poisonous Pigs."

"I did not ask for your opinion. Anyway, the time before that it was, what, this kind of, well, we did not have a chance to see them, as they were too fast for us. Too fast—"

"The Supersonic Sheep," the young soldier said.

"How do you know? They exploded on touch."

"One of them flew into a tar pit. The blast killed the sergeant right off. He was standing between it and me. Saved my life."

"Sergeant Zimmer? Really?"

"Oh, no, this was a few cycles ago, so it was Sergeant Johnny."

"What a coincidence, I am also a—" said Fux, but Roseneck cut him off.

"My *point*," he said loudly, "is that in all those times, we did not face an actual enemy but instead were attacked by mechanized forms of farm animals. And before that, from what I have heard, all sorts of mechanized . . . mechanisms. We have never seen an actual enemy soldier. What does that say to you?"

"That the enemy must be human, like us," the young soldier said. "They're luring us by making their machines familiar-like. Like, familiar to us."

"When was the last time that anyone here saw an actual live, natural cow?" said Roseneck.

That, to Bolon's surprise, was a rather good point.

"I saw one once," said Fux. "In my city of Praha in the—"

"Not now, Fux," Bolon said. "Please."

"I have another idea," said the young soldier, who was slowly advancing from his corner toward the food in the vain hope that Bolon wouldn't notice. "What if our enemies *are* the alien insects, but they're trying to fool us with what they think is common livestock?"

"Or common mechanisms," said Roseneck acidly.

"Not bad," Bolon said to the young soldier. "Here, you can have another half-sandwich. Just remember not to be too smart for your own good, yes?"

The soldier quickly took the offered parcel and put it in his mouth. He nodded.

"Good lad," Bolon said.

"But *my* point," said Mister Roseneck, "is that there is no actual *alien* enemy. Can't you see?"

"That's enough," Bolon said. "Mister Roseneck, even here in the barracks, you should keep your radical ideas to yourself, yes?"

"Huh," said Roseneck, still looking at the young anonymous soldier. "I am just stating, in favour of the broad education of some of the less experienced among us, that the obvious logical—"

"Mister Roseneck!"

The old man finally, defiantly, turned toward Bolon. "Haven't you heard?" he said. "I am no longer Mister Roseneck, sir. From now on, I am to be called Daisy."

"So *you* are the designated Daisy?" said Bolon, unperturbed. "I should have guessed. Also, I wouldn't make too much of it. It happens all the time, yes?"

"Poor Daisy," said Mister Daisy née Roseneck.

This, too, caused some hesitant nods among the present, for lack of a better word, company.

"And Johnny," someone said. There were some mumbled statements of agreement.

"Indeed," said Mister Daisy. "Poor Johnny."

"That would be me," said Fux.

The mumblings stopped. There was a general air of confusion in the barracks, with the exception of Bolon.

"That is," Fux added, "I think it would be me, or rather I be a Johnny, even though I told them that I suspect that it wouldn't."

"Intolerable," said Mister Daisy. "For shame!"

"I heartily agree, Mister Daisy," said Fux.

"What have you done, Fu . . . Johnny?" said Bolon.

"Well, sir," said Fux, "I pointed out that being a Johnny may be beyond my humble powers, sir."

The morale unit, listening quietly in the corner, decided that the conversation had just reached the required pre-set number of references to fallen comrades, making this a good time to intervene. It beeped, whined a bit, and found the proper song for such an occasion.

"Whatever happened," it sang, "to all the heroes?"

Strangely, this did not gain even its usual disgracefully low amount of attention. It was ignored.

"For shame," said Mister Daisy.

"Indeed," said Fux. "There surely must be someone other than me, someone more fit for being a Johnny."

"All the trooper-oes," the morale unit continued, somewhat louder than before. "They won the batt-*ul*, against the catt-*ul*!"

"I wish Johnny was here. He would be the best person to know who could be him," Fux continued. "Which is what I tried to explain to the honourable colonel."

"He was being an idiot again," said Mister Daisy.

"Certified, second-class, sir."

"Not too bad, not too bad," Bolon said. "Smart, even. And what did they say to that?"

"The honourable colonel was suddenly called to an urgent top-secret discussion at the venerable political headquarters office, sir."

"Whatever happened to the heroes?" sang the morale unit despairingly. It repeated this a few more times, to no one's benefit.

"Nicely done!" Bolon said. "Do you know what this means?"

"That he is a fool that should have been executed," said Mister Daisy bitterly. "Or at least have got the girly name and left me with the manly one."

"It means that your name changes were never finalized, yes?" said Bolon, his smile now genuine. "In all my years here, I've never seen anyone manage that."

"All our heroes win the war," the morale unit sang by

way of a chorus. But its voice noticeably dwindled. "All our heroes evermore," it added, but this time it was only a whisper.

"I was merely stating the obvious," said Fux.

"It is indeed obvious that you are a dangerous buffoon," said Mister maybe-Daisy.

"This dangerous buffoon," said Bolon with a laugh, "seems to me to be quite cunning, rather smart-going, yes?"

"Him?" said Mister Daisy bitterly. "Smart? This idiot?"

"Well," Bolon said, "seems to me that one of you is stuck with an unfitting name, and the other is not. Plus, one of you may have caused the name change to be void, and the other one—not. So, yes, if I had to point at the smarter person, it probably wouldn't be you, *Daisy*."

"Well!" the old private said.

"Just accept it," Bolon said with a smile. "Fux is probably the smartest person around here."

The speaker overhead emitted a rude cough. "Attention, Private Fux," it declared.

"They call him *Fux* again," the young soldier said from his corner. "So Bolon was right; he is smarter than he looks."

Sergeant Private Bolon immediately regretted his hasty words of praise.

"All our heroes, what a bore," the morale unit sang one last time, then turned itself off.

"Attention, Private Fux," the speaker repeated. "You are hereby requested to come to HQ at once."

And thus was Fux, by virtue of loyal friendship, put at risk.

17

FUX IS RECALLED

The commanding officer's most honourable duty is toward their underlings. The commanding officer's most critical duty is toward their superiors.

TO SAIL BEYOND THE SUNSET, A NAVAL
OFFICER'S HANDBOOK

COMMANDER KAPUST, while taking pleasure in Colonel Havock's discomfort, was still rather unhappy. Ensign Berserker's recent forced hospitalization and recalibration were still to be properly reported to High Command. This had to be done in a manner showing Kapust to be both innocent and competent—not a mean political, military, or literary feat. The presence of that miserable Corporal Kraut in the office was a sheer stroke of luck, and recycling him ensured that he would never testify in regard to Berserker or his venerable commanding officer. It also meant that Berserker could avoid recycling and merely get recalibrated. This was good news for Kapust since having one of your own people fully recycled was a serious smear upon one's already-tarnished political record.

Still, the difficulty of writing the report and the fear of its consequences hung like a cloud of ex-wives over Kapust's head. But even that was not as annoying as having to take upon himself the absent Ensign's duties, which he found to be not only incredibly numerous but also utterly unbefitting a dignified, high-ranking officer such as himself. Common among these were humiliating tasks such as dealing with official paperwork, answering communications from other units, plagiarizing encouraging speeches, and, most disgracefully, having to discover all by himself when's lunch.

He also had to listen in on random conversations recorded by the com system, looking for cases of betrayal, disloyalty, espionage, sabotage, and general failure to comply with whatever political line was currently in fashion. It was in this capacity that he had listened in to both the conversation in Colonel Havock's office and later, while waiting in vain for the colonel to appear, the soldiers ranting in the Mobile Infantry barracks.

If all that wasn't enough, and contrary to anything he had ever allowed himself to think, in his heart of hearts, Kapust missed the overzealous ensign who, after all, had *his* heart in the right place. Sort of.

Initially, Commander Kapust was not entirely sure this was the right time to invoke Lieutenant Lipton's strategy or— how horrible!—the secret backup plan suggested afterward by Lieutenant Commander Doctor Nightingale. However, this Fux matter had already proven politically volatile beyond even his wildest fears, and a pre-emptive strike had to be executed before any action by the no-less-volatile Colonel Havock. The innocent praising of Fux by poor Quartermaster Bolon was merely the last straw.

I knew it! Commander Kapust thought. *No one can be such a fool and survive here! It's all an act!*

On the surface of his desk, a timestamp display counted the seconds lazily.

Is he a spy? Kapust thought. *Or maybe just one of those untrustworthy foreigners? Eventually, the empire will have to deal with them, too. There's no room for such people, such* elements, *in proper society.*

Time passed.

Could it be that I'm beginning to think like Berserker? Kapust thought. *Could it be that . . . No! But . . . could it be that he was actually* right?

Eventually, his door, only recently fixed, moaned grudgingly and then slowly, reluctantly opened. In the last stages of this, it was assisted—that is, rudely pushed aside—by Colonel Havock.

"Well, Colonel," Kapust said, momentarily gazing up so as to signify the presence of a higher power. "Thank you for coming here on such *short* notice."

"Commander," said Colonel Havock, who seemed to be in a surprisingly restrained mood. "I am eager to promptly serve and obey our captain in any way I can."

Of course, Kapust thought. "A commendable trait," he said aloud. "I have summoned you here to discuss a certain, ahem, matter in connection with one of your soldiers."

"Oh?" the colonel said. "Who?"

"A person by the name of Fux, Colonel."

Havock gave Kapust a nasty look. "Is this the matter for which the captain issued a direct order, as you've implied?"

"The captain will have been made aware of a certain situation involving—"

"*Will have been made*, Kapust? Do you think I'm stupid?" Colonel Havock accompanied this by a rather good imitation of Kapust's previous upward gaze, conveying a clear understanding that the commander had used the captain's name in vain.

"The captain *will* receive a full report of the—"

"Two can play this game, Kapust, and you know it!"

"I certainly, ahem, have no idea what you may be talking about," said Kapust, trying and failing to avoid a flood of memories related to his last interaction with the colonel.

"I'm sure you do," said Havock with an evil smile. "I'm also sure I wouldn't like to stay here long, so just tell me what you want so that I can refuse and be done with it."

"I would like to suggest," said Commander Kapust, "that the, ahem, soldier, known as Private Fux, immediately end his term with the Mobile Infantry and be transferred back to the Navy without delay." The words "immediately" and "without delay" were the commander's secret weapons, for it was common knowledge that the colonel hated being given a deadline.

For a long moment, Havock just stared at him silently. "Well!" he said eventually. "From you, I expected no less."

"It is strategically imperative that Fux is transferred at once," said Kapust, continuing his onslaught of carefully measured Havock-teasers.

"Strategically imperative," said Havock, strangely unperturbed. "Such big words for such a humble political officer."

This was rather unexpected. The colonel's temper was still, somehow, mild. Cool, even. In light of this, Commander Kapust decided to use his doomsday verbal weapon. "I deem it is in the best interest of the Mobile Infantry," he said.

"*You* deem it," said Havock.

"So I do," said Kapust, staring Havock straight in the eye, an act which, considering each officer's temperament and combat ability or lack thereof, was actually rather brave.

"Well, if you so deem it," said Havock, "then it must be true."

"What?"

"You can have him."

"I say, Havock—"

"Is there anything else you would like to discuss, Kapust?"

"I . . . maybe—"

"Good. Private Fux will be in your office within the hour."

"But—"

"Good day, Kapust. Always a pleasure to serve and obey the captain."

COLONEL HAVOCK WAS ALMOST true to his word. However, instead of the promised hour delay, which Kapust planned to spend with a drink or two and maybe a short nap, only a few minutes passed before the sad creaking of the battle-torn door heralded the arrival of his least-favourite private. This deprived the shaken commander of his pleasurable plans and also of the time necessary to rearrange his thoughts.

"Honourable sir, Private Fux reporting for duty, sir!"

"I can see that," said Kapust gruffly, then spent a long moment staring directly and angrily at the offensive private, hoping in vain to break his insolent spirit. Fux, however, showed no recognition or understanding of the dire political mess which he had caused nor any awareness of the personal danger to himself. Instead, he merely beamed at his superior.

The commander broke first. "Do not think that anyone here is being fooled by your deliberately idiotic manners!" he said.

"No, sir!" said Fux. "I am quite sure, sir, that the only one fooled by that is my very own self, sir!"

"This word trickery will not help your cause one bit," Kapust said, "so you might as well stop it right now and start behaving like, ahem, like a normal person."

"Sir, I solemnly promise you that I will do my best, sir!"

"Good—"

"Also, it has occurred to me, sir, that in doing so, I might be helped by following the example of my superiors, sir."

"Not a bad notion—"

"And who is more superior than your very own honourable self, sir?"

Commander Kapust was as susceptible to flattery as any other senior officer. Still, after a short hesitation, his sharpened political instincts took precedence. *Just imagine,* he thought, *this piece of incorrectness running around and telling everyone that his shameless exploitations are his way of imitating* me.

"Thank you, Private," he said carefully. "This idea definitely has, ahem, some merit." Who knew who might be listening to what transpired in the so-called isolated political headquarters office? *I have no choice,* he thought. *Curse that Nightingale person; she was right.*

"I will find you a more fitting role model," he added.

"I am grateful, sir, even though I have already eaten."

"What?"

"I can save it for later," said Fux helpfully.

"Save what?"

"The roll, sir."

"I don't und—" said Kapust and then shook himself. "Be quiet, Private. No more interruptions."

"If I may ask, " said Fux, "what kind of roll is this model roll, sir? We used to have mushroom rolls and potato rolls, and mushroom-and-potato rolls, and sweet cheese rolls, sometimes with raisins too, and some would make chocolate rolls, even though—"

"Private Fux, shut up right now!"

"Yes, sir!"

"Not a word!"

Fux stood silently and did not answer. He was still smiling, though.

Eventually, we shall wipe that smile off your face, Kapust thought. *But first, let's wipe off someone else's smile.* He snickered, then pressed his thumb to his desk, which immediately beeped in agreement.

"Lieutenant Lipton, Lieutenant Lipton, report immediately to the political headquarters office!"

A long moment passed without any reply. Then a green rectangle appeared near the pressed thumb. Lieutenant Lipton, that smooth subversive slime, had acknowledged.

"That's it," said Commander Kapust, satisfied. "He's coming."

"I thank you, sir," said Fux suddenly. "I have great respect for Lieutenant Lipton, who was kind enough to interview me shortly after I . . ."

"Yes, yes," Kapust said quickly so as to avoid any mention of that sad incident in the airlock, which, having been somehow averted, had no business reappearing again on any ship log. "The lieutenant, your role model, is on his way. Be quiet."

LIEUTENANT LIPTON GAILY entered the political division office, his steps springy, his manner genial, his expression serious but with a hint of a smile. All this disappeared entirely when he noticed Fux. Commander Kapust immensely enjoyed this display. Silently, eye-bulgingly, the lieutenant's face steadily sank. It took him a while to get a hold of himself. Eventually, he faced Kapust and saluted.

"Sir!" he said.

"At ease, Lieutenant," Kapust said and then, just for the pleasure of it, waited.

"Sir?" said Lipton.

"Ahem?"

"I assume I was called here for an urgent reason, sir, considering the wording of the summons."

He's at it again, Kapust thought. *Well, let us see what mister smart-smooth has to say to this.*

"Present is Private Fux, recently released from the Mobile Infantry," he said. This caused some much-desired change to the lieutenant's expression. "He was just reassigned back to the Navy," the commander added, then paused again for effect.

"Yes, sir?"

"Therefore, and having put considerable thought into it," Kapust lied, "I hereby attach Private Fux to you, Lieutenant Lipton, to serve as your very own orderly."

Come to think of it, he thought as the lieutenant's expression promptly turned from slight suspicion into deadly shock, *this plan of Nightingale's is truly genius.* It was evident that Lipton, for once, was lost for words. *She should be watched. Being able to plan something this devious, she may pose a danger to others at some point. To me!*

"Sir!" said Lieutenant Lipton. His manner was clearly desperate. "I urge you to—"

"Venerable Lieutenant, sir!" said Fux. "I am honoured and gratified to the highest degree to be assigned to your noble command, sir!"

"I would like to suggest," said Lieutenant Lipton lamely, "that perhaps other, more productive pursuits could be found for the most industrious Private Fux here. It is well known that the life-support crew, of which I am in charge, has done quite well without the unnecessary burden of additional midshipmen, or—"

"Quite well?" Kapust said. He felt great. Better than ever. "Would you like me to go over the ship logs of recent events related to the life-support systems of this vessel, Lieutenant?"

"With all due—"

"For instance, a certain incident involving, ahem, one of the airlocks?"

"But—"

"How about the recent damage to the Mobile Infantry training ground?"

"But that isn't my jurisdiction; it's Colonel Havock's—"

"Avoiding responsibility, are we?" Kapust said. *I should do this more often,* he thought. *Maybe consulting with that Nightingale person, under strict limitations, of course, is not such a bad idea.*

"Sir!" cried Lipton in distinct, delightful distress. "You know as well as I do that Colonel Havock would never let anyone meddle—"

"That's enough," Commander Kapust said gayly, genially. The last time he had enjoyed himself this much was back in officers' school, where his untiring undermining successfully caused the recalibration of his best mate.

"Sir . . ."

"Lieutenant Lipton, I congratulate you for your, ahem, new command. Private Fux, I trust that you shall bravely and punctually attend to all your, ahem, duties as the lieutenant's orderly."

"I shall do my absolute best, sir!" said Fux. "Although some might say that my best in some matters leaves something to be desired, as my abilities are humble, not to say limited—"

Lieutenant Lipton's body sagged, but he still had some fight in him. "I would still like to offer," he said, "the more efficient option of—"

"—notwithstanding the fact that it is mostly I, Fux, who doubts said abilities, in view of—"

"Get out," Kapust said. By now, he was carelessly but unavoidably smiling. "Both of you. Out."

"But—"

"Out!"

And thus did Fux take another big step on his way to, as some might say, albeit reluctantly, greatness.

PART THREE
THE OUTRAGEOUS ORDERLY

18

FUX IS RECEIVED

Every three officers ranked lieutenant or lower are to share a single single-bunk cabin. Each officer is to be assigned a different shift so that at any given time, only one of them, if any, is in need of sleep. Surplus officers can be temporarily stored in the brig. Surplus cabins can be temporarily used for storing detainees.

TUNNEL IN THE SKY, A LIGHT FRIGATE COMMAND AND MAINTENANCE HANDBOOK

LIEUTENANT LIPTON'S cabin was too small to contain two adult humans, unless the pair huddled in the acceleration bunk. In happier days, that is until a few minutes ago, this had suited its occupant just fine. But now, as if the incredible political risk it entailed wasn't enough, the presence of his newly appointed orderly also threatened to rob Lipton of the privilege of sleeping with whomever he felt like. Or rather, that was the theoretical state of affairs, as it had been quite some time since any other kind of affair had come upon Lipton's door, not to mention bunk. But even sleeping alone without any company, pleasant or unpleasant—one's orderly, for instance—was a priceless commodity aboard the UPS *Spitz*. Once given up, it would be almost impossible to regain.

Lieutenant Lipton, furious, pushed Fux into the cabin and stood just outside, leaving the door open.

"Stay here and do nothing," he said. "And I do mean *nothing*."

"Venerable sir," said Fux, smiling upon his new commanding officer, "I am greatly humbled by your honourable trust. I hereby promise to do your bidding as loyally as I can, given the—"

"You will do absolutely nothing of the sort. That is, absolutely nothing at all. Hear me? Nothing. I'm going out now, and you will stand here doing nothing until I return. Understood?"

"Yes, sir," said Fux and, still smiling, saluted.

"Did I tell you to salute, Fux?" Lipton said. "Did I tell you to smile? Did I tell you to answer me?"

"No, sir. However, being your orderly, I respectfully—"

"Then don't. Stand here till I return."

"Yes, sir."

"And do not talk to anyone. I mean *anyone*. Got it?"

Fux, still smiling, did not answer.

"Good," said Lipton. "You're catching on."

Fux nodded.

Lieutenant Lipton sighed. It was not Fux, after all, who had raised his ire so. No, it was someone else who had caused this calamity, and Lieutenant Lipton had a rather solid guess as to who it might be. Fux, despite his proven record of mischief, was, in this case, an innocent bystander.

Innocent, thought Lipton. *What a strange theoretical concept. Not only for Fux but for all of us.*

"If you need some rest, you can sit on the bed," he said, then shut the door from the outside and left.

THE INSIDES of Navy Refrigeration Unit Mark VIII Number 37 had not improved one bit since Lieutenant Lipton's and Lieutenant Commander Doctor Nightingale's last visit. If anything, it stank even more of certain highly sought-after plant-related products.

"You really must do something about this," said Nightingale, breathing through her mouth.

Lipton, whose mood had seriously deteriorated during the walk from his cabin to the infirmary and then here, put his leg on one of the old polycardboard crates that randomly covered the floor and pointed a finger at the good doctor. It was shaking.

"Why did you do this to me?" he said.

"Did I?" Nightingale said. "I mean, what—"

"Stop it."

"Look—"

"I want to know why. What have I done to you, Nightingale? I thought we were together in this!"

"It would help if you told me what 'this' might be," the doctor said calmly.

"They stuck me with Fux," Lipton said. "With *Fux!*"

"Ah," said Nightingale.

Lieutenant Lipton looked at her with pure hatred and, unable to contain his rage, jumped up and stood on the crate.

"How could you?" he said.

"We did agree that there needs to be another angle from which to attack the problem of Fux," said Nightingale. "A backup plan."

"Pushing him at me? That's your backup plan?"

"Think about it. It's the logical conclusion."

"A logical conclusion," the lieutenant said bitterly. "A *logical* conclusion." His mouth twisted. "How is it any more logical than, for instance, *you* being stuck with Fux?"

"Obviously, since I was the one suggesting it to Kapust, I couldn't seem to have a personal interest in it, that's one," said Nightingale. "Also, I already have my own orderly, so I could not request another one, that's two. Also—"

"Since when is Medical Ensign Grippe your orderly?" said Lipton. He was gradually becoming aware of the awkwardness of his position on the crate but did not want to lose ground.

"In Kapust's eyes, he is. Kapust's opinion is the one that matters here, not yours or mine."

"What matters here is that you put it on me and that you didn't even bother telling me."

"That, too, was dictated by logic," said Nightingale. "You would not have agreed, that's one. Also, were you to know in advance, you might have done something to prevent it, that's two. Also, it was essential that Kapust never suspect that you are a part of this, that's three."

"There could be other solutions!" shouted Lipton,

ignoring an ominous creaking from the crate under his feet. "It didn't have to be *me!*"

"There's no one else who could be trusted with this."

"Flattery, Nightingale? Do you think flattery will get you out of this?"

"No. Just pure logic."

"How convenient," said Lipton. By now, he felt that his position was quite uncomfortable in terms of both pure logic and sheer crateness.

"Look, Lipton, you can throw a wild card out of your hand, but it will surely return, probably at the most inconvenient time. But if you keep it close to your chest—"

"Then *you* keep it close to *your* chest!"

"In a way," said Nightingale, "I am." To make things worse, she winked.

Lipton opened his mouth to answer vehemently and resolutely, applying the sternest logical arguments to expose the fallacy of Nightingale's reckless deductions, and discovered that no such arguments existed. He closed his mouth. There had to be something he could say. But there wasn't.

After a long and embarrassing moment, he stepped off the crate and carelessly sat on it. There was no point in resisting, he realized. The deed was done. And so was the future of a certain hitherto-promising lieutenant. The remainder of his life would be nothing but dark, fearful, lonely existence without joy or love.

At least, considering Fux's previous achievements, this period wouldn't last too long. Neither would Lieutenant Lipton.

"I will never forgive you," he said. "But for now, let's

hear your advice for handling Fux without both of us getting recalibrated. Or worse."

"Your guess is as good as mine."

"So now you're suddenly modest, eh?"

"No," said Nightingale, "just practical. Tell me: what were your first instructions to him?"

"Do absolutely nothing."

"Precisely."

"You can't seriously think that this will work."

"No," said Nightingale. "But it might help. It might also help if you went back to your cabin before he decides to obey your order in his own peculiar way."

"To Space with you, Nightingale."

"It's only logical that you are agitated right now," the good doctor said. "I won't hold this against you." She held out her hand for him to shake.

Lipton almost said that he would definitely hold this against her but then thought better of it. Reluctantly, he shook the offered hand. Nightingale's shake was rather firm.

GETTING out of the refrigerator unit was a great relief. The farther he walked, the more he relaxed.

Maybe the awful smell inside dulled my senses, he thought. *Maybe the situation is not quite that bad, and it's just me getting overexcited.* Alone in the long corridors of the UPS *Spitz,* he found himself reassessing his position. *Alone,* he thought, *everyone so busy with this pointless war, yet I still have time to be alone. What a privilege!*

Lieutenant Lipton's mind was racing in all directions

now. *Yes, the loneliness of command can be troublesome. And the lack of companionship. Oh, who am I kidding? The lack of a companion in my bed. How long has it been? The loneliness . . . if only Commander Aruhu was here. Why did she have to be transferred groundside? She was so beautiful . . . she had such . . . she looked just like . . . if only I could remember her face. Is that Ahuru's face I was just thinking of, or someone else's? Maybe Nightingale's? No, she doesn't belong here. She's just a doctor, albeit a beautiful one. But Aruhu, my lost love . . .*

A tear sneaked down his cheek, but Lipton was too engaged with his romanticized, mangled memories to notice.

But then, his mind continued, *but so, who else of my rank enjoys such a privilege? Who else has a bed all to themselves? Oh, fine, maybe Nightingale does, but I would rather, I mean, she's good-looking and everything, but honestly, she frightens the Space out of me.*

This rare admission of his innermost feelings took Lipton by surprise, but his mind rolled on, giving him no time to reflect upon this. *If she has a bed to herself, I will have a bed to myself,* he thought. *She won't share her bed with me, I won't share a bed with her, and I absolutely refuse to share a bed with Fux.*

Here he felt his spirit, despite the miserable situation, rising up. *I won't give up,* he thought. *There is a solution. There must be. And I will find it. And if I don't, Fux will find it for me.*

By the time he got back to his cabin and opened its door, he was—if only the good Doctor Nightingale could see it—smiling. Inside, on the lieutenant's bunk, lay the curled form of his new orderly, sleeping peacefully, emitting no more than the gentlest of snores.

Poor lad, thought Lipton. *He's been through a lot. Maybe not as much as I have, but still.* He pushed Fux gently toward the wall, then lay beside him on the meagre free space left on the bunk and closed his eyes.

Yes, he thought. *We will find a solution. Nightingale was right. Sort of. It's going to be fine. Just fine.*

Slowly, calmly, he fell asleep.

Only later did the strangely satisfied Lieutenant Lipton discover the pockmark on his right palm. The good doctor's handshake bore with it a hypersonic needle full of sedatives.

"HERE'S what we're going to do," Lipton said.

Fux nodded and smiled. He has been nodding and smiling a lot since waking up, a time that Lipton spent switching between awkward silence and screams of politically correct curse words aimed at the grossly over-cunning doctor, *may Space take her and her frigging medicines!*

"First order of things," the lieutenant continued. His voice was rather hoarse due to excessive shouting. He fleetingly considered treating this at the infirmary, then remembered who had caused his condition in the first place. Fux nodded again, and Lipton realized that he had stopped talking in the middle of a sentence.

"First order of things, then," he said, "is for you to go and find yourself a place to sleep that is not my cabin."

"I do find our cabin rather agreeable," Fux said. "Once,

back in the city of Praha, I had to share lodging with a couple of horses, and—"

"Be quiet. And it's not *our* cabin; it's *my* cabin. Make sure to remember that and behave accordingly."

"Sir?"

"You will find lodging upon this ship which is—pay attention, Fux!—which is, one, not my cabin, two, not the Mobile Infantry barracks, and three, unrelated to any of my equivalent officers. Do you understand?"

"Yes, honourable sir. It is just that in order to serve you best, it would be best if I were nearby at all times."

Lipton shuddered at the thought. "You will do no such thing," he said. "I don't care if you find lodging with the engine crew if they let you. Or," he smiled, "you could try the infirmary."

That will show her, he thought. And then, *no, I bet that she has a plan in place for this kind of thing. The bastard.*

"Do not worry, sir," said Fux. "I shall take care of that, have no fear. What is the second?"

"What second?" said Lipton, whose powers of concentration were still diminished due to recent unintended intoxications, not to mention a growing post-sedative headache.

"You said 'first order of things,' sir," said Fux, "so I assume there is a second order of things to follow the first order of things, sir, and maybe even a third order of things after that."

"Don't get smart with me, Fux!" Lipton shouted and promptly regretted it. His head was throbbing. "Now, get out of here and don't return until you've found a place for yourself!"

"Yes, sir!" said Fux, turned smartly about, and walked out.

I'm sure I could have handled that better, thought Lipton. *Though I'll be damned if I know how.*

And thus was Fux, under the strictest of warnings, released to do as he pleased.

19

FUX IS ACCLIMATED

That old proverb, "An army marches on its stomach,"
is obviously a defeatist lie.

NAVAL MAINTENANCE AND SUPPLY GUIDE,
POLIDIV CENTRAL

IT DID NOT TAKE LONG for the news concerning Fux's
reassignment to percolate down to the rank and file. It may
have originated in a careless remark by Lieutenant Lipton at
the Officer's Mess or a passing comment by the strangely
smug Commander Kapust. It may have even been Doctor
Nightingale and her machinations. In any case, word got
down to the petty officers, then to the midshipmen and the
ensigns, then to the remains of the 91st Battalion.

Meanwhile, in the armoury, the tormented Sergeant
Private Bolon was having a rather miserable time imagining
all the horrors that might have befallen his best friend, the

consequence of his, the quartermaster's, carelessness comments. "Cunning and smart-going," he mumbled to himself over and over. "What was I thinking? It would have been better if I had just hit him with a hammer straight in the head!"

Eventually, though, carried by a cook of the First Company who wondered why no utensils had been supplied for more than forty-eight hours, the reprieving rumour found its way to the quartermaster. And thus it was that, shortly afterward, a rather jolly yet slightly shameful Bolon greeted Fux upon his arrival at the armoury.

"I really cannot tell you how happy I am to see you," he said and gave Fux a short, awkward hug. "Please accept my apologies. I did not mean to put you in any danger."

"I am also happy to see you, sir," said Fux. "It was very kind of you to talk about me the way you did. I was never called 'cunning' before."

"Enough with the 'sir,' Fux, we're friends," said Bolon, who was still not sure whether Fux was carefully reproaching him or feeling genuinely flattered.

No matter: he had a plan in place to win back the heart of his friend. "To show my sincere regret and appreciation," he said, "I've prepared something for you."

He turned and fondled a small device, no larger than a medium-sized shoe, that squatted on his desk.

"I appreciate you too, Sergeant Private, sir," said Fux. "What do you have there?"

"A field oven," said Bolon. The device, an illegal piece of equipment predating the invention of the nutritomat machine, sported two short stubs on opposite sides. They were gently vibrating. "It will be ready in a moment or two. And then we can celebrate!"

"The oven will be ready?"

Bolon smiled. He was already used to Fux's turns of the tongue. "The *dish* will be ready," he said. "It's something special."

The machine beeped. The stubs stopped vibrating. Something clicked.

"Yes!" said Bolon. "Here it comes!" He opened a cupboard, took out two spoons, turned again toward the oven and, using the short stubs as handles, lifted it up. This uncovered its contents: a transparent jar filled with some grey-green material. Bolon smiled. "Here!" he said. "Your meal is ready, Mister Fux!"

"Private Fux, sir."

"Not anymore," said Bolon. "A naval orderly is always a Mister. It is almost as if he is not a soldier at all."

"I'm not sure I like that, sir," said Fux.

"Bolon, Fux. Bolon. Especially now that you've been assigned to your new position." He pointed at the jar. "Anyway," he added, "*this* you are going to like."

"What is it, sir?" Fux said. He sniffed.

"It is—" Bolon paused, savouring the moment — "a whole jar of liver pate!"

"Sir!" Fux said. "That is, Bolon! I am . . . I have not had liver pate since . . . I am greatly honoured, Sir Bolon!"

"I have to warn you, though," said Bolon, "that it's mostly eggplant."

"Ah," Fux said. His face fell. "Well, in this case, sir—"

"Still, it's the special stuff," Bolon said quickly. "It's what they give the officers when the admiral is visiting, to show

how well we take care of our own even in times of great danger."

Fux stared at him, slowly looked up to indicate one of the overhead cams, then turned his gaze back to the quartermaster. Bolon smirked.

"In repair," he said. "Some corrosive substance is eating the transmitters. I wish I knew what it was." This was true: the industrious quartermaster indeed wished he knew the exact ingredients of the corrosive goo he'd found in an old container somewhere in deep storage so that he could duplicate it and mess with more than merely his own local logcam. "Anyway," he added, "here it is." He held a spoon to Fux. "Dig in. You're going to love it."

"If that is your command, sir," said Fux, reluctantly taking the spoon, "I shall do my best to obey it with utmost—"

"Enough," Bolon said. "Oh, and before I forget, I also brought us something to complement the liver pate."

He pulled the cover off one of the surrounding armour suits and took something from under it. Proudly, he presented it to Fux. It was a full bottle of excellent Bohemian brandy.

"Ah!" said Fux. "Now I perfectly understand your meaning, Bolon!"

THE MAIN INGREDIENT of the liver pate was indeed synthetic eggplant powder. This, however, did not prevent the meal from being jolly in the extreme. So jolly, in fact, that halfway through the jar, not to mention the bottle of excellent Bohemian brandy, Bolon and Fux had already cemented their eternal friendship in no mean terms, and toward its end, they had decided to share all their possessions in this world, including Fux's precious blue Bohemia IV police-officer cap and Bolon's entire collection of faulty armour suits. Furthermore, they agreed that they would share the armoury as their sleeping quarters from now on.

"There's plenty of space here," mumbled Bolon drunkenly. "I'm sure no one would mind."

Fux nodded in agreement. Or so, at least, it seemed to Bolon. For, after they had finished that bottle of excellent Bohemian brandy, the quartermaster was hardly conscious, and the new naval orderly was, and had been for some time, fast asleep.

DESPITE SOME HALF-HEARTED regulations on the matter, unauthorized entry into the Mobile Infantry barracks was rather easy. No one in High Command had ever considered the possibility of anyone going there of their own free will. In this, it stood as a stark opposite to some other locations under the scrutiny of High Command, such as the armoury, the infirmary, and, most importantly, the kitchen. Therefore, when Corporal Clementine returned to the barracks from the First Company's compulsory morning-shift practice, she was only mildly surprised to find Fux waiting for her.

"Welcome, Mister Fux," she said, her smile belying the formality of her greeting. "Congratulations on your new position. How may I help you?"

"Hello, Corporal Ma'am Sir!" Fux said. "I just came to say goodbye."

"Goodbye to you too, Fux. It's been . . . interesting. Educational, even, I might add. I wish you luck in your new position. It seems to be a very satisfying . . . solution."

"Indeed it is, even though—"

The barrack's main hatch groaned mightily, creaked, then opened, admitting a small group of soldiers led by a familiar figure.

"You!" the familiar figure said.

Fux beamed. "Hello, Daisy!" he said.

"What are you doing here? Corporal, what is he doing here? He shouldn't be here! He should—"

"I came to say goodbye," Fux said.

"Ah," said Mister Daisy. "Goodbye. Yes. That is a fine sentiment. Absolutely. Goodbye, then!"

"Although, come to think of it," Fux added, "it is not a true goodbye, not really, since, in fact, I will not be very far away."

"A goodbye that's not a goodbye," Clementine said. "Of course."

"What blabbery is that?" asked Mister Daisy. "Is it a goodbye, or is it not a goodbye? It had better be a goodbye, a proper and pleasant and final, yes, absolutely final, goodbye."

"Yes," said Fux. "Very final, Daisy."

"Stop calling me Dai . . . never mind. Yes. Goodbye, Fux."

"Even though my new place of residence is not too far. Actually, I may see you from time to time, which makes me happy."

"But I thought you were Lieutenant Lipton's orderly?" said Corporal Clementine. "Isn't that so?"

"Indeed, sir ma'am, for which reason I will be sharing a cabin with my good friend Sergeant Private Bolon."

"What?" said Mister Daisy.

"The quartermaster?" Clementine said. "How did you manage to pull *that* off?"

"The armoury?" said Mister Daisy. "We have to share this stinking crummy place while you and your friend enjoy the whole armoury to yourselves?"

"That is a very correct and fair description," said Fux. "I could not have said it better myself."

Mister Daisy's face took a rather red tint. "You're doing this on purpose!" he shouted. "I'm going to kill you, you insolent—"

"Pipe down, Roseneck," Clementine said. She deliberately used the soldier's previous name. This had the desired effect, as it promptly muted Mister Name-in-Dispute. "Fine, Fux," the corporal added, "that's enough goodbyes for now. I'm sure we'll see more of each other."

"Certainly, ma'am sir," Fux said. "And if you need my help, you know where to find me."

"Your help," said old Mister Whatever. "As if."

"We shall definitely visit the armoury whenever help is needed," Clementine said. This, of course, meant nothing.

"Considering the future, sir ma'am, I would recommend it."

This remark was entirely too lucid for Clementine's taste. *The future,* she thought. *In which we fight and die, again and again, until no one remains.*

Or until we do something about it.

Which is basically what he's saying.

"Yes," she said. "Absolutely." She forced herself not to smile. "Though, of course," she added as gravely as possible, "as you know, the armour suits—"

"Are perfectly maintained," said Fux. He smiled, waved goodbye in a rather unmilitary fashion, turned around smartly, and left.

Clementine sighed. "Now, as for you, Roseneck—"

THE TIME that had passed since sending Fux on his way had been somewhat unkind to Lieutenant Lipton. At first, he attempted to distract himself by writing a long and fictional report describing the excellent condition of each and every naval team upon the good *UPS Spitz*, but his heart was not in it. He then tried to clear his mind by filling out all the urgent regulation forms that he had been famous for delegating to anyone of a lower rank than himself. This, for some reason, reminded him of the absent Ensign Berserker and thus effectively demolished his concentration.

Eventually, he decided to sleep and to his own surprise, succeeded, only to be shaken awake by the captain herself, who dragged him to the interrogation room, already occupied by his new orderly, accused both of them of high treason in general and the recent implosion of Commander Kapust in particular, and, having found them guilty as charged on all counts, promptly threw both of them out of the nearest airlock.

The cold vacuum of space turned out to be cold sweat as he woke up in his bunk. For a long moment, he could not shake the feeling that he was still in the void, his blood boiling and his body on the verge of exploding. This delicate state of mind was not improved in the slightest when the cabin's door opened, revealing Fux.

"You!" said Lipton, who was not fully awake yet. "You . . . the captain and you . . . the captain . . . you!"

"Yes, sir," Fux answered. "I would like to comment, however, that I have not yet had the honour of meeting our esteemed top commander, which, of course, I would be quite happy to do, though I am sure she is quite busy and may not have the time for such social calls."

"What? Who?" Lipton slowly started grasping that something was awfully wrong.

"The captain, sir."

This utterance, in a matter of seconds, magically transformed the lieutenant from half-drowsiness into full alertness.

"Mister Fux!" he said. "Is this any way for an orderly to stand? Is this any way for a Navy man of any rank to behave?"

"I was merely checking on you, sir," said Fux, in a tone as close to hurt as one could attribute to him. "You seemed to be doing fine until you mentioned the captain."

"I did not!" Lipton said and jumped out of his bed, unintentionally pushing Fux out through the door and into the corridor. "I absolutely did not mention the ca . . . the . . . I did nothing of the sort, not are you to imply that I have ever done anything of the sort, nor will you do anything of the sort, nor any other sort of thing, or I will make sure that you are . . . sorted out!"

"Yes, sir," said Fux solemnly. "I promise not to do this

sort of thing, or any other sort of thing, in the future or in the past, sir."

Lipton inhaled and exhaled a few times, then shook his head. "Good," he said eventually. "And make sure never to mention . . . you-know-who."

"Yes, sir. The captain."

Lipton felt his heart momentarily stop in his chest. If the political controller received and processed this conversation correctly, he would be as good as dead.

He stepped outside and joined Fux in the corridor. "Get in there," he said, pointing at his own bed.

"Sir?"

"Get there, close the door, go to sleep, or remain quiet until I return."

"But, sir, I have found myself a proper accommodation."

"I don't care, just . . . oh?"

Fux nodded. "Yes, sir," he said. "I will be sleeping with Quartermaster Bolon in the armoury."

Lipton felt his mind spinning. The armoury! He might be saved, after all!

"Well done, Fux," he said.

If the controller raises the alert on me, I can always say that Fux's behaviour is a result of the undisciplined manner of the quartermaster, he thought. *Who belongs to the Mobile Infantry. Great!*

"I am proud to have caused you satisfaction, sir," Fux said.

"Yes," Lipton said. "Satisfaction. Right. Now get out of here, and stay in your new dwelling until further notice."

And thus was Fux, to the envy of every soldier who ever lived, left to his own devices.

20

FUX IS ESTABLISHED

There's nothing more dangerous than bored personnel with access to specialized equipment. Keep your soldiers busy, no matter what. Put them through as many drills as possible, yet avoid exhausting them completely. When rest is absolutely required, let them maintain their equipment. While they're forbidden from the deep technical knowledge required for any serious work, simple tasks such as cleaning and shining are acceptable and highly recommended.

DOUBLE STAR, A MOBILE INFANTRY OFFICER'S
HANDBOOK

THERE CAME AGAIN one of those brief periods of deceptive relaxation, common to most wars, fondly remembered despite their insignificance in comparison to whatever came before and, especially, afterward.

For a few shifts in the cramped officers' mess, Lieutenant Lipton calmly endured his colleagues' jabs in regard to his new orderly. This eventually subsided, replaced by the usual thinly veiled gossip regarding who had slept with whom and what influence this had on their chances of promotion or, in some cases, survival. Lipton spent the rest of his time in the usual manner, faking reports so as to preserve an all-is-as-usual stance with Top Command, in the same way that Top Command itself presented all matters to whoever was even more, well, Top. This kind of behaviour was in no way unique to the lieutenant, although it was agreed by many that he was exceptionally good at it. Furthermore, to make a show of employing his new orderly, he called the armoury and requested the presence of Fux in his cabin at the next morning shift at exactly nine of the clock.

"Mister Fux," said Lieutenant Lipton when this had eventually transpired, at exactly nine thirty-five of the clock, "from now on, you shall report to my cabin every morning shift at exactly *nine oh-hundred* of the clock to receive your daily orders. Do you understand?"

"Yes, honourable sir!" said Fux. "I shall endeavour to be my usual punctual self, sir!"

"Get out of here," said Lipton, who could feel that pursuing the matter of punctuality would result in nothing but a headache. "Return tomorrow as ordered."

"Mister Fux," said Lieutenant Lipton at their second such meeting, which had occurred at exactly nine twenty-seven of the clock, and thus was considered by him to be a step in the right direction, "have you anything to report?"

"Yes, sir," said Fux. "I dutifully report that my friend, the honourable Sergeant Private Bolon, had a bad stomach this morning owing to eating too many of those sausages we got on loan from the Infantry noncom kitchen."

"Your *friend*," said Lipton bitterly. As of late, he had felt that, as far as he was concerned, friends were somewhat of an endangered species. In particular, some so-called friends turned out to be undeserving of the name. A certain Lieutenant Commander Doctor came to mind.

"Mister Fux," said Lieutenant Lipton at their third morning meeting, "how is your dear friend Bolon doing?"

"Oh, much better, sir; thank you for asking! Between you and me, I think it has a lot to do with the attention of that nice cook, Corporal Fenny. She and Bolon get along famously . . . well, not so famously because it is a secret, and no one should know about it, even you, though, of course, you are my commanding officer, and therefore I have no secrets from you, but still, it is a secret, so maybe not famously at all, if you get my meaning, sir." To ensure the proper delivery of said meaning, Fux winked in a somewhat disturbing manner.

"Famously," said Lipton bitterly. Discussing matters of the heart, or at least the bedsheets, was still painful to him. *Oh, Commander Aruhu, where have you gone?*

"Mister Fux," said Lieutenant Lipton at their fifth morning meeting, "the burden of command is a lonely one. You don't realize how lucky you are, Fux, having your friends, having a place where you're accepted, no great decisions to make—"

"Loneliness," said Lieutenant Lipton at their seventh morning meeting, "can crush your heart, Fux. To have loved and lost, Fux, do you know what this means?"

"I may have heard about it, sir," said Fux, and Lipton

noticed a certain hesitation in his manner, as if he wasn't sure that this subject of conversation was allowed.

"Don't worry," said Lipton. "As long as you're not doing anything strictly forbidden, matters of the heart are safe to discuss." That was indeed the case. Otherwise, as High Command had realized the hard way years ago, there would have been no one left to run the ship. Or to fight. Or to do anything at all.

"I am honoured by your trust, sir," said Fux.

Lipton nodded.

"Have you ever seen a woman so beautiful that your heart just stopped in its tracks?" said Lieutenant Lipton at their ninth morning meeting. "And then lost her in the most unjust way possible? Has this ever happened to you, Fux?"

"Sir, I would not say so, sir. But you tell that story of yours so passionately that I would not mind listening to it again, sir."

And so it continued in a very tranquil and easygoing fashion. Barring the occasional burst of an unrelated story from the city of Praha, Fux turned out to be a good listener. Lieutenant Lipton, to his surprise, enjoyed the morning sessions so much that he even considered, briefly, apologizing to Nightingale.

MEANWHILE, the good doctor enjoyed a few more pleasurable visits by Engine Master Chief Maguro, none of which were interrupted. When in the infirmary, she spent a considerable amount of time fighting and cajoling the new main controller into at least a semblance of the behaviour of the old one. This required fending off all inquiries by her patients, whom she was quicker than usual to release, and by Medical Ensign Grippe, who came dangerously close to being released, too, though in a slightly different manner, probably involving an airlock.

This surge of brisk recuperation and forced health resulted in the prompt and surprising recovery of the infirmary's most frequent visitor, Second Lieutenant Big, who was quickly sent back to the First Company. Soon, the only remaining patient to distract her from the controller was the current occupant of the recalibration bin. He was pushed from the correctional closet into the infirmary after receiving about twelve times the recommended dosage, with standing orders to keep him there until further notice, which never came.

Therefore, in an act of kindness, Nightingale took Ensign Berserker out of the bin, put him into full cryogenic sleep, and stowed him in the infirmary's medicine cold storage under the floor. Her calculations showed that she might get into trouble for this, but not as much as for any of the other options.

THE ABSENCE of said patient had left the political division embodied entirely by Commander Kapust, who spent that time concentrating on ways and means of procuring another underling so as to free himself from performing duties that he found distasteful, e.g., all duties whatsoever. The political controller's periodic report kept showing nothing more than the usual murmurs of dissatisfaction among the troops, never crossing the level of direct interference. Kapust was vaguely aware that the replacement controller was not all it was supposed to be and that, therefore, its reports were probably created by that horrible Nightingale person or perhaps even an underling. He had absolutely no idea what such a situation called for and therefore decided to ignore it. In the meanwhile, he treated the reports as if they were the true work of a well-functioning machine, and their regularity and normality in this time of war made him alternately quite happy and rather suspicious.

DOWN IN THE BARRACKS, the First Platoon and Company et cetera was practicing daily, having meanwhile gained a few new draftees taken—or, as some called it, kidnapped—from the Navy by the ever-forceful Colonel Havock. These new pre-privates made Sergeant Zimmer a happy man. Their bad soldiery and reluctance for action were exactly his cup of tea, or rather his sea of creatures, whose names he gleefully bestowed upon the heads of deserving and undeserving alike.

It never occurred to the sergeant that at least some of his subjects were not entirely truthful when demonstrating their abilities. A series of seemingly random absences, explained only as unnecessary visits to the uniform dispenser or the kitchen, did not make the sergeant suspicious in the least. Even when, one by one, each of his flock disappeared for a shift at a time, the sergeant was still content and unconcerned.

A new zero-grav shift and FTL hoop crossing created

new opportunities for gambling and practical jokes among the common soldiery. When gravity returned, there were numerous uneducated guesses as to where they were going next. This behaviour, Sergeant Zimmer knew, was perfectly normal. Everything was as it should be.

IN THE ARMOURY, unbeknownst to anyone but themselves and the loyal Sergeant Private Bolon, Mister Fux started accepting visitors. This, for some reason, occurred every first shift at exactly ten of the clock. The political logs claimed that it was nothing but a surge of eagerness on the visitors' part to better maintain their equipment. No alarms were raised.

A less evident aspect of this was the sudden popularity of certain working tools among the troops, anything from the most advanced memory burners and carbon shapers to the primitive ancient screw-inducers and laser cutters. Vast amounts of moleglue were procured by mysterious means, and the secrets of their proper usage spread by whispers and rumours, and sometimes by smell alone.

The Infantry barracks started resembling a giant workshop. When the officially recuperated Second Lieutenant Big returned there, even he noticed the unusual activity. His half-hearted question on the matter was cunningly answered by Corporal Clementine, who had spent a considerable amount of time preparing for just such an inquiry. In essence, she explained, the soldiers greatly dreaded and respected their commanding officers and had therefore decided to make an extra effort, and that was as far as she got before The Big turned away and entered his cabin and closed the hatch.

No other officer upon the UPS *Spitz* noticed the slightest of discrepancies. This was partly because anyone who could afford to ignore the barracks did so rather industriously and mostly due to the machinations of Sergeant Private Bolon. The quartermaster had converted a part of the armoury into an improvised garage in which more and more armour suits were treated in ways that were forbidden by their manufacturers or the captain, or both. Another section was dedicated to suit operation practice. As this was potentially quite dangerous, the cunning sergeant found the perfect place for it: the quadruple-fortified bomb storage hall. The bombs themselves, he argued, were absolutely safe as long as one didn't arm them. Fux, innocently enough, inquired how this was done, just so that he would make sure to avoid it. In all the days of their friendship, this was the one thing Bolon had refused his comrade. It was probably the right thing to do.

All this was keenly watched by the armoury's single logcam, which happened to be strangely yet conveniently dead.

The soldiery activity surge was not limited to the areas designated for the Mobile Infantry. All across the ship, small pieces of equipment went missing. The closest that anyone got to noticing was Lieutenant Commander Doctor Nightingale, who caught an unfamiliar soldier attempting to pry a part of the infirmary's backup power unit out of a nearby wall. Upon seeing her, the culprit fled. Initially, she was of a mind to take this up with someone in the Mobile Infantry, but then thought better of it, in view of the identity of whomever that someone might be. Instead, she instructed

Medical Ensign Grippe to install another logcam outside the infirmary. This task had the combined advantages of fitting the ensign's abilities, that's one, and relieving Nightingale of the burden of his company, that's two, and for once in her life she could not think of a third reason and therefore got back to the controller and quietly forgot about the whole thing.

ALL IN ALL, it was a time in which everyone of note was, as much as such a thing is possible in such places and times, happy, or at least not too disgruntled. Alas, just like a sunny day on an innocent planet soon to be approached by the imperial fleet, the period of calm was not destined to last.

The planet they were approaching, though, was not innocent. At least, not officially so. Launch pods were prepared, armour suits shined, and lengthy speeches conceived, forcefully delivered, and mostly ignored by their recipients. Even the rebellious Mister Daisy had learned that his efforts to enlighten his superiors always ended the same way, i.e. himself running around the parade ground to everyone else's delight.

No one in the barracks, on the parade grounds, and eventually inside the launch pods made even the slightest mention of Fux. But in the minds of most, he was never absent.

And thus it was that, in the chain of highly irregular occurrences shortly to come, Fux took a large part almost entirely, to use a forbidden expression, in spirit rather than in body.

21

FUX IS NOTED

All complex machinery used by the Navy is specifi-
cally designed in a distributed way so as not to give
any one person access to all its components. This is
most prominent in the case of spacefaring vessels,
where propulsion, navigation, and life-support
systems typically consist of numerous sub-systems and
energy sources scattered and spread over as large an
area as possible. This ensures no unauthorized action
can take place without disrupting several system
components and raising various alarms.

Furthermore, to keep vessels ideologically safe, the
sole authority for structural modifications is given to
neither the captain nor the chief engineer: it safely lies
in the hands of the political officer.

TUNNEL IN THE SKY, *A LIGHT FRIGATE*
COMMAND AND MAINTENANCE HANDBOOK

THE FIRST INCIDENT caused by Fux in his absence did not take place inside the *UPS Spitz*. Instead, it transpired upon the surface of yet another nameless planetary body and came to pass courtesy of the First Company of the Mobile Infantry.

The launch pod, still sizzling from its forced entry through the atmosphere, was immediately attacked by weird flying creatures emitting projectiles and radiation beams. So far, this was nothing out of the ordinary. Then the pod's officer's nook opened, emitting Colonel Havock and Second Lieutenant Big at high velocity. Both took on the attacking flyers, using the heavy weaponry included in their suits. This was slightly more efficient than usual, but nothing worthy of special attention when later committed to regimental histories.

What happened next, however, was a first of its kind, as far as anyone remembered. The First Company marched quickly out of the pod, took positions behind it and, by way of the perfectly maintained armour suits, released a coordinated fire strike. This resulted in the prompt decimation of more than half of the floating enemy.

On the common com channel, a happy voice strangely reminiscent of Corporal Clementine's shouted, "Up and up!"

The entire company obeyed, jumping up in the air and taking aim at the remaining flyers, which, up close, looked like deformed deflated birds.

"Fire!" the joyful Clementine shouted. Eight heavy-duty grenade launchers and ten energy weapons sang in response.

A moment later, the sky was empty of flyers. Unless, that is, one counts the hovering armour suits.

The successful execution, despite following the exact battle plan devised by Corporal Clementine, surprised everyone involved, including herself. This, however, was dwarfed by Colonel Havock's astonishment, a heartfelt annoyance which soon transformed into rage. Shortly after returning to the ship, he made a point of expressing his feelings to the entire, strangely unharmed, body of soldiers. Addressing the troops in his usual fierce manner, he stressed the importance of using weaponry only by a superior officer's command, then vehemently delved into the sins of unauthorized battle plans. Between the lines, by way of fire-breathing tantrum, his actual meaning became clear: where the Space did you people get operational armour suits? And why the Space did nobody tell me? And battles should never end without casualties; otherwise, what's the point? Where's the sport in that? And who the Space gave you permission to deprive me of my well-deserved fun time behind enemy lines?

He would have continued in this vein for quite some time were it not for an interruption by the powers above, namely Commander Kapust. The political officer spent the duration of the combat making sure that the parade grounds ceiling speakers were both fixed and mightily fortified. Now he made gleeful use of those wise preparations by delivering one of his usual victory speeches with the volume control set to maximum. Colonel Havock, initially shocked to hear the speakers he had so deliberately destroyed, soon made an honest attempt at re-demolishing them, only to discover that energy weapons had no effect whatsoever and that, having

used his entire supply on the planet's surface, he was totally
out of projectiles.

THE SECOND INCIDENT caused by Fux in his absence,
much like and in direct relation to the newly operative
armour suits, had to do with propulsion. While not as satisfying as the former to some, in the long run it helped spread
Fux's name and influence far beyond his regular circle of
acquaintance.

The UPS *Spitz* did not have an engine room. While it
definitely, according to the laws of both state and physics,
had an engine, that vital part was designed to be as inacces-
sible as possible. It was cast into a solid sphere of some super-
hard polymer, which itself hung in the middle of a graphene
spider web inside a hollow, fortified space that consisted of
the entire rear quarter of the ship, sealed with a combination
of tough materials not only totally impenetrable› but also a
tightly kept state secret. The only opening was for the main
power supply shaft, which itself was similarly sealed and
protected up to the very point it split into about a dozen
immense cables, each, in turn, splitting into numerous thick
tubes transferring power from wherever it was stored. The
whole apparatus was remotely controlled, and even the
control units were cast in tough security boxes, just in case.

The goal of this heartwarming arrangement was the
complete prevention of anyone from tampering with the
engine or even studying its work. The only way to fix the
thing was total deconstruction and overhaul in a naval dockyard, Class A. This, as everybody knew, was a far-fetched

scenario, especially in comparison with likelier incidents, e.g., the ship being lost along with its entire crew. And so the engine, just like the captain, God, and history, in that order, became one of those subjects which one did not discuss if one knew what was good for one's health and status and everything else.

It was for this reason that almost no one dared to comment when, shortly after the great and unexpected planetary victory, and right upon the navigation crew setting a new course and remotely ordering the sealed engine to execute it, absolutely nothing happened. The ship failed to move. Gravity failed to return. Instead of accelerating the ship in its quest toward a new top-secret and hopefully unsuspecting target, the mighty engine of the UPS *Spitz* was wrapped in ominous silence.

All over the ship, soldiers clung to whatever half-official explanations were delivered by their officers and also to whatever zero-grav equipment they could find. The best items were magnetic boots, which were in demand despite the general lack of metal in the ship's structure, pulleys and wires, and, most desirable of all, self-sealing bunk covers, allowing one to sleep without floating away due to stray air currents or one's humour-prone colleagues.

The only people who could not avoid discussing the situation, at least to some degree, were those of the engine crew, headed by Engine Master Chief Maguro. Gathered in the telemetry chamber, an emergency title given hastily to Chief Maguro's personal cabin and, due to its insufficient size, also to a part of the corridor outside it, they spent a whole shift performing confused and frantic tests.

The engine-error telemetry insisted that there were no

engine errors. Nor could they find any other kind of error. All their efforts proved beyond any shadow of a doubt that the engine was in perfect working condition, its power transmission was in perfect working condition, its power units were in perfect working condition, and the engine crew was in perfect working condition, except for slowly but surely losing their minds to perfect mortal fear. There was no need to explain to them that this kind of failure was militarily and politically impossible, and therefore its occurrence meant, for everyone involved, either recalibration or recycling or, if tortured memory served some of the more veteran crew members right, plain ejection out of the nearest airlock.

"I don't care how, I don't care why, I don't care who, I don't care nothing, we are going to solve this thing," said Engine Master Chief Maguro, surrounded by green system graphs depicting a perfectly operational propulsion infrastructure. At first he was confident, then confused, then despairing.

Eventually, this led to the solution, though not in a way the master chief would have imagined.

"Sir," said his most junior crew member, a spaceman apprentice named Aubergine, leaning in from his place in the corridor through the narrow cabin door. "In regards to 'who,' sir—"

"Yes?"

"It might sound silly to you, sir—"

"Spit it out, Aubergine. Right now, there's nothing that I wouldn't try."

"Sir," the apprentice said, "as you may know, when I first came aboard I was assigned to the Mobile Infantry. But shortly afterward I was declared unfit, through no doing of my own, and was replaced by a person named Fux."

"Continue," said Chief Maguro, who found that name somewhat familiar, accompanied by a vague memory of mischief.

"This Fux is the one who made the trouble at the airlock, sir."

"Ah!" said Master Chief Maguro. "He's the purple-alert fool."

"Sir?"

"The next time you fail to remember what a purple alert is," Maguro said, "will be the last time. Don't try me, Aubergine."

"Sir, purple alert is the airlock being opened during engine operation or engine preparation for operation, sir," said another crewmember, Apprentice Boyle, who was famous for being a pain.

"Shut up," Maguro said and turned back to the painfully slow Aubergine. "Anyway," he added, "I know this person. Of this person. Sort of. So?"

"So rumour has it that he . . . I mean to say . . . the Mobile Infantry armour suits, sir?"

"Yes?"

"He made them work agai . . . that is, he made them *perfectly maintained*, sir."

"He did?"

"Of course, they were always perfectly maintained, but—"

"Oh, Space," Chief Maguro said. "Oh, sweet Space."

"Sir?" said Aubergine.

"Is it purple alert again?" asked Apprentice Boyle, in

innocent defiance of standing orders. But Master Chief Maguro was too terrified to address this lack of discipline.

"Oh, sweet, loving Space," he said. "That must be it. He couldn't have. He must have. How could he have?"

Maguro shook his head, got hold of himself and turned back toward the expectant engine crew.

"Thanks, Aubergine," he said. "Everyone, come with me."

They all realized that he was dead serious. It was probably because he didn't bother snapping at Apprentice Boyle.

They hovered single-file in the narrow corridor leading away from the engine telemetry cabin and shortly reached the closest blue, round hatch, one of many spread all over the ship, signifying the presence of an in-wall power unit. Or, as they now discovered, the lack thereof. In its stead, there was a tiny wire patch, which Maguro identified as a primitive control circuitry override, sending out a series of fake positive messages so as to avoid error reports and alarms. It was familiar to him because, like any crew member who ever dealt with the engine, he had had to build and install similar patches in the past to ensure the perfection of the hardware maintenance reports in a spitefully imperfect universe. But those were special cases, and he knew each and every such patch upon the ship, and this was not one of them. Nor was the one replacing the next missing power unit. And the next. And the next.

There were one hundred and twenty engine-dedicated power units embedded in the walls of the *UPS Spitz*. Of those, ninety-six were actually operational. Of those, as the engine crew soon discovered, there currently remained three.

Master Chief Maguro sent his crew back to the telemetry cabin with a firm order not to leave for any reason whatsoever until his return. Not even for the mightiest engine telemetry error. Not even for a purple alert. He then took the great risk of rushing in the corridors, even though this kind of behaviour was highly irregular and tended to result in uncomfortable questions being asked—but not even close to the magnitude of the questions involving an inoperative engine.

Maguro fast-floated all the way to the Mobile Infantry barracks, burst inside, and demanded to see Fux. This resulted in an unexpected show of lack of discipline among the troopers, there being no officer or noncom present. A grumpy bespectacled old man told Maguro that Fux was no longer with the Infantry and good riddance. Others suggested inquiring with Lieutenant Lipton, for whom Fux was now supposed to be an orderly.

Disregarding the unlikeliness of this statement, and strangely feeling put upon, Maguro, cursing under his breath, still climbed ship-up all the way to the naval officers' quarters, only to find both lieutenant and underling to be missing. Desperately, he went to the infirmary, hoping for enlightenment by the sharp intelligence of Doctor, not to mention lover, Nightingale. She, alas, seemed to be entirely occupied with dissecting a mechanical monstrosity that he surprisingly recognized as a political controller and curtly brushed him off. Her ensign, a snotty skeletal thing, gave him a strangely knowing look, but deciphering it would have to wait for later. First and foremost, he had to find Fux.

He could not have done this alone, Maguro thought in desperation. *Someone must have helped him. Someone . . .*

The captain is going to make an example out of me. With her own hands. She . . .

But there must be someone else, someone who can . . .

Ah.

It did not take him long to reach the armoury.

IT SHOULD BE NOTED that the first incident was bad enough: an unplanned battle plan causing an unplanned victory would have alerted any captain in the, for lack of a lesser word, fleet. The second incident was even worse: no captain in her right mind would ignore any issue of any sort involving the propulsion system. After blind loyalty to leader and empire, blind obedience to military regulations, and blind deference to one's superiors, the engine was as close as anything could get to being holy. It would be considered by some to be, along with the rest of the ship, one of the captain's actual bodily parts. No one aboard the *UPS Spitz* could have imagined anything worse than messing with the captain.

And thus, one may find mild interest in the fact that those two horrendous incidents were easily dwarfed by a third one.

22

FUX IS HELPFUL

It is the political officer's duty to closely monitor all interpersonal communications between his charges. It is of utmost importance that those transactions remain informative, practical and cordial. Anything more than that is strongly discouraged.

I SHALL FEAR NO EVIL, A POLITICAL OFFICER'S HANDBOOK

LIKE PROPHECIES OF OLD, as told in ancient and strictly forbidden writings eagerly read in secret by every youth in the empire, Lieutenant Lipton's impending calamity was heralded by numerous signs of varying magnitudes. First among those was an unpleasantness during a second-shift lunch at the Officers' Mess, where he found himself the focus of nasty stares by a young officer of the navigation unit,

Second Lieutenant Klar. Of this negative attention, he felt himself undeserving, for while indeed considering Klar a fine officer and a handsome young woman, he was certain that those thoughts were never expressed to her face or to anyone outside of his own head. After a few uneasy moments, he decided to boldly approach her and inquire as to this behaviour. This resulted in Second Lieutenant Klar boldly hissing in his face, accompanied by bold and hateful glances from two of her companions, which in turn led to Lieutenant Lipton's immediate and no less bold retreat.

Upon returning to his cabin, he found an encrypted message blinking on the desk. It was, he saw, from one Corporal Clementine of the First Platoon of the First Company of the First Battalion of the 91st Regiment of the Mobile Infantry.

Why all that formality? he thought, putting his hand on the table, then his eye on the scanner, then letting the table prick his finger for some blood, then showing his face to the cam, then to the verification cam. All this was slightly more difficult than usual due to the ongoing lack of gravity. Shouldn't the engine have started already?

No matter. Now, that corporal. He had nothing but a vague recollection of her. She was non-naval and a noncom, and he could not fathom what issue she might have with him, much less one requiring encryption. Eventually, yet reluctantly, the desk accepted his identification and projected the contents of the message. Lipton hovered over it and read:

FROM C. CLEMENTINE TO L. LIPTON IN REPLY TO YOUR REQST ABSOLUTELY NEGATV

REPEAT ABSOLUTELY NOT REPEAT ABSO-
LUTELY DENIED PERIOD. PLEASE REFRAIN
FROM ANY FURTHR SUCH REQSTS OR ANY COM
PERIOD. HOW DARE YOU PERIOD. YOURE LUCKY
IM ENCRYPTING THIS PERIOD. NEXT TIME ILL
MAKE IT PUBLIC PERIOD. SIGNED C. CLEMEN-
TINE 1ST PLTN 1ST CPNY 1ST BTLN 91ST RGMT
PERIOD.

He merely stared at the offensive communication,
uncomprehending. *What request?* he thought. *Is this
Corporal Clementine who I think she is? Could I be mixing
the names? Or the faces? Is it someone else? Someone I've
requested something from? But who? And what?*

He read the message again. It did not seem to make any
more sense than it did the first time around.

I requested a report from Corporal Kohl, Lipton thought,
*regarding the current condition of the airlocks, but that was
some time ago. And also, he's dead now. Recycled. Poor
bastard.*

Another light started blinking on his desk. He ignored it.

*Could it be that Kohl has changed his name? To Clemen-
tine? No, I distinctly remember a Corporal Clementine of the
Mobile Infantry. Maybe he changed his name to Kraut. But
Kraut is also dead. But . . . Clementine?*

His powers of concentration were not as they should be.
Could this be a late effect of the drugs inflicted upon him by
Nightingale? *No, don't change the subject. Deal with
Corporal Clementine.*

The light on his desk was now accompanied by a penetrating sound, of the kind that usually implied urgency.
Indeed, it's quite urgent that I find out what's going on here,

the lieutenant thought. *There must be, as* she *likes saying, a logical explanation.*

The light dimmed, the sound stopped, and the cabin door screamed and opened on the quickest possible manual override, revealing the *she* of Lieutenant Lipton's recent thought, i.e. Lieutenant Commander Doctor Nightingale.

"I was just thinking of," said Lipton, but Nightingale, propelling herself into the cabin, was quicker.

"Don't finish that sentence, Lieutenant."

"But, maybe we should, er, should be checking the status of Refrigeration Unit Number Thirt—"

"Nothing of the sort, Lieutenant," said Nightingale, who now hovered uncomfortably close to him. By now, Lipton had managed to regain enough of his mind to focus on her exact wording.

She, too, is suddenly official. What happened?

"I am about to show you a certain medical supply manifest document," Nightingale added. "I would like you to take some time and compose your thoughts *before* you comment on it."

Medical supply. Nice touch. I wonder . . .

But when Doctor Nightingale made the desk show the document in question, wonder promptly became the furthest thing from Lipton's mind.

*Dear and Honourable Madam Lieutenant
Commander Doctor Nightingale,*

*I am hereby, most venerable ma'am, delighted to
declare my long-lasting and eternal admiration and
attraction, not to mention love, to you. In the reason-*

able and most satisfying hope that our feelings are mutual, I would like to suggest visitation by you of my spacious cabin so as to discuss our future together and/or consummate our everlasting love to everyone's benefit.

Honourably and gracefully yours,
Lt. Lipton, Naval Officer (Honourable)
UPS Spitz, Cabin #1437
Anytime after ten of the clock, morning shift

The supposed author of this gentle communication had just discovered that it is very difficult, if not impossible, to collapse in zero gravity. Pushing himself away from the desk, he felt the cabin swimming around him as if in a dream. But the effect was real, as in his haste he forgot to balance himself and started rotating gently. He felt the blood rushing to his cheeks, the tips of his fingers, his toes, his head. His lungs burned, and tears came to his eyes, slowly flying away due to the gentle centrifugal force of his spinning. His stomach lurched and might have gone on to a more demonstrative performance were it not for Doctor Nightingale, who grabbed his hand and stopped him in his tracks, and not a moment too soon.

His breathing was fast and painful. Talking was almost impossible. Still, he tried.

"I . . ." he said. "I . . ."

"Lieutenant Lipton," said Nightingale. She was still holding his hand, fixing him to his place. Her gaze said what should best not be uttered aloud: *Get a hold of yourself.*

He forced his breathing to slow down. Inhaled, exhaled. "I did not—" he said; inhaled again. "I could not—"

"Are you sure?" said Nightingale. Her voice seemed strange to him. But so did everything else.

"I would absolutely never," he said, "not even in the slightest. It's not even my writing style. 'Venerable ma'am?' Who writes like that? Who speaks like that? What kind of a person, what kind of a buffoon, what kind of an *idiot* would even dream of *OH MY SPACE!*"

"Ah, yes," said Nightingale, and suddenly Lipton realized that he was right; there was a strangeness to her voice: she was trying hard to stifle a laugh. "I trust that you are now aware of the true nature of the situation," she added.

Inside Lipton's mind, something tore up. It was the carefully cultivated political awareness and response mechanism that he had been perfecting since his earliest days in school or even kindergarten.

"Fux!" he shouted, his face even redder than before. "I'm . . . I'm . . ."

"Easy now," said Nightingale. "This sort of issue should be considered carefully, as is our habit."

"Space be my witness, I'm going to bloody kill the bloody—"

"Yes, you're going to kill the *problem*," said Nightingale, and now there was a warning in her tone. "Killing problems, or rather eliminating them, is what you and I do best."

"I will . . . I . . ." Lipton said. He knew that Nightingale was right. He also knew that, no matter what had caused Fux to betray him in such an insane and deadly manner, his treacherous orderly was going to die painfully, in indescribable agony, by the lieutenant's own hands, even if it was the last thing Lipton would ever do. His blood was still wildly pumping in his ears and his body. He looked around but could not decipher what he was seeing. Everything was red. Everything was bad. *To think that I actually liked him!*

Doctor Nightingale's voice easily sliced through his confused thoughts.

"You've got to think this through," she said. "I assume this isn't the first evidence that you receive of this kind of issue, that's one."

Lipton remembered the cryptic message from Corporal Clementine and then the weird incident at the officers' mess. He nodded.

"And so, there's a system to this, that's two," Nightingale said. "And so, it would be unwise to assume that all the occurrences of said phenomenon have already been . . . exposed. That's three."

"Unwise," said Lipton woodenly. *Does she mean there's even more? Did the bastard pen love letters to every woman on this ship?*

"I would hope," he said, feeling some of his old spirit return, "that there's some limit to the scope of the matter so that it can be prevented from bothering those of us who are too important to be interrupted by such trifles."

"I share the sentiment," Nightingale said. "However, for safety's sake, one has to take into account the possibility of this already having happened."

"Let us all hope that this is not the case," said Lipton, and even as he was speaking, realized that there's no way this would not be the case, that this *had* to be the case, that there was no way in which the universe, and in particular its representative in the form of Joseph Fux, would let this not be the case. Still, for a long and confused moment, he completely and utterly failed to grasp the sheer scope of said case. Then his desk coughed, blipped, chimed, and declared, "Lieutenant Lipton! You are hereby requested to report immediately to the captain!"

And thus had Fux's loyalty found its proper reward.

23

FUX IS TAKEN

Good captains must instill fear in their crews. Good political officers must instill fear in their captains.

STANDING GUIDANCE, UNITED PLANETS
IMPERIAL NAVY POLIDIV CENTRAL, TERRA

THE *UPS SPITZ* did not have a bridge or a combat information centre per se. Those honourable institutions of naval past were replaced by a single chamber populated by a single occupant: the captain.

Common knowledge upon the *UPS Spitz* was that the captain was not a person to trifle with, in the same sense that a yellow sun is not a good place to hang your boots to dry. This analogy, originating long ago with an anonymous naval officer who was No Longer With Us, was well-known but rarely used, for the mentioned hanging and drying were, alas, not entirely fictional and also unrelated to boots. They were also, to Lipton's horror, the only things on his mind at the expense of everything else. As he was pulling himself frantically along the command-level corridor, trying in vain to slow himself down, he knew that, in all probability, by next shift he'd be just another anonymous naval officer who was No Longer With Us.

When he reached the first security hatch, a new thought popped into his mind. *Maybe,* he thought, *there's going to be another malfunction. The engine is down; why not the hatches? The captain will be literally locked behind bars, at least for the time being.*

The hatch, smoothly and noiselessly, opened.

Hanging and drying, Lipton thought. *In space, everyone can hear you scream, because the com is on up until the end, making sure that you're setting a good example.*

Another hatch opened.

I'm going to keep my dignity until the very end, Lipton thought. *I'm going to go honourably, quietly. She will not make a blabbering example out of me!*

He reached the last stretch before the captain's chambers. The massive hatch on its far side slid open. It did so silently, but in Lipton's ears it was accompanied by the moaning of the rust and blood of a thousand lost naval officers.

Who am I kidding?

IN ADDITION to being the most dangerous person on the *UPS Spitz,* the captain was the most mysterious. While her few public appearances presented nothing more than a severe-faced grey-haired pale woman of arguable age, in the crew's minds she took strange and various forms. Some said she was a living brain embedded inside the ship, the woman's body merely a cunningly constructed robot. Others claimed that, while originally a human being, she was now technologically enhanced and could kill with a glance. Yet others claimed she was the result of a genetic experiment that rendered her a vastly deadly being, poisonous at will. Other rumours were even stranger.

The only concept agreed upon by everyone was that of the captain's own hands, which occasionally took a crucial part in mandatory televised educational programs such as throwing offenders overboard, pushing offenders into bio-reclamation chambers, mutilating offenders, dismembering offenders, and other gruesome activities. It should be noted, though, that the hands in question were not the ones naturally—if one believed she wasn't a robot—attached to the captain's torso. Instead, they were a pair of specially trained guardians, their entire bodies, heads and faces included, covered with thick, shiny black material. No one had ever seen their eyes or mouths or even their skin. Or perhaps no one had lived to tell the tale.

It was one of those pillars of the community that poor Lieutenant Lipton, in his desperate haste to cross the command hatch, had accidentally bumped into. Or, rather, this would have been the case had the captain's hand not taken the liberty of grabbing Lipton by the throat.

It was exactly like being strangled by a rubberized vice. Alas, Lipton's current mental state did not allow for such comparisons, while his respiratory state did not allow for anything but, barely, survival. The hand and its cargo swiftly turned around and started walking toward the inner captain's quarters, each step ringing loudly in the metal hull. A tiny part of Lipton's mind noted that this should have been impossible considering the current lack of gravity, then gave up due to a current lack of oxygen.

There was movement; there was a momentary shadow, then a light, then a sound. The floor smacked Lipton's feet. The vice left his throat. Breathing deeply, desperately, he leaned over. This only served to disconnect his feet from the floor. His body wasn't entirely under his control. Something pushed him back in the direction officially known as down. Eventually, still loudly wheezing, he managed to bring himself into a semblance of standing at attention.

He was in the middle of a softly lit cabin, its walls barely visible in the shadows. It was almost entirely devoid of furniture. The only exception was a simple black desk, merely three or four times the size of a Refrigeration Unit Mark VIII. There was nothing on it except for the weak light emitted by a document on display. Behind it sat the captain.

"LIEUTENANT LIPTON," the captain said eventually.

"Yes, Captain."

"I have to give it to you, Lieutenant; this one is a first."

"Captain, I can explain the—"

"Silence."

Lipton's mouth snapped shut so fast that he bit his tongue. The captain smiled. Or rather, the edges of her mouth rose slightly in an entirely humourless way. A hidden light source softly illuminated her face. It did not help at all.

"Your logs do not show the slightest tendency toward such insolence," the captain continued. "Mild political unsteadiness, for sure, but that applies to almost everyone."

Somehow, Lipton managed to prevent himself from replying.

"Casual treachery, absolutely," the captain said, "but then again, I've yet to meet a soldier who's not basically a traitor waiting to happen."

Lipton concentrated on breathing. *Control yourself!* he thought.

"But sending me a *love letter*, Lipton? An actual love letter? What were you thinking?"

Lipton's breathing turned into hyperventilating.

"Under different circumstances, I would have commended you. Your silly sense of humour isn't without bravery."

Lipton's throat started burning. His hyperventilating was now accompanied by unbecoming gargling.

"Silence, you. Next time you speak without permission, I lose my patience. Got it?"

This was probably in Lipton's best interest, as without consulting him, his body inhaled sharply and then stopped breathing.

"Good. So here's how it goes, Lieutenant: I can recycle you, same as everyone else. Easy. If I may say so myself, it's the humane thing to do."

Humane! the lieutenant thought. He was starting to feel the lack of oxygen. He tried exhaling as quietly as he could. Luckily, the captain was too engrossed in her own speech to notice.

"But satisfying," the captain added, "it isn't. Not at all."

Lipton's hard-won political survival instincts saved him from opening his mouth, but just barely. Utilizing every bit of self-control that he could muster, he stayed perfectly rigid, still slowly exhaling.

"I must admit," the captain said, "that this is my own doing. I don't punish enough, especially not in truly meaningful ways. Can't be good for morale, that. An efficient crew requires a constant state of fear."

In principle, Lipton heartily disagreed with every aspect of this statement. In practice, right now, he would do anything, absolutely anything, with perfect efficiency, more than perfect, even, whatever it took, no matter what, for him to avoid the bio-reclamation chamber.

"Problem is, people can get used to anything," the captain said. "Even to their friends getting recycled. Even to the possibility of being recycled themselves. Crazy, eh?"

Lipton invested all of his remaining energy in preventing his teeth from shaking. His ears were filled with the sound of his own frantic heartbeat.

"So what we have here is general indiscipline. Unacceptable," the captain said. "Totally unacceptable. First, because it means I need to interfere, which in turn means I need to take my mind off my own occupations to deal with this muck." An almost imperceptible turn of her head pointed, Lipton noticed, at a piece of dirty cloth hung on a frame at the far corner of the cabin. He glanced at it. It seemed to consist mainly of blood-red smears over an off-white background. Could this be a painting of some sort? But of what? Whatever else it might have been, pretty it was not.

"But more importantly, Lieutenant: if any word of this

somehow gets beyond this ship, it has a direct effect on my *political position*. Do you understand what I'm saying?"

Lipton, feebly, nodded. He was trying in vain to ignore the smeared red thing in the back, which on second glance indeed turned out to be an awful unfinished painting depicting . . . could it be a creature of some kind? Perhaps an animal being tortured?

"So here's your choice, Lieutenant . . . look at me when I'm talking to you!"

Lipton's head turned back so fast that his neck almost cranked.

"The easy way is for you to die in a very public manner, just like everyone else around here. The recycler's too good for you, but it'll have to do. Can't be bothered to find a better solution."

Lipton stood in his place, fighting to keep his silence. *Oh please oh please oh please oh please . . .*

"The other way is," the captain said, "*you* find me a better solution."

Against Lipton's direct wish, his mouth gained a life of its own.

"Yes, Captain!" it said. "I promise you, I shall work tirelessly, day and night, to find a solution! I will dedicate my whole being—my life!—to finding a proper way to do it! First thing next shift, I'll deliver a detailed report with various ways of creative punishments and preserving discipline; just let me—"

"Wrong, Lieutenant."

"Captain?"

"You find a better solution, or I use the regular final solution, yes. Within the next sixty seconds."

Lipton felt as if his spirit had left its physical dwelling. He watched, in a strangely detached way, as his own body lost control and started dancing madly in front of the captain. This, he slowly became aware, was accompanied by a sound. Or rather, a scream. The body was shouting. Quite loudly, now that Lipton's distracted mind took note of it. One might even say, crazily.

"Fux!" the body roared. "It was Fux! Not me! It's Fux! Bring Fux! Fux Fux Fux Fux Fux!"

Then the body rolled over, curled into a ball in midair, and Lipton's mind sank into darkness.

THERE WAS AN AWKWARD SMELL. Slowly, carefully, Lieutenant Lipton inhaled. Yes, a distinct smell of . . . something. Other than that, his senses were muted, disconnected. He was embedded in darkness, in silence, in softness. It was relaxing. It was perfect. It was just what he needed.

The smell, however, wouldn't go away. Something had to be done about it.

Gradually, so as to avoid challenging anyone, Lipton opened his eyes. The world was a blur. This was a relief. He was probably dead. Nothing in his education had prepared him for such an experience. Blurriness, therefore, was welcome. It meant that whatever it was that he was supposed to deal with, being dead, was either nonexistent or had not arrived yet.

Still, the smell. It was rather penetrating. It did not befit his current condition. Being dead should be more . . . dignified. Yes. Either that or . . .

Or could it be that he wasn't so dead after all? But then, he did not want to jump to hasty conclusions. If, indeed, by some exceptional occurrence, he was still alive, there was no need to press the matter, for someone might take notice and decide to correct it. The smell, now that he put more thought into it, was much stronger than it had any right to be. Could it be . . . onion soup?

The blurry vision twisted, or rather retreated, and focused into a face. A familiar, smiling one.

"Fux!"

"At your service, honourable sir!" said Fux, for indeed, it was him.

"What are you doing here?"

"The honourable doctor ma'am told me that you were summoned to the captain, and so—"

"The captain," said Lipton weakly.

"Right here, Lipton."

The lieutenant made a feeble attempt at jumping to attention. Luckily, in his weakened state, combined with the weakened state of the local gravity, this amounted to nothing much. He was still, he saw, in the captain's chambers. In fact, it seemed almost exactly as it was during his last coherent moment: the captain was still sitting behind her desk, one of her black-clad hands was still standing to the side, and the awful red painting was still quietly menacing in the background. The only change was the presence of Lipton's incredibly, infuriatingly, insanely duplicitous orderly.

"So," the captain said. "Clearly, one of you is guilty of high treason."

"Yes, Honourable Captain Ma'am," said Fux. "I wholeheartedly agree."

This simple statement jolted Lipton into immediate rejuvenation.

"Captain," he said hurriedly, "please disregard Mister Fux, who, being somewhat feeble in mind and also a foreigner of questionable Bohemian origins, does not mean what he just said in the way that you or I would surely expect of—"

"Silence, you," the captain said. "Mister Fux, did you mean what you were saying?"

"I usually mean what I am saying, though sometimes I'm saying what I'm meaning," said Fux. "I admit that I may be unsure which is which, me being a certified idiot, second-class, ma'am."

"Stupidity isn't an excuse when it comes to treason," the captain said. "Or, as long as I'm in command," she added, "to anything else."

"Hear, hear!" said Fux.

"Are you making fun of me, Mister Fux?"

"I would not dream of it, Honourable Ma'am Captain! The fact of the matter is that I adore you, ma'am!"

Lipton, who until now had strongly felt that there was no fate too bad for his orderly, was suddenly struck with regret.

He is *an idiot,* he thought. *He really did not mean any harm. And she's going to mash him into pulp. No one deserves that.*

"Captain," he said, "may I suggest that we continue this conversation without the presence of Mister Fux so as to avoid wasting your valuable time and promptly solving the—"

"Bore me one bit more, and I'll recycle you just on principle," the captain said, then turned toward Fux. "Explain yourself, Mister."

"Yes, ma'am," Fux said. "I was born in the city of Praha in the county of Czek in the state of Bohemia, not far from the river Vlt. Even as a child, I was recognized as exceptionally—"

"If you think that by telling me your life story, you're going to prolong your life by even one minute, think again."

"Yes, Ma'am Captain," said Fux and closed his eyes. There was a long and awkward silence. Lipton fought the urge to say something and was on the verge of losing when the captain saved him.

"What are you doing?" she said.

"By your command, I am thinking again," said Fux without opening his eyes.

"Mister Fux," the captain said, "listen very carefully. You will now tell me, in regard to this ludicrous so-called 'love letter' that I have received, and also in general, *why* you think I was right in saying that one of you is guilty of high treason, which means *who* it is who's guilty and *what* it is that makes him guilty. Do you understand?"

"Yes, Ma'am Captain. It is, I have to admit, a bit shameful, ma'am."

"Out with it!"

Now it was Lipton who closed his eyes. There was nothing to do. Fux would talk himself into oblivion and will take his commanding officer with him. It was going to be that simple.

"Honourable Captain, there is no easy to say this," he heard Fux say, "but in fact, the letter that you have received was sent by myself."

Lipton discovered that, without his consent, his eyes were open again, and his mouth was in a state of speaking, to wit, "I told you!"

The captain ignored him.

"To be clear, Mister Fux, you're admitting to being the traitor," she said. "You, not your commanding officer," she added. "Are you sure that, out of some misplaced loyalty, this admission is not a miserable attempt to cover for him?"

"I had a cover once," Fux said dreamily. "It helped me pass several winters back in Praha. It was made of Sumavska wool. It had lilacs drawn on it."

He seemed lost in thought, and Lipton had a fleeting thought that this, on Fux's side, was rather unusual.

The captain, however, showed every sign of not sharing this sentiment. "I suspect that this so-called stupidity of yours is nothing but a so-called clever performance," she said.

"I wish it was," said Lipton.

"Silence, Lipton. Fux, suppose I told you that nothing you say will save Lieutenant Lipton here? Would you stick with this story of yours?"

"Ma'am, I am just, as you say, saying what I am meaning," Fux said. "It was I who sent you the letter, ma'am."

"Then why'd you send it under Lipton's name?"

"I was shy, ma'am. I was afraid that my tender feelings were unworthy of the attention of someone as honourable and admirable as yourself, ma'am."

"Tread carefully, Mister."

"Ma'am Captain, it is not an easy saying, but it is what I am meaning: Ma'am Captain, I am in love with you!"

The captain, for the first time ever, as far as Lipton knew, lifted her right eyebrow.

"That's not special or shameful," she said. "Everyone loves the captain. Always. It's in the naval officer's handbook, chapter one."

"Yes, ma'am, but I meant more than that," said Fux. "I have tender feelings toward you, ma'am."

The captain raised her other eyebrow. Lipton suspected that she did not know the meaning of the words *tender feelings*, together or separately. But Fux, once started, was not one to stop for such trifles.

"I have been lying in my bunk every night shift, ma'am, thinking about you, imagining you, admiring you," he said. "It is not every day that someone of my stature finds such a match, fitting body and soul, ma'am, to be present in his vicinity."

"Fux!" Lipton said.

Fux pointed at the local logcam, which Lipton hoped was off and not, as he suspected, connected to some private log accessible only to High Command.

"And so, as my honourable commander and everyone else are my witnesses, I would—"

"Fux! Enough!" said Lipton. If footage of this conversation became available to anyone higher up, even the captain might not be safe, not to mention himself.

"Yes, sir," said Fux and made a rather good imitation of kneeling down in zero-grav. "And so, honourable and beloved captain," he added, "I would like to offer you my hand in holy matrimony."

THE UNIVERSE SCREECHED and tore itself into dark fragments that, like the ravens of ancient, forbidden rhymes, encompassed Lieutenant Lipton right above the captain's floor. *I am dead; I'm nevermore.*

Or maybe it was just a momentary lapse of, for lack of a better word, reason.

"LIPTON," the captain said after a few hours of confusion, which probably translated into a second or two of real time, "get out of here. Right now."

"Yes, ma'am!" the lieutenant said. "Absolutely. I'll take care of this. Come, Fux, we're going. Right now. No more smart talk. No excuses."

"No," the captain said. "He stays. You—out. Now. Before I recycle you and him and everyone else on this miserable ship. Now!"

"But," Lipton said, then made the wise yet cowardly choice, shut his mouth, and pulled himself quickly toward the door, which was mercifully quick to open and then close behind his back.

The last thing he heard before the seal cut all sound from inside was the captain saying, "As for *you*, Fux . . ."

IMMEDIATELY AFTERWARD, and for the remainder of the shift, absolutely nothing happened. No one was recycled, nor were there any pompous declarations released by the captain. Lipton visited the infirmary but found nothing suspicious on the premises, with the exception of the stowed and frozen Ensign Berserker.

Knowing full well that this was not a good idea, Lipton eventually decided to visit the political division. To his surprise, Commander Kapust seemed glad to meet him. Or maybe that wasn't exactly the case. Relieved, perhaps? But why?

"How can I help you, Lieutenant?" Kapust asked, his manner suspiciously polite.

"I was wondering, sir," Lipton said, "what has become of my orderly."

"Your, ahem, orderly?"

"Yes, sir. You know. Mister F—"

"As I reckon," Kapust interrupted, "you have always objected to having an orderly. Isn't that right, Lieutenant?"

"Yes, sir, but it was you who—"

"I was and, ahem, still am in absolute agreement with you on that particular matter. You do not require an orderly, nor should you have one, nor are you worth the effort of recruiting and training one."

"Sir?"

"Therefore, Lieutenant, I would like to make it absolutely clear that you never had an orderly and, ahem, it is highly unlikely that you will have one in the future."

Lipton stood silently and stared at the political officer. This was one of those things that could have happened back home, where people would disappear without leaving a trace. Or, at least, such were the tales that some people used to hint about when they thought they weren't being logged, which was never. But in the fighting forces? Here, where military-inflicted death was so much easier?

He now realized that Kapust's strange mood was not relief, nor was it happiness, exactly. It was gloating, mixed with a pinch of dread. A total erasure of a person isn't an easy thing to handle, even for an old political officer, even when said officer hates said person and everything about his existence. Lipton was fleetingly tempted to inquire as to Fux's actual fate, but of course, Kapust would never let him know. Or, more probably, had no idea himself. It was safe— what a miserable word!—to assume that Fux's fate was terrible beyond belief.

He had it coming, Lipton thought miserably. *He was deranged; he was annoying. He couldn't shut his mouth. Insufferable.*

I'm going to miss him.

And thus did Fux vanish and cease to exist or, rather, ceased to have existed in the first place.

All consumables on board must be pre-packed by authorized military suppliers so as to fit a standard-issue kitchen nutritomat; see Appendix C, list of approved ingredients. In case of special circumstances, such as emergency replenishing on a soon-to-be-conquered settlement without proper military suppliers, use only ingredients that require minimum treatment before being processed by the vessel's nutritomat. To clarify: anything that requires manual cooking is strictly forbidden.

TUNNEL IN THE SKY, A LIGHT FRIGATE
COMMAND AND MAINTENANCE HANDBOOK

UPON ENTERING THE ARMOURY, Engine Master Chief Maguro was greeted by a pleasant, yet strong, smell of cooking. It emanated from a large wire-studded and knob-decorated spherical contraption anchored to three of the walls by thick cords. These, the chief recognized, were regular-issue Naval Cables Mark I, taken out of commission half a century previously on the grounds of being sensitive to sudden changes in temperature. The thing in the middle, though, was even worse in that it was absolutely and eternally forbidden: an impromptu zero-grav boiler.

"Pea soup," said Sergeant Private Bolon, who, Maguro now discovered, was hovering behind the thing and gently stroking the fluid inside with a chunky, half-melted waldo. "Just the thing for this time of year, yes? Also great for morale. Want some?"

"Fux," said Maguro.

"The best way to make it," Bolon said, "is to add some sausage. You have to do it at the proper time so it doesn't get overcooked and lose its texture, yes? Of course, it also has to be a proper sausage."

Maguro, who by his own admission was never the most observant as far as people were concerned, still noticed that while Bolon's words fully conformed with his usual jolly disposition, his face did not. The master chief had never spent much time in the company of anyone in the Mobile Infantry, quartermaster included, yet he was convinced that this behaviour was unusual. Or worse. Still, the engine came first.

"I know about Fux," he said, "and I believe I know who else is involved. Do you understand me, Bolon?"

"If you knew about Fux," said Bolon, who, to Maguro's amazement, had tears in his eyes, "you would have joined me in making this soup." He stirred the thing some more, perhaps a tad too forcefully. The waldo emitted a tired creaking sound, but he did not seem to care. "Maybe it needs a bit more sausage," he added.

"Don't give me this cookery, Quartermaster," said Maguro. "I want to see Fux, and I am going to see Fux. And if I don't get to meet him in a minute or so, I'll have to settle for second best. Do you understand? *Second best*, Bolon."

"Come to think of it," Bolon said, "I distinctly remember Fux telling me that it *was* second best. I mean, the sausage."

Maguro came close to thinking that Bolon's state was at least partly interesting. However, in addition to being fully occupied by the missing power packs and the culprit who took them, he had no capacity for handling the phenomenon described in Navy regulations as *an emotional state*.

"I definitely *do not* mean the bloody sausage, Quartermaster! Get a hold of yourself!"

"Ham," Bolon said and stirred the soup again. "'Ham,' he said. Ham was better than sausage, he said." More tears rolled down his face. He did not bother wiping them. The boiler emitted a nasty slurping noise.

Maguro, who started suspecting that Bolon was perhaps a bit sad, decided to stick to more familiar ground.

"Stop messing with it," he said and pointed at the spherical soup. "It's boiling already. That's enough to make the fluid stir itself. You should lower the heat."

Bolon stared at him, then shook his head. "Ham," he repeated. "I have no idea what that might be, but Fux promised it was better than sausage."

"Enough with the sausage!"

"No, the sausage is fine," Bolon said. "Sort of. It's the ham that's missing. Missing. Missing!"

He lifted his hand off the waldo and turned one of the

boiler's big knobs in what Maguro could have sworn was the wrong direction.

"What are you doing?" the master chief said. "Stop this right now!" He pushed himself closer to the quartermaster and grabbed his hand. "That's it," he added. "You're coming with me."

Bolon, with agility far surpassing what one would expect from a person his age and proportions, shook the master chief off him and jumped ship-up, toward the ceiling.

Taken by surprise, Maguro found himself pushed toward the floor. However, like all naval technical personnel, he was heavily trained in zero-grav and easily regained his balance. He promptly pushed himself ship-up, toward the strangely rebellious quartermaster.

"Stop it!" he said. "What's wrong with you?"

A thick grey tubular container for spare parts ran along the length of the ceiling, and Bolon pulled himself over it and hid behind it. "Ham!" he shouted. "I'll never find out what ham is!"

Maguro was on the verge of actually considering whether this statement carried with it any amount of meaning before his military education caught up and put a stop to it. "This behaviour will not go unpunished, Quarter-master," he said aloud, slowly approaching the tubular container from below.

"Unpunished!" wailed Bolon from above. "Fux was taken, yes? I'll be taken too, yes? Who is going to be left here to be unpunished?"

"Taken?"

"I thought you knew all about Fux," Bolon said, his voice echoing from behind the container. "The captain took him, and I don't care who hears this. He's gone! There's no Fux anymore!"

This, like any other mention of the vessel's top commanding officer, stopped Maguro in his tracks. But, being an engineer above anything else, he was better equipped than most to handle such situations. That is, his mind naturally put aside all matters human, especially human nature, in the face of a pressing problem of a technical nature.

"All right, no one is going to take you," he said. He had no idea how true this statement was, though it was safe to assume that if the engine wasn't fixed very soon, everyone on board would be taken too, whatever that might mean.

"I need your help," he added. "Right now."

"No," said Bolon. "I'm going to sit here and make my soup, and eat my soup, and . . . and make another soup, maybe. That's all I'm going to do."

"The soup!" said Maguro, who by now had managed to position himself near the ceiling, right beside the quartermaster. "Go down there and turn it off before the damned thing explodes on us."

Sometime in the very near future it would occur to Engine Master Chief Maguro that he might be suffering from a certain repeating pattern, it being his recurring tendency to identify problems of a technical nature only after the damage was done. This realization would be greatly assisted by the fact that the soup boiler chose this very moment to sizzlingly yet wetly, forcefully yet miserably, explode.

It would also occur to Maguro that by luring him to reach his position behind the tubular container, Quartermaster Bolon had saved his life. While it was obvious that the latter was also responsible for the thing from which his life was saved, i.e. a lethal sphere of glowing, hissing, boiling green pea soup in zero-grav, Master Chief Maguro could not avoid, from then on, a weird feeling of gratitude toward the quartermaster.

STRANGELY ENOUGH, sharing a near-boil experience with Master Chief Maguro seemed to have shaken the quartermaster out of his misery, if not entirely, then at least enough to help the former in his hunt for the lost power units. Recognizing the urgency of the matter, Bolon spent merely an hour alternately kicking and seducing a dusty lump of polycardboard into life, eventually sending it to fend for itself in the muck-covered armoury, which it immediately started to lick into some kind of imagined cleanliness. After this, there was no point in staying there, especially in view of the intense aroma of crushed peas. And so, at long last, Master Chief Maguro found himself revisiting the Mobile Infantry barracks, this time with Bolon by his side.

"Oh, look," said one of the troopers, "it's Mister Looking-for-Fux, again."

"Shhh!" said someone else. "Don't mention that name!"

"Maybe he's in love?" suggested another.

"Lovely person, Fux," said yet another. "Absolutely worth it."

"Quiet!" said the one who was against mentioning names, who seemed to be older than the rest of the troopers and had some sort of primitive eyewear stuck on his nose. "We were specifically told that—"

"I will specifically tell you something, Daisy," said one of the others, "if you don't shut up right now."

"Maybe not really tell, eh?" said someone else. "Maybe more like shove."

Maguro was about to say something, but before he managed to decide what it might be, Quartermaster Bolon shouted, "Attention!"

This seemed to take the troopers by surprise. What's more, it definitely drew the attention of someone who had not participated in the conversation thus far, a menacingly big soldier who, up to that point, had been hovering idly farther back in the barracks, facing the other way. Now, turning around, she started moving toward them. She was wearing the stripes of a corporal. As she drew near, Maguro, who was born and raised on a remote and socially-backward planet upon which women were still considered weaker than men, was nevertheless considering a careful retreat.

"Corporal, ma'am!" said Bolon. "I did not mean to—"

"What are you doing here, Bolon? And . . . sir?"

While acknowledging the presence of a superior noncom, the underlying message was quite clear. *You Navy people have no jurisdiction here.*

"Corporal," said Maguro, "I am Master Chief Maguro of the engine crew. We need to discuss an urgent matter."

"All matters are urgent," the corporal said, as per regulations, yet still conveying the same sentiment as before.

"Indeed," said Maguro. "So, Corporal . . .?"

"Clementine."

"Clementine. Yes. So, This *truly* urgent matter has to do with the power—"

"The armour suits, ma'am, yes?" said Bolon quickly.

"The suits?" the corporal asked rather stiffly.

"Yes, ma'am," said Bolon. "The suits."

The corporal raised an eyebrow. "What does the naval engine crew have to do with our armour suits? Which are, of course, perfectly—"

"Exactly, ma'am," Bolon said. "It has to do with the question of . . . of . . . how exactly they came to be *so much* perfectly maintained."

She's in on it, Maguro thought. *Of course she is. Fux would never have managed to do it all by himself.*

He felt something close to admiration. *In their place, would I have done the same thing?* But then he remembered the silent engine awaiting him and its implications. *Bastards!* he thought. *Thieves!* The more he thought about it, the angrier he became. He was thinking of a proper reply, one which would convey his rage and also the captain's when she found out how the engine was shut down and who the criminals were, and, alas, who failed to prevent it. Luckily for him, before he could deliver this politically incorrect, not to mention outright dangerous, speech to his interlocutors, he discovered that they had already been trying to attract his attention for some time.

"Sir!" said Corporal Clementine. "Sir?"

"Corporal?"

"This calls for immediate action, sir."

"I agree, sir," said Bolon.

"I also . . . agree?" Maguro said.

"However," the corporal said, "one must take into

account that a few of the units in question, due to certain factors which at the moment are beside the point, are currently very temporarily in a slightly less than nominal status."

This kind of language was common in the Navy as much as in the Mobile Infantry, and therefore in Maguro's head, it smoothly translated into, *At least half of my power units are dead beyond repair.*

Bastards!

"What did you think those units were for? Why did you take them?" he asked. His anger made him a bit careless.

"Honestly, sir, we didn't," the corporal said. "Think, that is. We just needed them. Like that book says: need a space-suit, get a spacesuit."

This sounded both familiar and sensible to Maguro, though he was not ready to admit it. Also, the engine . . .

"Ma'am," said Bolon, showing a surprising streak of literacy, "it is, actually, *Have Spacesuit, Will Travel.*"

"Nah," the corporal said, "that's just stupid."

"Ma'am!"

"Enough!" Maguro said. "You and your... people... you are going to return all my units. Right now."

"All the nominal units," the corporal said.

"All the bloody units! Ninety-three of them, you hear me? Each and every bloody unit! All of them!"

"Yes, sir."

"And then you people and my people are going to put them to . . . nominal use, just in the way they were . . . nominally used before!"

The corporal sighed. "Well," she said, "if you choose to ignore the actual condition of—"

Bolon cut her off, which, Maguro thought, was a rather brave thing to do. "Sir, ma'am," the quartermaster said, "you may want to consider some other possible sources of nominal units."

"I'm not sure—" Clementine said.

"I don't care," Maguro said. "Ninety-three units!"

AND SO IT WAS THAT, come mid-shift, a swarm of troopers and engine technicians spread in the corridors of the good old UPS *Spitz* in what was preemptively logged as an in-ship combat exercise. This manoeuvre included, for some reason, replacing and fixing faulty engine power units, and if anyone noticed that said units were not in existence before being replaced and that some other units were taken from places that were not designated as belonging to the engine, there was no sign of it.

And thus was Fux, even while officially not in existence, still very present in spirit upon the UPS *Spitz*.

25

FUX IS MISSED

Note that the person in charge of the smooth operation of the political machinery is not yourself: this falls entirely within the responsibility of the chief medical officer. You are in charge of people, not machines.

I SHALL FEAR NO EVIL, A POLITICAL OFFICER'S HANDBOOK

SHE'S GOING *to turn us all into pulp,* Lieutenant Lipton thought, pulling himself along the main corridor. *Or jelly. Or worse.*

There was only one way to avert the horrible fate sure to befall everyone on board the *UPS Spitz*, but decades of proper imperial education made it incredibly hard to imagine. The one thing, the only thing, said education could not overcome was pure, sheer, utter desperation: knowing full well the axe would go down not only on one's neck but also on everyone else's. And so, in Lipton's mind, one of the most forbidden officially-inexistent words ever suddenly made an appearance.

Mutiny.

He was shaking. *Mutiny,* he thought again. Nothing happened. No axe fell on his neck. No flame came out of the captain's quarters to burn him alive for this atrocity. *Mutiny.* The crew, Mobile Infantry included, could overcome the captain's hands, powerful as they were, and subdue the captain herself. She might be powerful, but no one was *that* powerful.

Maybe she is, he thought. *After all, there must be a reason for her being the captain. She must have some power we don't know about. A device. Or maybe she is a cyborg, after all. I saw no evidence that she is not.*

The lights in the corridor were dim, even dimmer than usual. *Why?* he thought, and then, *why should I care? We're all going to die anyway. If we rebel, it'll be brave and heroic and incredible, and no one will ever hear of it. All of us will just disappear. And if we don't rebel, well, we'll disappear anyway.*

It occurred to him that this line of thought might have been followed countless times in the past, obviously to no avail.

But the thought would not leave him. *Mutiny.* Suppose they did it. Suppose all the captain's powers were mere propaganda. Like so many other things one notices upon joining the Navy. Or the Army. Any kind of fighting force. Suppose, then, that this crazy scheme succeeded. Then what?

Well, for starters, the crew of the UPS *Spitz*—whoever remained of it—would never see their homes again.

Do I even remember what home was like?

They'd be hunted. No place would be safe. Every naval vessel would fire at them on sight. There might even be a small hunting fleet. It wouldn't be the first one.

What an honour, having a whole fleet dedicated to me. Dedicated to catching me, admittedly, but it's kind of the same.

They'd need to find a habitable planet, somewhere far enough, marginal enough. But the UPS *Spitz* wasn't equipped for identifying and analyzing planetary bodies.

We'll have to run away, always run away. Until they find us. Or until we die of natural causes. Such as starvation.

For a time, he busied himself thinking of all the other jolly ways a renegade crew of a renegade ship might find its end.

Even if we survive, chances are we'll never leave this ship.

We, he thought. *Plural. As if there's anyone else here who thinks like me.*

Someone appeared at the edge of the corridor, slowly dragging himself toward the lieutenant. As it got closer, it was revealed to be a moustache of sorts, carrying behind it a corporal of sorts.

"G'evening, sir," the apparition said and quickly saluted.

"At ease, Corporal . . . ?"

"Kartoffel, sir," the corporal said.

"Do I know . . . ?"

"No , sir," said Corporal Kartoffel. "I'd've remembered meeting sir, sir."

Maybe he didn't need everyone to agree with him. Maybe, with the help of only a select few, he could overpower the captain. "Corporal," he said, "have you ever given thought to our current condition?"

"Of course, sir. All the time, sir. Way I see it, if it works, don't touch it, sir."

"Works?"

"Yes, sir. Perfectly so, sir. If it works when you don't touch it, touching it will mess up its working, so don't touch it. I'd've known if t'was otherwise, sir, which it can't be, sir, due to it working perfectly, sir."

Of course, Lipton thought. *As if anyone here could behave differently.*

"Carry on, Corporal," he said.

"Yes, sir," the corporal said and lightly hovered, moustache and all, past the lieutenant toward the other end of the corridor.

But why is it only me? Why can no one else see this? Am I so special? Too sensitive? Or am I just overreacting? But the captain, the captain herself . . .

Why did you do it, Fux? Why?

Something was off. Fux was behaving illogically. Idiot or not, it was just too much.

Or maybe it is I who's illogical about this?

He could see no fault with his logic. Admittedly, though, he wasn't purely objective. He had suffered serious emotional stress in the past few shifts. Maybe his reasoning was impaired. Maybe his thinking wasn't as straight as his turbulent mind insisted.

Logic.

He knew only one person who could untangle such

conundrums. He just needed, somehow, to overcome his rage and forgive her.

THE CORRIDOR LIGHTS turned even weaker. Lights were the responsibility of the life-support crew. His crew. Himself.

Now they blinked. That shouldn't be happening. But then, compared to the enormous list of other things that shouldn't have happened . . .

Lieutenant Lipton could not bring himself to care. Slowly, haltingly, despairingly, he pulled his way forward in the slowly darkening corridors.

An alarm sounded. Even in his shaken state, he knew it to be the grav-return warning. *So at least one crew was lucky,* he thought and instinctively grabbed one of the corridor safety rungs with both hands. Over the alarm, a mechanical voice was intoning, "Five, four, three—"

Who cares? Lipton thought. *Just do it already.*

". . . two, one, ignition."

Nothing happened.

"Ignition," the voice repeated.

Still nothing.

Well, maybe that other crew wasn't so lucky after all. Lipton could not find any consolation in that. *We're doomed, the lot of us,* he thought. He noticed that he was sweating. The air-circulation system was probably overdue for maintenance. He should see to it. If he, or anyone, remained alive after this horrible shift.

He shook his head, momentarily let go of the safety rung,

and wiped his brow with his right sleeve. The paper cloth was immediately soaked with sweat. Totally unpresentable. As if anyone cared.

"Ignition," the voice repeated. Lipton, left hand still holding to the safety rung, waited for something, anything, to happen. *Some people just can't gracefully accept losing the game,* he thought. *That engine is probably gone. Like everything else around here.*

This is ludicrous, standing here waiting for nothing, he thought and took his hands off the rungs. The corridor was quick to respond by way of vibrating, shaking, and violently lurching upwards. The engine did start, after all. Gradually, grudgingly, gravity returned. The good ship *UPS Spitz* was on its way again.

And so, by the time Lieutenant Lipton finally reached the infirmary, his state of mind was somewhat altered, his grievances magnified by his newly broken nose.

LIPTON'S only plan of attack involved being very firm and making it absolutely clear that he meant business and that this was no time for a certain medical officer's bizarre sense of humour. Therefore, he applied an emergency override that opened the infirmary's hatch without requiring confirmation from inside, and immediately, before anyone could stop him, said in a loud and clear voice, "Werrr havrr torr tarrk."

Someone yelped. It was, he discovered, the medical ensign, who stood too close to the hatch when it opened and was now rapidly retreating toward the back of the cabin. This hasty move revealed the woman in charge.

Here she is! thought Lipton. *She can't run away. Now we're going to have that conversation!*

Lieutenant Commander Doctor Nightingale took one look at her returning visitor, held a finger to stop him from further talking, lifted something out of a nearby drawer, and shoved it straight into Lipton's face. He howled, but the sound that came out was stifled and, embarrassingly, wet.

"Whrrr rrr yrrr doinrrr?" he gargled. This wasn't as satisfying as his original inclination, i.e. tearing the doctor apart with his bare hands, but he discovered there was nothing else that he could do.

"That's better," the doctor said, grabbed him with both hands and pushed him into a medichair. "This is a bit of a surprise," she added. "I thought you, of all people, would not be caught off-guard on-grav."

Lipton gargled again, achieving nothing but further frustration. The pain in his nose was dull now, but he could still feel something there being awkwardly off-axis. Another something was definitely loose inside. His throat made a sound, though he wasn't sure it was intentional.

"Not a good idea, speaking," the doctor said. "Let's fix your nose first; then we can talk."

The medichair extended one of its mechanical arms, which in turn extended two flexible fingers, which in turn extended straight into Lipton's nostrils. Before he could express his feelings properly by jumping out of the chair, demolishing everything in sight, and murdering the doctor, there was a strange feeling inside his nose and throat, something airy yet wet and cold.

She poisoned me! he thought as the strange freezing material entered his lungs. *Again!*

Something was definitely moving inside his nose. Maybe even digging. Yet somehow, this wasn't such a pressing matter, especially in comparison to being, again, a victim of Doctor Nightingale's toxins.

Actually, his mind continued, *this is not surprising. I should have expected this. It's a neat solution: blame everything on poor Lieutenant Lipton, then get rid of him. Smart. Cool. Awesome. I like it. It solves not only her problems but mine too. Everything will be fixed when I'm gone. Everything will be fine. Being dead is the best way to get on with my life.*

I wonder what I should do afterward. I've been an officer for so long. Maybe I could go for something creative. Knitting? Too complicated. Poetry? Too dangerous. Well, I don't have to decide right away. Being free of this life, I've got all the time in the world . . .

He was so busy figuring out his posthumous future that he completely failed to notice falling asleep.

IT WAS A RATHER MODEST WEDDING. It took place on a cliff rising above the seashore, although this effect was slightly ruined by the lack of gravity. The bride was dressed in a simple white orb and was glowing with happiness and maybe the slightest hint of smugness. The groom wore a plain dark suit with only a single, shining decoration, merely the platinum star, the top imperial badge of honour. Both hovered gently in front of the high registrar, who was dressed in pretty much nothing, as was his custom, him being a robot. All of it was quietly dignified and proper.

"You may kiss the bride," the registrar said softly. The lovers smiled. Their gazes locked. It was pure tenderness, yet very passionate. Their hands touched, pulling themselves toward each other. Her grip on his hand was strong. Her smile grew bigger. Maybe even, how strange, wolfish. No matter, love conquers all.

"My love," he said, "my one and only love." He raised his left hand, touched her cheek, and drew her closer. She raised her right hand, her smile revealing white, even teeth, then grabbed his arm.

"Not so hard, my love," he said.

She let go of him, looked deeply into his eyes, and sharply smacked his wrist.

"How feisty you are, my love," he said.

This time she slapped him in the face. It stung. "There's no calling for that right now, my love," he said good-naturedly, "even though I might admit that I'm open to such experiments when we finally get to our wedding bed." He smiled, rather fetchingly, he thought.

The lovely bride slapped him again. He blinked. The background abruptly changed. Gone were the cliff and the seashore, replaced by metal walls and a vague impression of machinery. The only thing left intact was the lovely bride.

"Welcome back, lover boy," said Doctor Nightingale.

HAD ALL this happened in normal times, as much as any of those existed upon the *UPS Spitz*, Lieutenant Lipton's embarrassment would have all but incapacitated him. But in light of recent events, he now found this to be almost comical. To fall in love with Nightingale, how ludicrous! Indeed she was, he thought, rather striking and exceedingly smart in that nasty way of hers, but *love?* He'd sooner fall in love with a Mobile Infantry armour suit!

He felt that this might not be his final conclusion, but the object of his absolutely-not-love promptly cut short any attempts at further brooding.

"Now that you're all right," she said, "in a manner of speaking, what was it that you wanted to see me about?"

This quickly flooded Lipton's mind with his most recent line of extremely dangerous thinking. It also made him notice the dull pain in his nose, which served to stress the danger. Naturally, his thoughts couldn't be discussed freely. Nor did he know how one could go about suggesting mutiny without exposing oneself to terrible and immediate punishment.

"The reason I came here," he said, "is that after further consideration, I think we should re-examine the storage conditions of—"

"No need for the bloody fridge again," said Doctor Nightingale. "You can speak freely here."

"Of course, doctor, one can and should speak freely anywhere on board the—"

"The controller is off, and so are the logcams, that's one," Nightingale said. "And I sent Ensign Grippe on some errand, and he should be returning soon, so stop wasting time; that's two. And eventually, I will lose my patience with you, Lipton, that's three."

"The controller?"

". . . is off. Well, not precisely off, but we never managed to make it fully functional again. We're missing some parts."

"But—"

"No, using parts from the controller affected by Fux is not such a good idea."

"I'm not sure that—"

"It's safe, it that's what you're worried about. The only danger is, again, me losing my patience. Come on, Lipton, out with it."

This robbed Lipton of the time required to develop any strategy of delivering his point in a reasonably—or even slightly—safe manner. He was left without a choice. His mind was locked in a loop, showing his recent encounter with the captain over and over. The captain, and himself, and Fux. Horrible Fux. Poor Fux. Poor Lipton. Poor everyone. Nothing was safe anymore, anyway. No point in delaying.

He took a deep breath, held the air inside, then quickly, just to get this over with, said, "Mutiny."

"Crap," said Nightingale. She seemed mildly surprised but strangely far from being as perturbed as Lipton had expected.

"I'm serious!" he said.

"I bet you are."

"Believe me, I spent a lot of time thinking about it," said Lipton. It seemed to him, in his current state of mind, that he had hardly ever thought of anything else.

"Double crap," said Nightingale. "I hate it when you do this."

"What do you mean 'do this'?" said Lipton. He knew for a fact that no one on board had ever approached this subject of conversation. Not even slightly. Not even indirectly. Nightingale must be confused. Maybe it was the shock of hearing him say the word in such a direct manner. "I said *mutiny*," he added.

"Yes," said Nightingale. "I heard you perfectly well both times. Now, what caused you to arrive at such a conclusion again?"

Poor Nightingale, she still did not grasp it. *No matter. Shortly she will. A matter such as this may require a few repetitions. It's to be expected. Some people need time to accept the horrible truth.* "Again," Lipton said, "I am talking about mutiny. Mutiny. Do you understand? Mutiny!"

"Just assume for a moment that I did not understand," said Nightingale, "and that it's absolutely imperative that I understand and that the only way of making me understand would be a detailed explanation on your side in regards to the history, the motives, and the logic of what you're trying to say."

"But you said that you *did* under—"

"But *assume* I did not."

"But—"

"From the beginning, Lipton. We haven't got much time."

So Lipton told her. He almost managed to avoid crying.

"WELL," said Doctor Nightingale after patiently listening to Lipton's tale. "It is a serious matter indeed. I should have seen it coming. I shamefully admit, though, that this time around, your story is on the verge of being enjoyable, original, even refreshing, and so—thank you. But most of all, it's sad, and I am sorry."

"This isn't about being sorry! It isn't about our feelings!" said Lipton. *What a time for Nightingale to discover her tender feminine emotions,* he thought. "I am done for," he added, "and so are all of us. We are in grave danger!"

"Yes," said Nightingale. "In grave danger. Or, one could say, in a grave. To a certain degree. I wouldn't make such a fuss this time, though."

"This is not the time for metaphors either," said Lipton. "This is real!"

"To a certain degree," said Nightingale.

Lipton wondered whether this was just another dream, less pleasant than the last one. This would explain Nightingale's strange illogicality and even stranger emotional discourse. But the inside of his nose still ached, and he strongly felt that this kind of thing was a sure mark of the realm of reality, albeit a bizarre one. He looked at Nightingale questioningly.

"You should pay more attention to details," she said. "You know me, and you're familiar with my exact articulation. Still, you ignored it."

"Ignored?"

"Twice, in fact."

"I don't—"

"I'll say it again, in a simplified manner. Do try to pay attention," said Nightingale. "So: this is not the first time."

"The first time of what?"

"Of you approaching me with the idea of mutiny."

I was mistaken, thought Lipton. *This is a dream after all.*

Either that, or she's completely lost her mind. Which is even more impossible than . . .

"You're going to say that this is impossible," Nightingale said, "and I'm going to explain how it isn't, and you are not going to believe me and suggest that you might be dreaming, and I'm going to have to explain everything again, this time from the beginning—"

"How did you know—"

"And you will get it this time," said Nightingale, "which still, in the grand scheme of things, isn't going to do anyone any good either."

"But how did you—"

"Because, Lipton, this is not the first time that we're having this conversation."

"Impossible!" said Lipton. "I would have remembered talking about . . . about . . . I mean . . . there's no way—"

"Do you remember a certain commander named Aruhu?"

"I . . . sure . . . what does it have to do with—"

"Do you remember precisely what happened between the two of you?"

This was too surgically low even for Nightingale's questionable moral standards. Especially after the recent exposure of her emotional side. "I don't see how any of that is any your business!"

"Do I need to remind you that I outrank you? This is a direct order, Lipton: tell me what you remember of the incident with Commander Aruhu, the one that ended your relationship."

"I still don't—"

"Tell me!"

"It's too painful! And you can't just—"

"Tell me, or I shall recalibrate you right now!"

"I . . . she . . . we. . ."

"Yes?"

"I . . ." Lipton said. "I can't remember."

Nightingale pressed her lips into a thin smile. "Precisely."

26

FUX IS INDOCTRINATED

They don't have to be happy or content. They can be overworked, exhausted, endangered, and harshly treated. There is only one limit: never let them reach the point of despair. The desperate are dangerous.

GLORY ROAD, MEMOIRS OF AN IMPERIAL ADMIRAL, AUTHOR UNKNOWN

"DO you know what this vessel is, Fux?" the captain said.

"I'll tell you," she added. "Just so that it's clear that you've made no real change here. Merely accelerated it.

"It is a hearse," she continued. "One big, bloody hearse. Always was, currently is, soon will not be. That is, it will continue being a hearse, but not for us. We're finished. Done for.

"It's not your fault. It's not even mine. It being a hearse, that is. It's the way things are. I just hoped for some more time.

"You think I'm a horrible person, and that's how it's supposed to be. But that's for your own good, for everyone's. Also, it's fake.

"No, don't interrupt; you've talked enough."

The captain looked at her guest, shook her head. "Here's the thing about serving in the military," she said, "the thing that most of you people never realize: no matter what rank you have, you are never truly in command. There's always someone higher up. Even those at the very top have someone to answer to. If they don't—they're not in the military anymore. That thing that is called *command* is actually nothing more than being stuck between an asteroid and a planet. You can punish whomever is below you, but it's always too late: their actions already reflect on you, and soon, you will be punished for their behaviour.

"I will be punished for your actions. All of us will. Even High Admiral Frosch of Top Naval Command, my direct commander. The bastard. But I won't be enjoying his punishment as I should. Also, he won't be punished as thoroughly as us.

"It's funny; you people don't really know what true punishment is. All you know comes from what we show you. Seeing is believing, eh? Stupid.

"You think that this is about your ludicrous offer of marriage. It isn't. Not on its own. It's the combination of everything you've done. It's as if we were a puzzle and you've solved us.

"Do you know what you've done, Fux? Do you realize?

"No, don't answer me.

"The airlock we could have lived with. Also, the mess with the political controller. Machinery can break down; it can be explained. In fact, we'd be in a bad spot if it didn't malfunction from time to time. It gives us excuses so that we can explain to the higher-ups why the universe refuses to comply with their idiotic plans. Oh, if only it was merely broken hardware.

"But then we've won a battle. That's serious. That's something that should never actually *happen*. Not without proper planning from above. What's more, it's unheard of. It's a first.

"Still, on its own, even that could be dealt with. Troopers come and go. Mostly go. We could have fixed it. But your name got into it, even though you weren't there. Somehow, you were logged as being the cause of victory. You like that, don't you?

"Space damn you, Fux, now is not the time for false modesty!

"Anyway, then there was the engine. Its mysterious stoppage isn't a mystery at all, once all the ship logs are combined, even if the controller is broken, and it has to be done manually. No mystery here, then. Also, it's clearly connected to the not-so-mysterious victory, which is, again, clearly connected to you.

"Even this was fixable. Explainable. A spy, a rogue element, working quickly under the noses of the loyal crew. There'd be some punishment, but nothing serious. Some transfers, some recalibrations, maybe even a recycling or two, nothing the crew isn't used to.

"Do you know what true punishment is, Fux? I'll tell you. It's not death. Death is quick and merciful: one moment you're here, the other you're not. Maybe there's some pain in the middle, but the final result is the same. Even if you're tortured—and we don't have the time and resources for that—it's relatively short compared to the total duration of your life.

"No, true punishment is being alive, but without being yourself.

"You think you know what I'm talking about. You have no idea. But soon you will. You idiot.

"The crew, even the officers, are simpletons. Recycling isn't easy, but it's not as if they had great and amazing personalities to begin with. They're riffraff. They're the unwanted remains of society.

"But me, Fux, I'm a real person, Space damn it! I cannot be recycled! Not even once!

"Why do you think I never leave this cabin? I'm the captain, I'm the absolute ruler around here, my word is command, and my command is death. But only here. Up there, there's High Admiral Frosch and every interaction I have with you people can be used by him against me. In fact, almost anything on this ship can be used against me. I can avoid it only by eliminating direct contact.

"And then *you* came and did *exactly* that, damn you and damn that lame Lipton person for letting you. We are connected now, you and me. Did you want marriage? Here it is. Till death do us part. Part of what, we'll never know.

"Here's the best, well, part: the direct cause of our death isn't you. It's Chief Maguro. He fixed the engine you've disabled. Good for him. Bad for us. Now we *will* arrive at the rendezvous point. And do you know what happens at the rendezvous point?"

"Don't try guessing; that's insulting.

"Ship logs are transmitted to the local transponders, that's what. Automatically. And they, in turn, transmit it to High Command for analysis. Which is neither here nor there, really, unless something extraordinary has happened.

"Now, it may take them some time to realize that such a thing has happened. The logs are huge. But there is *one* thing that will trigger an immediate alarm. Can you guess what that is, Fux? Any clue? No? No smart ideas all of a sudden?

"Being *late* to the rendezvous point, that's what it is, you idiot.

"Are you an idiot, Fux? Looks like everything you've done was calculated to ruin us but also yourself. There was never a chance that you'd get away with it. You must be aware of that.

"Why am I even having this conversation?

"It's been so long since I've had one, that's why. I wish it could be someone else. If we're all going down, the least I could ask for is having a decent conversation with a decent person.

"Well, sure, there are no decent persons to be found here, not really, but at least I could be talking to someone who's not a complete idiot.

"Are you an idiot, Fux? Are you?

"Answer me!

"Answer me, damn you!"

But no answer came. Fux, sitting in a chair bolted to the floor on the other side of the huge desk, merely stared at the captain and, insolently, did not reply. Somehow, he managed to remain completely inert. The captain, for the first time since beginning her speech, stared directly at her remarkably silent audience. Clearly, weirdly, her words did not achieve the dread she had expected.

Then realization hit her. "Ah," she said and gestured toward her desk. The elastic arms holding Fux to the chair retreated, and so, with a wet sound, did the gag. As the disgustingly moist red ball retreated into the depth of the chair holding Fux, the latter slowly smacked his lips, moved his tongue within his cheeks, and smiled.

"Ma'am Captain," he said eventually. "I totally and wholeheartedly agree with almost everything that you have said."

"I've read your file, you know? Not the arrests; that's superficial. Not the robo-pets or the other criminalities; that's just foolishness. Not the drunkenness and rude songs. No one cares. But I know the other part. I know what happened to you during the imperial occupation."

"Ma'am?"

"It's too late to pretend, Fux. I know what happened to your family."

Fux's face fell.

At last, the captain thought, *something is getting to him. He's not completely impenetrable, after all.*

"Of course, ma'am," Fux said. He seemed to be immersed in his old memories. "I loved Velbloud and Kun very much," he added, "I truly did. But when the honourable imperial forces landed, there was a crucial shortage of all sorts of things and especially high-quality motor oil, and Velbloud had a bad leg, and Kun's neck ball bearings haven't been greased in years—"

"Fux!"

". . . and so I had to sell them quickly before their value

decreased, and this old lady in Czichneka Number Seven gave me a fair price, and so—"

"I'm not talking about your bloody dogs, Fux!"

"I am sorry, Honourable Ma'am Captain," said Fux, "but you did."

"I was talking about your *family!* I know what happened to—"

"Well, ma'am, that's it. Unless you mean my house-keeper. But, in all honesty, we were never that close, ma'am."

"You know what I mean, Fux."

"No, ma'am," said Fux and smiled.

Was he recalibrated before coming here? Recycled, even? the captain thought. *There's nothing about it in his file, but then, if files were perfect, we'd all be perfect. Perfectly dead. Which is exactly what's going to happen anyway. Very soon.*

"Oh, never mind," she said. "It doesn't matter. Not after being late to the rendezvous point. Definitely not after they read our ship logs."

"Ma'am Captain," Fux said, "in regard to that, I think it is important to arrive on time, and it is bad to be late, but also that sometimes being late can be excused, or at least deserve only minor punishment, especially if you promise to make things right afterward, or even before it."

"*Promise?*" the captain said bitterly.

"Take, for example, the honourable ship logs, ma'am," Fux said. "They are broken, but maybe they can be fixed?"

"Fixed?"

"The engine was broken, and Chief Maguro fixed it, ma'am. Maybe someone could fix the logs, too."

The captain, by reflex, glanced at the logcam, then sharply turned her eyes back to Fux.

"Do you have any idea what's going to happen to us if we are caught tampering with the logs?"

"We shall be dead, ma'am, and rightfully so, too. The honourable High Command will have every right to do so."

"Do you *want* to die, Fux?"

Fux did not answer but merely gazed at her with terribly innocent eyes.

Can this idiot be right? We can't change the logs, but what if we sabotage them? Erase them completely? And find an excuse for both this and our delay?

Well, no. There's absolutely no chance that it'll work. Admiral Frosch will never let this go. What's more, he will enjoy it. The bastard.

But then, what other choice do we have?

"Space damn you, Fux," the captain said. "Stand up. On your feet."

"Ma'am?"

"Silence. You're going to get what you wanted. Now listen. Carefully."

And thus it was that Fux convinced the mighty captain of the UPS *Spitz* to boldly go where no captain had gone before.

27

FUX IS CONSEQUENCED

While naval officers cannot be instructed concerning matters of the heart, regulations dictate that tender feelings should be shown only toward an absentee. Affairs involving persons sharing a location, a unit, or a vessel are strictly forbidden.

TO SAIL BEYOND THE SUNSET, A NAVAL
OFFICER'S HANDBOOK

"THERE NEVER WAS A COMMANDER AHURU," Nightingale said.

"Don't do that," Lipton said. He was shaking. "You can't do that to me."

"By now, you must have suspected it, or at least that something was seriously off. You've had a love affair, you know you've had it, you're absolutely certain that you've had it, but can't remember anything about it. Why? Because Ahuru never existed."

"I loved her!"

"Yes, you did fall in love," Nightingale said, "but not with her. You were very spectacular about it. It was enough to get you recycled."

"I don't remember being," Lipton said, then stopped. "Wait," he said. "*Recycled?*"

"Yes."

"Recalibrated, you mean. I'm still alive, am I not?"

"Do I usually say what I don't mean to say, Lipton?"

He managed a wry smile. "All of us do, now that you mention it."

"True." He wasn't a bad sort, really, this Lipton, Nightingale thought. If only he could keep his feelings to himself or get rid of them altogether like everyone else. "But we're not playing political games now. The fact is: you were recycled."

"But I'm—"

"Have you ever watched a recycling up close? Have you ever been in the room when someone was being recycled?"

"Well, no, but I've seen it."

"That's right, but only twice, and you wouldn't remember it. My point is, what you do remember is mostly for show."

"Wait, how do you know? And why are you telling me this? Are you playing with me? Is this another trick? Haven't you caused me enough pain by now? What have I done to you?"

Nightingale sighed. "Do you know the reason I'm here, Lipton?"

"Excuse me?"

"I had a great position, a wonderful job in a top-ranking medical institute. At a top-ranking *political* medical institute. On Terra-actual itself, no less. Do you have any idea how lucrative that is? How privileged?"

"What does that have to do with anything?"

"I was happy. But clearly not happy enough. Or maybe happiness wasn't enough. I wanted more. I wanted to climb the ladder, to get to the top."

"You don't seem the type," Lipton said, "and also, what does this have to do—"

"Problem was, the top was already occupied. No place for anyone new, anyone young, and especially not a young, ambitious smartass such as myself."

"I don't see—"

"But where there's a will, there's a way. And so, one of the old doctors gave me some useful advice. 'Get enlisted,' he said, 'somewhere not outright dangerous, maybe in a military hospital or the Navy, so you're not doing any actual fighting. Spend a year or two like that, then get back to us. No one at the top has a military record of any kind, and they're too old to gain it. You'll have an advantage. In a few years, this place will be yours.'"

"A year or two?" Lipton said. "Since when does the military let you go after—"

"But I didn't know that, did I?" Nightingale said. "And so, here I am."

And he thinks I am the one who tricks others, Nightingale thought bitterly. *It would've been funny if it wasn't my life.*

"But what does that have to do with me?" Lipton asked.

"It's an act of mercy on my side," she said. "I'm giving

you the big picture so that the person that you are now will have it before . . . before ceasing to be that person."

"Is this some kind of—"

"No, I'm not threatening you. Now, let's talk about another young and promising person, that's one, and about my position here, that's two, and about a sad, unavoidable conclusion, that's three."

"Why do you have to enumerate everything?" asked Lipton. "It's insufferable."

"That's your *current* opinion. Anyway, some years ago, there was a young and promising lad, also born on Terra-actual, who was rather gifted in his studies but sadly entertained greater aspirations. Like many young persons, he felt that the world could be a better place, though without any clear vision as to how this might be achieved. Looking for more than just a life of honest, boring servitude, looking for a higher cause, it occurred to him to investigate the past. He knew that history was best kept to state-approved scholars, but his urge was too strong.

"He searched, and soon enough, he found. It was almost too easy. Right there, in his school's local storage, there was a collection of old poems. Ancient poems, forbidden poems, strong, exhilarating, exciting, moving poems. He read them over and over again. If only everyone else could read them too, understand them, be moved by them, the same as him! But it was clear that any attempt to spread the word would end quickly and harshly. Then, the young lad had a brilliant idea: he would write such poems himself. Camouflaged, of course, fitting the spirit of the time, going right over the heads of the stupid imperial truth enforcers and ideologists, but just enough for an intelligent, aware, inquiring person to understand.

"He was very careful, of course, using only his personal, octo-encrypted logbook. He took special care to disguise his message of love and liberty to all with cunning, seemingly politically correct metaphors. And sure enough, the day after his first two poems were committed to storage, he was forcefully drafted into the Navy."

"I think I've heard of that," Lipton said, "though I'm not sure where."

"The young person's name was Lemons," said Nightingale.

"That also sounds somewhat—"

"It was you, you idiot."

This time Lipton didn't answer.

"Well, not precisely you," Nightingale said. "It was you before I made you the man you are today."

Lipton just looked at her.

"Or rather," she added for the sake of precision, "it was the man you were before I made you the man you were before you were the man you are soon not to be."

The hurt in his gaze was almost as piercing as the last time this happened. *That's to be expected,* she thought. *The last time, he had an even better reason to feel betrayed.*

"I had to recycle you, Lipton. That is, at first, I had to recycle a foolish young man named Lemons and reconstruct him in the form of Lieutenant Lyons. Then I had to recycle a foolish young Lieutenant named Lyons and reconstruct him in the form of Lipton."

Lipton still failed to answer.

"The first recycling was by order from above," Nightingale said. "Standard Navy procedure. But the second one was my own doing. I am sorry, Lipton, but you forced my hand. That is, my hand was forced by Lieutenant Lyons. Can you guess why?"

She hoped that Lipton's expression meant that he was slowly understanding.

"He fell in love with a superior officer," she said, "and in his despair over an affair that was never to be, concluded that it was the system, the Navy, the whole military, the entire empire which were to blame. And so—"

"Mutiny," said Lipton.

"Precisely. Enter Lieutenant Lipton."

"But," said Lipton, "if you recycled me, how come nobody saw it? What about the displays?"

"I was just coming to that," Nightingale said. "But first, a question: what is it that I'm in charge of on this ship?"

"Why are you changing the subject?"

"I'm not changing anything except for you, but that comes later. Now, you were going to say that I am in charge of everything medical on board this ship. And you'd be right."

"But," said Lipton. He seemed slightly more composed. Not bad for someone in his position. Or maybe he was just sliding into a more stable state of shock. What a waste.

"But, indeed," Nightingale said. "But—and that's the part which almost no one here has fully grasped—these days, there's no real difference between 'medical' and 'political.'"

"Political? But Kapust—"

"Knowing Commander Kapust, would you put him in any meaningful position? Do you know anyone who would?"

"But he is—"

"Any position whatsoever? Any responsibility whatsoever?"

"Well—"

"Precisely."

"But . . . you?"

"Think, Lipton: who's in charge of the controller machine? Who's in charge of recalibrations? Who's in charge of recycling?"

"But I never saw you on—"

"No, you never saw me on any public recycling, and that is because those, as you should have concluded by now, are fake. That 'bio-reclamation chamber' you see is as real as your Commander Aruhu."

Lipton lowered his head and did not answer. This was probably due to mentioning his fictional object of love. If only he wasn't so sensitive.

"In answer to your question," said Nightingale, "recycling is just another kind of recalibration. It's the kind where your entire mind is wiped out and reconstructed. So, in a sense, it's a kind of death. Even if, as you've just demonstrated, much of your essential character remains unchanged."

Lipton raised his head and looked her in the eyes, still saying nothing.

"I am really, truly sorry that I have to do this to you again," said Nightingale. "There's no way to avoid it. The only other option is true death at the hands of the captain. Most of those are fake, too, but not for mutiny. For that, they will be real enough."

"I thought we were friends," Lipton said.

"We were. Sort of. I trust that we will be again."

"I hate you."

Doctor Nightingale sighed. "Don't worry," she said. "Not for long."

She initiated the preparation sequence on the infirmary's main control board. The medichair groaned, emitted a few restraining arms and grabbed the unremitting Lieutenant Lipton.

"For the last time," Nightingale said, "I'm sorry."

Lipton opened his mouth and made a rather strange sound. There was something mechanical about his voice. In fact, it couldn't be his voice. Especially, Nightingale realized, as it came from behind her.

The Lieutenant Commander Doctor turned around. The infirmary's hatch was open. What it revealed made both Nightingale and the shackled Lipton inhale sharply at the same time.

There, framed by the open hatch, stood the very familiar yet officially-inexistent Private Fux.

PART FOUR
THE RAMBUNCTIOUS REBEL

28

FUX IS REINSTATED

A light frigate, like any other United Planets vessel, requires absolute obedience and dedication in order to operate. Its design prohibits any rogue operations. The amount of organization and cooperation required to modify or disable any of its major systems is, given our systematic political control, inconceivable. It is absolutely rogue-proof.

TUNNEL IN THE SKY, A LIGHT FRIGATE
COMMAND AND MAINTENANCE HANDBOOK

"FUX!" said Lieutenant Lipton. "You're alive!" He hesitated, then added, "Aren't you?"

Doctor Nightingale didn't say anything but was strangely smiling. Lipton, for the first time since the beginning of this miserable affair, felt a surge of hope.

"Yes, sir," Fux said. "As far as I can remember, I was

never not alive. Though I could be if you commanded me to, or at least I would tell everyone that I was not, I mean, not alive, sir, if that was absolutely required by yourself, sir."

"Stop blabbering, Fux," Lipton said warmly. He hadn't realized how much he had missed his well-meaning yet deranged orderly.

"Yes, sir," the latter said. "And honourable ma'am, too."

Doctor Nightingale was still smiling. "As happy as I am to see you, sort of," she said, "I suspect that your arrival here has more to it than just reuniting with your, for lack of a better word, *commanding* officer."

Lipton found this remark to be rather unfair, especially considering recent revelations regarding his history and Nightingale's part in it. But before he made up his mind as to the proper way of expressing his earnest feelings on the matter, his ex-orderly answered.

"I do not know what a better word might be," Fux said, "but essentially, ma'am is absolutely correct: I was told to come here. With respect to both sir and honourable ma'am, and I am sorry in advance for this, and it was not really my idea, even though some would say that I did have something to do with it, though, of course, I am too insignificant to be of actual—"

"Get on with it, Fux!" Nightingale said.

"I was told," said Fux, "that, only this once, it is me who has to tell you what to do and not the other way around."

Despite the seriousness of the situation, Lipton still managed to enjoy the expression on Nightingale's face. Immensely, even. Alas, this did not last for long.

COMMANDER KAPUST COULD NOT BELIEVE his eyes.

"You!" he said. "You cannot be here! You cannot be anywhere! How can you be? You cannot! Go away!"

"Absolutely, honourable sir!" the apparition said, yet made no evident effort to obey.

"You do not exist, do you hear me? You were officially erased! Your existence is in direct violation of military protocols!"

"I most certainly agree," said Fux. "I have been told many times that I am in violation. This reminds me of a funny thing that happened back in my hometown of Praha when I was young and yet unattached, much like today. It involved this fetching lady, some years my elder, who favoured me for some reason, very much so if I may say so myself, and afterward, some people also said that I was in violation, or rather that I violated something, though now that you mention it, I am not sure what it was."

"You bloody . . . you . . . you . . . I will kill you!" Kapust said. He was mortally afraid of mentioning the idiot's name, which would put him in violation of protocol himself.

Fux nodded in agreement. "That is also what her husband said."

Kapust rose up from his chair. "Get out!" he screamed. "Get out before I call the captain!"

"Funny you should mention her, sir," Fux said. "For, in fact, she had also mentioned you."

Fux's calm and smiling manner utterly failed to prevent Kapust from losing his balance and falling back into his chair. But this was merely the beginning. Being mentioned by the captain, the commander soon found out, was by far the least disturbing thing that his impossible guest had to say.

COLONEL HAVOCK WAS HAVING A RELATIVELY quiet time in the officers' mess, attacking a generous portion of a supposed meatloaf, slurping a mercifully unidentified beverage, and deliberately ignoring the miserable Second Lieutenant Big, may Space have no mercy on his soul. The latter was an ongoing reminder of some uncomfortable recent events, a disgrace to the uniform.

Like everyone else, he had noticed the engine failure, a lucky occurrence that would surely divert High Command's focus from the Mobile Infantry's unexplainable tactical mishap on Planet Whatever. But then, despite the common soldiery's obvious reluctance to communicate with him, word of some other naval debacle had reached the colonel. There were even some whispers of troopers cooperating with naval personnel in order to either cause some unfortunate failure or to fix it. This was, of course, impossible. They wouldn't dare. Especially now that what's-his-face was safely out of Havock's jurisdiction and back in the Spacedamned Navy.

It was for this reason that Havock received a nasty shock upon seeing that same what's-his-face person entering the officers' mess in complete contradiction to standing orders and also the state of the colonel's stomach. Before anything could be said or done, the miscreant approached, gave the most undignified salute the colonel had ever seen, and said something that the roar of blood in Havock's ears completely prevented him from hearing.

A trained trooper of the highest degree, Havock reflexively stood up, grabbed what's-his-name by the throat, and was preparing to be done with him once and for all, logs and bloody Kapust be damned, when someone politely tapped on his back. He half-turned, still holding his intended victim in an iron grip, to find that the source of the interruption was his disgraceful second-in-command.

"Sir," said Second Lieutenant Big, "I'm sorry, but we have to listen to him, sir." His voice was way too whiny for an officer of the Mobile Infantry. Something would have to be done.

"Shut up," Havock said and turned again toward what's-his-name.

"But, sir," Big said behind his back, "he said that—"

"I don't care," Havock said. "Pipe down before I pipe you down. Know what? I'll pipe you down anyway, right after I finish with this one."

"Yes, sir," Big said meekly. To think that this person was actually commanding troopers. Shameful. Horrible. "Only, sir," the second lieutenant added, "he said that he was sent by the captain."

SERGEANT PRIVATE QUARTERMASTER Bolon was having a most wonderful dream. In it, his best friend and colleague, the fabulous Mister Fux, had somehow returned from the dead, his sins against leader and empire miraculously forgiven, or at least unmentioned. Everything returned to just the way it was before, except for the armoury lying in shambles after a few shifts of complete negligence, not to mention a sad incident involving thirty litres of exploded soup.

True to character, the recently returned dream-Fux brought with him a slab of so-called cheese that he had liberated from the regimental kitchen and, while they were both consuming it, embarked upon a detailed yet vague story. This quickly turned out to be a scheme, a plot with which the quartermaster's assistance was required and which in some way involved the captain. Bolon promptly agreed. He did not want the dream to end.

It occurred to him that, in comparison to most of his other dreams, this one was rich with smells, tastes, and plot details.

"Am I awake?" he asked eventually.

"I wouldn't presume to say, Sergeant Private, sir," said Fux with a smile, took something out of his pocket, and handed it to Bolon. It was a small jar filled with some grey material. Bolon opened it and sniffed. The smell was unmistakable: liver-flavoured eggplant pate.

"It *is* you!" Bolon shouted and rushed to embrace his long-lost—well, short-lost—friend.

Eventually, after much hugging and crying, things quieted down enough for Bolon to consume the pate and for Fux to repeat his previous briefing. The plot still sounded weird. It still involved the captain. Bolon accepted it without hesitation. If Fux could return from the never-existence, anything was possible.

SOMETHING really nasty must have happened inside the circuitry of the morale unit of the Mobile Infantry barracks. For the past hour or so, it had continuously repeated the chorus of an old imperial hymn, driving everyone around it to the brink of insanity.

"Freedom!" it shouted, and then, pretending to use another voice, *"You won't let us down."*

They tried to turn it off, but the morale unit was designed with just that kind of thing in mind and remained unaffected.

"Freedom! *You will not give us up* . . . Freedom! *Have some faith in the leader!*"

One of the younger troopers suggested shooting it. This caused a major argument about the dangers of using live ammunition inside the barracks or a spaceship in general. It was rather academic and, to a degree, interesting. It was also utterly useless, as Corporal Clementine made it clear that the first one to use any kind of weapon would have to answer to her.

"You've gotta give for what you take . . . *The leader deserves everything I've got!*"

Someone suggested short-circuiting the thing, but this required opening it, which turned out to be impossible. The atmosphere in the barracks became quite heated. The repeating hymn was, by this time, unbearable.

The only person to remain unaffected was Mister Daisy, sitting quietly in his corner and smiling to himself. While he didn't like the awful hymn any more than the others he found his colleagues' distress rather entertaining. He was hoping that someone would notice his expression and ask him about it, giving him a chance to demonstrate his moral and mental superiority, but in vain. No one paid any attention to him. This was disappointing, but not as much as the sudden wail emitted by the morale unit, which soon turned into an insufferable screeching noise, and then into ominous silence.

On the other side of the barracks, near the hatch, someone choked. Mister Daisy raised his gaze and, over the heads of the other troopers, saw a familiar face entering the premises. It was that useless quartermaster person carrying some parcel on his back. Someone emitted a short, surprised cry. Mister Daisy couldn't imagine why Bolon would cause any excitement whatsoever, but then, as the quartermaster took a step forward, the person behind him, who was, in fact, helping him carry the parcel, was revealed.

"Fux!" shouted Mister Daisy in unison with the rest of the platoon.

Corporal Clementine rose from her bunk and, as shameless as Mister Daisy always suspected she was, gave Fux a hug. A wave of joy spread through the barracks. Mister Daisy found this absolutely uncalled for, not to say treacherous. The fool was supposed to be done with! The fool was erased! But no, here he was, and everyone was happy about it. This was, Mister Daisy thought, terribly unfair.

"What's to be happy about?" he said aloud. "This obscene person shouldn't be here! Wait until I tell the—"

Only then he noticed that his voice was rather too loud and clear since everyone else had stopped talking. Or emitting any sound whatsoever. They weren't looking at him. They were ignoring him. Even more than usual, that is. They were gazing at the hatch, mesmerized.

"Listen to me, you bastards," he said into the suspicious silence, "or you'll be sorry!"

He was immediately proven right in that there was sorrow to be had and, in particular, his very own, as another familiar figure appeared behind Fux's smiling face. It was holding a still-glowing energy gun. It was Colonel Havock.

AT THE PARADE GROUNDS, Sergeant Zimmer, waiting for his very late and extremely insubordinate trainees, was torn between rage and relief. The very idea that the soldiers under his so-called command would dare behave this way was impertinent beyond belief. On the other hand, considering the soldiers' recent unfortunate history, and especially the resultant consequences in regard to his own wellbeing, he kept hoping for some miracle that would keep them away. Not that any of it greatly mattered or was any cause for excitement, for he was still under the powerful calming influence of his recent recalibration.

Despite his condition, Sergeant Zimmer was about to experience a series of mood changes of a rapidly increasing magnitude.

At first, he was mildly disappointed to notice that the missing troopers had finally arrived, meekly entering the parade grounds in a relatively orderly manner. Then, he was slightly alarmed to notice they were carrying their close-combat energy weapons, which should have been locked in the armoury until right before boarding a combat launch pod. Then, he was marginally relieved to notice Corporal Clementine among the soldiers, albeit similarly armed, which meant that she could safely be blamed for any resulting mishaps. Then, he was somewhat distressed to see Second Lieutenant Big, who had no business being there. Then, he had a certain bad premonition, noticing the ship's doctor and another unfamiliar officer, a Navy lieutenant, completely out of place there, where only real soldiers train. This soon turned into fear in the form of Colonel Havock.

Zimmer instinctively started preparing a list of excuses but got interrupted by the arrival of a heavyset person whom he recognized as the dreadful Commander Kapust. A political officer inside the parade grounds! This was not only serious but horrible. It could not be.

Alas, this wasn't the end of Zimmer's inner turmoil. His mounting fear and confusion were soon turned into sheer mortification. This occurred just as he noticed the next person to enter the barracks.

It was the captain.

In his dizziness, he lost his footing and sat down clumsily. Someone shouted, "Attention!" Everyone around him obeyed. He saw only a forest of feet in crumpled green one-time paper uniforms of various hues and levels of decomposition. Which is why, perhaps blissfully, he did not notice the last person to enter the parade grounds.

That is, until the captain herself said, "Come here, Fux."

AS FAR AS Zimmer was concerned, the rest of this strange and frightful gathering passed in a haze. Initially, someone shouted at him, and someone else grabbed his collar and pulled him up to a standing position. The captain, after a short hushed conversation with the ship's doctor, turned to the troops. Then, Colonel Havock shouted something about the Mobile Infantry code of honour, but the captain cut him in mid-sentence.

"It's as phony as everything else about you," she said. "Do shut up, Havock, before I reveal some of your true fake combat histories right here and now."

This had the desired effect on the colonel but, for some reason, seemed to encourage Commander Kapust, who, compared to his numerous televised appearances, seemed rather pathetic.

"Dear, ahem, Captain," he said, "I would not advise, for reasons of troop morale and well-being, to employ this kind of language; that is, the usage of that particular word, 'fake.' In fact, let us avoid it altogether by calling it 'the f-word,' if you will, and even then—"

"Look who's talking!" the captain said. "Fake indeed!"

The political officer visibly deflated. Zimmer found this to be both hilarious and awful. Nothing in his experience had prepared him for any of this.

Having dealt with the two senior officers, the captain stepped back and let the doctor come forward and start talking. Zimmer did not understand most of it but had the impression that she was discussing the ship logs. In particular, how to dismantle them. Zimmer had never suspected that this action, or even thinking about it, was possible. This was high treason. Right in front of the captain.

No, by *the captain.*

"All right," the captain said eventually. "You know what you have to do. It's either that or we're all gone. So, in groups of three, officers and soldiers, get out of here and do what needs to be done."

"But, ahem," said Commander Kapust, "surely top officers are exempt from such—"

"*Officers* and soldiers, I said!" the captain retorted. "Are you an officer, Kapust? Would you like to continue being an officer, Kapust? Would you like to continue being a *Kapust*, Kapust?"

The political officer stood to attention faster than anyone would have thought possible. "Yes, ma'am!"

"I'll take him," said someone else. It was Colonel Havock. He was smiling. It was not a pretty sight.

Everyone quickly divided into groups and marched out. Soon, only Sergeant Zimmer remained. Unchosen. Uncared for. Ignored.

He was almost surprised to realize that he preferred it that way.

29

FUX IS FOLLOWED

The existence of an army must be balanced by the existence of an army-worthy opponent. Hence, the creation and continuous operation of the counter-combat committee. In this, our leadership took inspiration from the famous scientific principle: for every action, there is an equal and opposite political reaction.

THE PUPPET MASTERS, A POLITICAL
INTRODUCTION FOR TOP-LEVEL MILITARY
PERSONNEL, CLASSIFIED

"I STILL DO NOT UNDERSTAND," said Commander Kapust.

"That's the problem with you Navy types," said Colonel Havock. "You're always highbrow. You always ask questions. True soldiers don't ask questions. True soldiers do as they're told. But then, you were never a true soldier, were you, Kapust?"

"I'm your superior officer, Havock! You will not speak to me that way! I shall log a formal complaint! Even someone like you must know what this means."

"It means nothing, you wimp," Havock said and pointed at the third member of their group, the disgraceful Second Lieutenant Big. The young officer, doing his best to pretend this conversation was not happening, was fiddling in vain with a service latch on the wall marked LOGMEM 112 / ADMIRALTY ONLY / NO TAMPERING / ON PAIN OF RECYCLING.

"So suddenly the political division means nothing to you?" Kapust said. "Well, well, well. We shall see about that."

Havock's smile grew enough to be in danger of leaving his face altogether. "Correct," he said. "Without the logs, you're nothing, Kapust. Absolutely nothing."

"The word of an officer and a gentleman—"

"Means nothing without a supporting ship-log entry. Which is exactly why we're here," Havock said. "Also—you, a gentleman? Ha. Pathetic."

Before Kapust could find a proper reply to this atrocity, the colonel jabbed the second lieutenant's neck.

"What the Space is taking you so long, Big?"

"Sir," the young officer said, "this thing isn't built to be opened, sir." His voice had a whiny undertone that even Kapust, who was used to this kind of behaviour, found to be insulting.

"A fine example of, ahem, an officer," Kapust said.

"Mind your own business," said Havock without turning around.

"Oh, but everything on board this ship is my, ahem, business," Kapust said.

Havock, who was notoriously incapable of holding lengthy discussions, did not reply. Instead, he pushed aside the worthless underling and took his energy weapon out of its holster.

"I say!" blurted Kapust, who still vividly remembered that horrid encounter in his cabin. "There's no need for violence! Remember what happened last time—"

Havock aimed his weapon and opened fire. For the briefest of moments, there was no sound or visible effect. Then, with a proper sizzling sound, the wall, hatch and all, melted in a cloud of smoke.

"Sir!" said the miserable fine example of an officer. "We were told to leave no visible marks of this, sir!"

"What marks?" said Havock. The smoke evaporated, exposing the storage chamber it was enclosing. From the other side of the wall, a rather surprised spaceman-apprentice was staring at them, holding an absolutely illegal bowl of instant broth, a noodle dangling stupidly from his mouth.

"I don't see any marks," the colonel continued. "Do you see any marks, apprentice?"

The interrupted eater shook his head obediently, promptly and, to Havock's evident satisfaction and Kapust utter disgust, fearfully. This caused the hanging noodle to dance around his chin in a most inappropriate way.

"See?" said Havock, ignoring the undignified aspect of this performance. "No wall—no marks!"

Kapust sighed. *I shouldn't care,* he thought; he's *not my problem. Let the captain eat what she's cooked.*

As they were moving toward the next LOGMEM, Kapust idly wondered whether his own existence would last long enough to include any cooking whatsoever.

His concern was, eventually, proven justified.

"I STILL DON'T UNDERSTAND," said Lieutenant Lipton.

"You'll have to be more specific," said Doctor Nightingale, pushing some sort of unidriver into LOGMEM 86. "Is this about your personal situation, or why we're doing what we're doing, or Fux?"

"All of the above," Lipton said. "Plus everything else."

"Well, you're actually better off, sort of, now that Fux has done what he has done. I won't have to recycle you, even though there's a good chance of all of us getting it for what we're doing right now. Now, please stand back."

Lipton retreated, and the latch clicked and opened. There was the typical pressure-equalizing hiss and a small cloud of vapour.

"I'm probably done for either way," Lipton said from his new place behind the doctor's back. "If I'm lucky, the next me won't remember any of this. Which, come to think of it, doesn't help me at all. It's confusing."

"Here's a thing for you to consider, though," Nightingale said. "Actual recycling always takes place after the televised one. It happens in the infirmary. It involves a complete rebuild of the personality. We're not talking here about mere recalibration; that one's easy enough to do in the brig. At least, the simple variety. But full recycling requires something heavy. Can you guess what kind of machinery would be complex enough to perform such an operation?"

"I assume you mean the main controller."

"Indeed," Nightingale said, sticking her hand into the cavity in the wall. "Now, do you remember what happened to it?"

"It got messed—"

"It got *Fuxed*. Do you realize what this means?"

"I . . . no?"

"The main controller is a learning machine. That's the only way you can rebuild a personality without turning the person into a vegetable: you need to read the mind, then analyze it, then use that information in a . . . let us say, in a non-linear way, to achieve the desired effect. This means that the controller is, to a degree, affected by the person it works on."

"That doesn't seem to be wise in the long term," said Lipton, who found this kind of academic discussion to be much more relaxing than its relevance to his immediate future.

"There are built-in filters and barriers, ensuring that the controller's basic neural structure is never damaged or overridden."

"Sounds wise, in the long term," said Lipton, delighted in his newly gained freedom to express outright sarcasm.

"But then, there's Fux," said Nightingale, twisting hard at something inside the LOGMEM cavity. A loud click followed. She pulled her hand back, holding a small box. "I've spent quite a lot of time working on the controller after Fux. And what did I find?"

She stuck her hand into one of her numerous pockets, then into another, and pulled out something which, to Lipton's untrained eye, seemed to resemble one of those toilet pumps you can encounter on some of the more primitive planets. This, she pressed onto the unit she had taken out of the wall. Something beeped.

"Well?" Lipton asked after some time.

"Just a moment," Nightingale said. Soon, there was another beep. "Right," she added, putting the pump thing back in her pocket. "Total feedback."

"Excuse me?"

"Total feedback. It's as if, instead of the controller spreading the desired personality all over Fux, Fux spread his personality all over the controller."

"But you said there are filters—"

"It should be impossible. Except that it happened."

"So how—"

"I can only guess that there's something in his personality that the machine wasn't built for. That it couldn't take. You have to admit that he's quite special."

"Definitely," Lipton said, with almost no bitterness at all. "Special. Absolutely."

"Still, if I had to guess what kind of personality would be able to resist the machine, not to mention overthrow it, I wouldn't have considered anyone like Fux."

"None of us considered anything like Fux," Lipton said. "Yet, here we are."

"He's too jolly," Nightingale said. "He's just not the right type."

"Type?"

"Maybe not precisely happy, but too . . . satisfied."

"As opposed to?"

"Total despair. Someone who's completely unaffected by anything, any future event, because the worst possible thing has already happened. Traumatized, perhaps. Just the opposite of Fux. I would even go as far as saying—someone who wishes to die."

"Hmm," Lipton said. "Interesting."

"Indeed," Nightingale said. She pushed the small box back into the wall and twisted it, then closed the hatch.

"The interesting thing is," Lipton said eventually, Nightingale having failed to be lured by his suggestive tone, "that Fux sort of fits the bill."

"I don't see how," said Nightingale.

"I'm disappointed in you," Lipton said with a smile. It wasn't every day that one got a chance to prove the doctor wrong. "Consider all the information you have: he began by attempting to open an airlock and finished by asking the captain—*the captain!*—to marry him."

"So?"

"So if all that isn't suicidal—what is?"

After that, they worked in silence for some time. Both felt that this needed some contemplation, and further discussion could wait.

In this, they were mistaken.

"I STILL DON'T UNDERSTAND, MA'AM," the skinny old trooper said. He was ludicrously dressed in an ill-fitting one-day uniform that had to be at least a month old and awkwardly bespectacled, to boot. He was fighting the lock of LOGMEM 42 and, so far, losing.

The captain was enjoying this, in addition to her newfound, if surely short-lived, opportunity to participate in a true conversation of any kind. "Don't you know what a hearse is?" she asked.

"Yes, ma'am."

"And?"

"And I do recognize the connection to our current situation, ma'am," said Mister Daisy, whose new name was also quite entertaining. "But you say it has always been this way."

"If I remember right," the captain said, "you've had some original ideas about our enemy."

"How did—"

"I, too, have to pass the time somehow. Monitoring the barracks is, let's say, a hobby."

Mister Daisy gave her a fearful glance. She did not bother telling him that it didn't matter, nor that he was selected to accompany her here for his sheer entertainment value. "You think, correct me if I'm wrong,"—*as if he'd ever dare to*—"that the insects are merely a metaphor for another human culture, one that the empire is determined to obliterate."

"I knew it!" said Mister Daisy. "I was right!"

"About the metaphor, you were."

"I wish they could hear you say it! They gave me serious Space about it. They laughed at me. The fools! I knew I was right all along. I knew it!"

"No," the captain said. This was, she felt, like a truly great last meal. Destined to die, the doomed can still enjoy themselves.

"But you said—"

"That it's a metaphor, yeah. In a way. But no, there's no other human culture, just our own."

"But if—"

"Exactly."

"Right," said Mister Daisy with an obedient nod. He attacked the LOGMEM one more time, then stopped. "No, but, ma'am, I don't—"

At this rate, the captain thought, *we're all going to be recycled before he gets the hang of it.*

"Step aside," she said, "and give me that unidriver."

Mister Daisy promptly obeyed.

"There's no other culture," the captain said. "Therefore, the enemy is, well, ourselves." She pressed the unidriver into the designated slot inside the latch. It required quite a bit of force. Nothing that a proper trooper should find hard to do. *Which,* she thought, *just goes to show.*

Mister Daisy was nodding but clearly without understanding.

"The Mobile Infantry and the Navy serve the same goal," the captain said. "Getting rid of potentially dangerous, subversive, tainted, or otherwise substandard persons, for the betterment of the empire."

"Getting rid of you, Captain?"

"Me being here means that I'm nowhere else," the captain said. "That I'm out of the way. Same goes for all of us in the Navy. Which is still better than you people, set to be regularly consumed in fake combat."

"I *was* in combat, in *actual* combat!" said Mister Daisy. "I mean, ma'am. I was there! It can't be fake! I saw the cows, I saw the—"

"You wouldn't expect the empire to waste real, valuable resources on you people, would you? The counter-combat committee has never enjoyed a huge budget. When they ran out of proper mechanical monsters, they had to improvise. Hence what you call 'the insects.' It's a general enough name."

"Counter-combat ... committee?"

"That's who you've been fighting. You'll be happy to know that they, too, answer to High Command."

"But they killed us!"

"Admittedly, their transition to automated self-replicating hybrid robo-animal contraptions went a bit too well. Too efficient. You may even say that it got a bit out of control. But, of course, you can't report anything like that. Politically speaking, being faulty or too efficient or out of control are all the same thing: unacceptable, impossible. So, the counter-combat committee got too good, and the Mobile Infantry got too crippled, and the reports reflected nothing of this, and, well, you saw the results."

"Crippled?"

"Of course. The Mobile Infantry had to be slightly crippled, by design, for the insects to have any chance at all. Initially, that is, before the insects got too good at it. Remember your perfectly maintained armour suits, soldier? Remember how, up until recently, they weren't so perfect?"

"But Havock has a working suit!"

"As he must. We wouldn't want to lose him. There aren't too many Havocks around. He has just the right amount of infantile aggressiveness and combat readiness. It's a rare combination."

"Does . . . does he know, ma'am? I mean, about the insects, the. . . the counter-combat committee?"

"That's your first good idea, Daisy. I should tell him. He should know who it was that he was fighting. And that it never mattered. Yes, I want to see his face when he learns it. Should be entertaining."

To the captain's pleasant surprise, Mister Daisy, despite the recent unrooting of his worldview, managed a smile.

"I would like to see that," he said.

Maybe, after all, there was more to him than met the eye.

It was a pity, she thought afterward, though not that much later, that this idea would never be realized.

"I DON'T UNDERSTAND," Bolon said, "or maybe I just don't fully understand, yes? But also, I sort of don't want to understand."

Fux smiled and quickly opened LOGMEM 128. "This reminds me of a funny thing that happened back in my hometown of Praha," he said.

Bolon enjoyed the story very much. It involved a turkey and a piece of ham. It lasted seven LOGMEMs.

It was only afterward that Bolon thought to ask about the mysterious ham thing. It was obviously a foodstuff, but of what kind, exactly? Was it solid or fluid? Did it come in a jar? Was it edible on its own, or perhaps some kind of spice? But by the time these important questions occurred to Bolon, it was already too late.

"I DON'T UNDERSTAND," said Master Chief Maguro. This related less to the lack of understanding of his fellow ship-mates and more to the fact that the recently restored engine had, unprovoked, stopped working again. Even more embar-rassing was the fact that gravity on board the ship had failed to comply with this failure, preferring instead to obey Navy regulations and remain in existence.

The engine crew was frantically going over the teleme-try. Everything was in the graceful green, except for the thrust, which was in the embarrassingly absent.

"They couldn't have taken the power units again," Maguro said.

"Sir," said Apprentice Boyle.

"They wouldn't have dared," Maguro said.

"Sir?"

"And so quickly, too. It took them much longer last time it happened."

"Sir!"

"It must be an engine telemetry error," added Maguro after some thought. "But then, why don't we see the engine-error telemetry on this?"

"Maybe the engine-error telemetry also has an error?" said Apprentice Aubergine.

"Sir!" said Apprentice Boyle.

"Shut up, Boyle," Maguro said. "Aubergine, if the engine-error telemetry had an error, then we would see some engine-error-telemetry-error telemetry."

"So maybe the engine-error-telemetry-error telemetry also had an error?"

"That," Maguro said, "is just ludicrous."

"Sir!"

"What the Space, Boyle?"

"We've got a purple alert, sir."

"You and your purple alert! Can't you let go of the purple alert? Space damn you and your bloody purple alert!"

"Sir," said Apprentice Aubergine, "he's actually right."

He was.

"I wonder," said another crew member, "how we can have an airlock-opened-while-engine-active alert when the engine is clearly inactive."

"The engine is active," said another.

"But there's no thrust."

"But it's turned on."

"But no thrust."

"Shut up, the lot of you!" Maguro said.

"Actually," said Boyle, "there is another explanation, kind of."

"He told you to shut up," said Aubergine, ungracefully gleeful.

"It could be a system override," said Boyle. "A higher-ranking system locked to ours."

"I am a higher-ranking system locked to your mother," said Aubergine.

"The next person to say anything whatsoever gets sent to POLIDIV!" Maguro shouted. "Shut up and let me think!"

They obeyed, which was a small mercy, a very small one, compared with the next thing that happened. That next thing was the instant proof of the higher-ranking system theory by way of the sudden and forceful entrance of three unfamiliar troopers wearing strange black uniforms, followed by a large person wearing white from head to toe, marred only by a suspicious amount of decorations.

Master Chief Maguro and his crew were described at some point, by a certain *UPS Spitz* top officer, as fine examples of politically degenerate personas allowed in the Navy only for their marginal engineering skills. Even so, each and every one of them immediately recognized the chubby invader, who was now taking a considerable percentage of the meagre remaining space of the engine telemetry chamber. They had all seen him on numerous public informaticas.

It was High Admiral Frosch.

"Attention!" someone shouted.

"At ease!" the High Admiral said. His voice, Maguro noticed, was high-pitched and nasal, quite different from the Admirals' televised appearances. "Turn off the engine!"

Maguro nodded at Apprentice Boyle, who happened to be the closest to the control panel. Boyle opened his mouth but then, seeing Maguro's expression, snapped it shut and made the necessary move. Gravity, as before, remained unchanged. Master Chief Maguro saw, in his mind's eye, the Admiral's huge flagship surrounding the *UPS Spitz* and carrying it under its own acceleration. Or deceleration. Who cared? This was the end. Total and unconditional despair.

"Now, Master Chief," the High Admiral said, "take me to your captain."

30

FUX IS AFTERMATHED

Recycling, while admittedly an extreme measure, is nevertheless quite common. This is no cause for concern but rather a logical outcome of our harmonious political reality: the stress of military life can break, over time, even the best of officers, to say nothing of the common soldiery, which naturally consists of lesser-quality individuals.

Therefore, while recycling a person should be the last measure, it should not be feared or avoided. Not only is the procedure safe and quick, but the accompanying virtual demonstration of torture and death helps keep the recipient's comrades in check. The individual, slightly changed in appearance so as to avoid raising undue questions, can easily be programmed to assume a new identity, erasing in the process any forbidden thoughts and the entire near-term memory. The basic personality itself, however, remains mostly unchanged.

THE LIGHT FRIGATE *UPS Spitz* was a mere speck of dust in comparison to the vessel engulfing it. This was the mighty *UPS Ermordung,* Navy flagship, home of Top Mobile Naval Command. The crew of the smaller ship was made aware of this situation by a neat audiovisual recreational informatica projected on every wall, floor, and ceiling, followed by a lengthy set of instructions, essentially meaning *return to your cabins and do absolutely nothing until further notice.* This was mercilessly repeated even within the cabins so as to ensure that their occupants were too distracted by it to actually do anything.

The only place spared from this menace was the captain's chambers. Lieutenant Commander Doctor Nightingale, standing in one corner, felt sorry about that. The informatica would never be as boringly pompous as High Admiral Frosch.

The admiral had spent a considerable amount of time describing in detail the offences performed by the crew, officers, and captain of the *UPS Spitz.* This was mixed with gloating over their stupidity in assuming that the LOGMEMs weren't protected from tampering by transmitting each such attempt directly to HQ. One could almost think that this precautionary measure was his very own idea, which obviously wasn't the case. From time to time he would ask for the reasons for the listed atrocities, but could never hold himself from speaking for long enough to listen to any answer.

Eventually, he seemed to have sufficiently vented his grievances. Or just ran out of breath. Or so Nightingale hoped. But in vain.

"To be honest," the admiral lied, "my request for an explanation has nothing to do with punishment. It is merely a way for you to contribute to our glorious empire one last time, helping us make sure that this kind of thing never happens again."

"Well," the captain said, "there's this soldier named—"

"No," said Nightingale. She had already reached a certain conclusion as to what was about to happen. She didn't want the captain to ruin it by alerting the admiral, even though the latter wasn't as sharp as one would have expected.

"Silence, you," the captain said.

"No."

"What's the meaning of this?" said High Admiral Frosch in his High Nasal voice.

"Silence, I said," the captain said, "or I silence you for good."

Nightingale smiled. "You and what army?"

"Be quiet, the two of you!" the high admiral shrilled. "I gave you a direct order! Explain yourselves!"

"Here's the thing, Frosch," Nightingale said. The high admiral visibly stiffened upon hearing this direct, undignified form of addressing a superior officer. "This kind of thing *will* happen again. It will happen again even if you recycle us all."

The captain, who was about to say something, probably

quite loudly, froze, then lowered her head. She seemed to be deep in thought.

"You're dead," Frosch said flatly.

"Not yet," Nightingale said. "And it *will* happen again, and it will happen to *you*, and eventually, it will happen to *everyone*."

"It is evident, sir," the captain said, looking directly at the high admiral, "that here stands the source of our troubles." But something about her tone of voice sounded off. Nightingale glanced in her direction and saw the captain's lips pressed together. What was she doing?

Was she suppressing a *smile*?

"I can see that," the high admiral said. "Though this doesn't lessen your criminal negligence one bit, Captain."

"I am ready to take any punishment laid upon me by High Command," the captain said, keeping her flat expression.

"True," the high admiral said, "and, indeed, you shall. As for you, Lieutenant Commander, in the spirit of mercy, I'm giving you one more chance to explain yourself."

"Of course," Nightingale said.

"Well?"

"Oh, I was just idly agreeing with your self-description as a merciful person."

"I could torture you first, you know," the high admiral said.

"You *are* torturing me first, Frosch."

"One last chance!"

"You want an explanation? Fine. Here it is: this is going to happen over and over again, simply because the system you people have erected, the system I was a part of, and therefore am as guilty of as anyone else, the system we call 'the empire'—that system cannot survive."

"Have you degenerated that much? Plain rebel talk, is it, Lieutenant Commander? Is this supposed to be your 'my recycling wasn't in vain' speech?"

"There's one thing the system cannot take, Frosch. And it's not me, or you, or any rebel. It's the bloody truth. The system cannot take the truth."

"Fine words for someone put in charge of the political logging system," the high admiral said. "The highest of high treasons."

"That's precisely the systematic problem," Nightingale said. "The truth being high treason. Therefore, the system is set to eliminate the truth. Therefore, eventually, the truth shall eliminate the system."

"I would kill you myself, even though recycling is more painful. Really. If I wasn't under strict orders to recycle every so-called capable person here, I swear I would."

From the corner of her eye, Nightingale saw the captain's brief smile. She hoped Frosch didn't notice.

She knows, Nightingale thought. *She must have listened to us in the infirmary. The Fuxed controller.* She knows!

"You can kill me and everyone else here," she said. "It won't help. The truth you're trying to eliminate isn't some high and noble principle. It's just a simple fact: that all of us, you included, are merely human. There's nothing you can do about that."

"We have eliminated religion," the high admiral said. "We have eliminated gender and racial differences. We have eliminated cultures and traits and nations and rogue states and whatnot. We have eliminated belief of any kind except in ourselves. We can eliminate whatever we choose to eliminate."

"Not the truth, you can't. Not *that* truth, at least."

"What are you, a child? We *are* the truth!"

"I'm quite interested in reading your report to High Command, Frosch. I bet it'll contain the exact details of this unfortunate incident, including your very own responsibility as our captain's direct commander. I am sure you'll take upon yourself the *full* responsibility. I'm sure your report will contain nothing but the actual *truth*."

The high admiral's face turned bright red. "What I say is true by the very fact that it is *I* who say it! It *becomes* the truth; it *is* the truth, the whole truth, and nothing but the truth!"

"We shall see about that," Nightingale said.

"*We* shall," the High Admiral said. "*You* won't."

The captain, even as the black-clad soldiers came and took her and Nightingale away to the brig, kept smiling.

THE REPEATING SET of instructions was, at last, replaced. The new informatica was much shorter: everyone upon the UPS *Spitz* was to be considered under arrest and wait in their places until called for. Meanwhile, a medical crew from the flagship took over Nightingale's infirmary. The passage tube between the ships was locked and guarded in case some rogue elements decided to infect the UPS *Ermordung* with their deranged, diseased ideas or personalities. Unfamiliar armed troopers stood in every corridor.

Few on board the UPS *Spitz* entertained any thoughts of

surviving this situation. And even those lost all hope when the general broadcast started calling people by name, ordering them to the infirmary.

HAVING PERSONALLY OVERSEEN the recycling of each and every crewmember of the UPS *Spitz*, High Admiral Frosch returned to his own ship. While most of the recyclees would be spread among other naval vessels, never to serve as one unit again, a few were still too valuable for that. Therefore, Frosch cunningly took the opportunity to augment his own crew with a few carefully chosen blank new personalities. The UPS *Spitz* itself would be towed to the nearest dockyard, receive some basic maintenance, a modest crew and a colossal new name, and eventually sent on its way to fight another day. There were never enough ships to feed the war machine.

Still, High Admiral Frosch felt that despite his excellent efforts and perfect execution, as properly reported to Terra HQ, something was missing.

THE ONE THING no one missed lay still and frozen in a forgotten chamber under the UPS *Spitz* infirmary floor. This state of affairs continued uninterrupted for a suspiciously long time.

31

FUX IS VICTORIOUS

And so, we have established beyond all reasonable doubt that this kind of mental disruption, of which the subject, Fux, Joseph, is a prime example, is not only highly dangerous in itself but also extremely contagious.

SECRET APPENDIX TO A REPORT BY SERGEANT
K. ČAPEK, MUNICIPAL POLICE HQ, PRAHA,
BOHEMIA IV

LIEUTENANT JOHNNY, the new life-support officer, demonstrated his questionable qualities in a most splendid and satisfactory manner less than an hour after setting foot upon the light frigate *UPS Schmal*. This feat, in the form of a sharp and horrible stench that quickly spread everywhere through the ventilation system, was marked by everyone who happened to smell it as a record of some kind.

The captain had to interfere. The new lieutenant was quickly set to be recycled. In the infirmary, he briefly met another recyclee, a strange moustachioed corporal officially named Johnny, who insisted upon being called Kugel. During their brief pre-treatment period, they became the best of friends. No one in the infirmary understood how said friendship survived their recycling, though it should be noted that the medical crew was largely preoccupied with previous pressing, smelly matters. Eventually, the ventilation system was cleaned. Everyone literally breathed a sigh of relief.

It was premature.

CORPORAL DAISY, a new transfer to the 75th Regiment of the Mobile Infantry, demonstrated her questionable qualities in a most splendid and satisfactory manner less than a day after setting foot upon the light frigate UPS *Schlau*. This feat involved a mechanized armour suit, which was supposed to be perfectly maintained only metaphorically. The resulting incident tore a new hole in the officially impenetrable body of the ship.

The corporal was quickly set to be recycled. There was some talk among the troops, but no one cared. No one of rank, that is. Not immediately. A few other recyclings followed, perhaps slightly more than usual, but nothing to worry about, so no one worried.

No one of rank, that is. By the time the medical officer discovered that something was off with the main controller machine, the newly recycled had already become the majority of the ship's personnel. There was no way to explain this to High Command, and so no such attempt was made.

MASTER CHIEF JOHNNY, a fine addition to the long-suffering engine crew of the long-suffering *UPS Sonde*, splendidly demonstrated his qualities before the end of his first shift on the vessel. He did this by disabling the engine-error telemetry system and the engine-error-telemetry-error telemetry system in the guise of installing a new engine-error-telemetry-error-telemetry-error telemetry system. After some initial confusion, the captain decided to avoid any risks and promptly recycled him. This caused some sighs of relief, both among the crew and, strangely, by the culprit. *Never mind,* the captain thought. *Recycling fixes everything.* Only later did she find out that she was, literally and quite painfully, right.

PRIVATE DAISY DEMONSTRATED her questionable qualities before ever setting foot upon the light frigate *UPS Zapfen*. This was done by her very presence, as she was obviously of the male persuasion and quite vocal about it, to boot. The local political officer, while finding no regulations forbidding this kind of thing, still felt it to be annoyingly wrong. He tried to resolve the issue peacefully by reminding the fool that he should be a Private Johnny rather than a

Private Daisy, to which the pervert answered that he was, in fact, also not a private but rather a mister.

This resulted in a quick and hasty trip to the infirmary without even consulting the captain. This, in turn, had a quick and nasty effect upon the political officer's relationship with the captain in the short term. In the slightly longer term, it was moot.

DRILL SERGEANT JOHNNY had a somewhat shaky start to his service on board the UPS *Macht*, having trouble distinguishing the officers from the common soldiery.

"Don't answer me, you vulture!" he shouted at a lieutenant who had tried to inquire. "Don't even let it ever be thought that you are worthy of talking to me, you degenerate parrot!"

This might have quietly passed as an acclimatization hiccup were it not for the arrival of the local Mobile Infantry colonel, who received an even harsher treatment, including at least a seagull, a wagtail, a starling, and a thrush. For a short time afterward, the regimental lieutenant had to take company drilling upon herself. She didn't enjoy it.

She enjoyed what followed even less.

LIEUTENANT COMMANDER DOCTOR DAISY did not cause any trouble at all during her time as a secondary medical officer on board the mighty UPS *Ermordung*. The only irregularities were some minor fiddlings with the main controller and the occasional visit from the high admiral, who, it seemed, was forcefully gloating yet strangely depressed.

Meanwhile, in the brig, a certain Commander Johnny, a beefy man who was rumoured to be a retired political officer of some sort, had to be chained and gagged due to excessive talking. His only companion there was an unnamed high-ranking officer stripped of her insignia yet, despite her dangerously serious situation, constantly smiling.

This tranquillity lasted all through the vessel's long trip to Terra HQ, to which the admiral was called in order to discuss the strange incident on the now officially inexistent *UPS Spitz*, and especially its influence on the high admiral's career, well-being, or even being at all.

A shuttle carried Frosch and, by way of evidence, the medical officer and the two occupants of the brig down to Terra-actual. By the time it landed, Frosch had managed to convince himself that whatever disciplinary action might be taken against him would be mainly for show. A warning, perhaps even a stern one. If worse came to worst, a remark in his personal political file. That would be nasty but still manageable. And quick. He had no doubt that the time of trouble would soon be over.

He was wrong in every possible way.

PRIVATE JOHNNY and Sergeant Private Quartermaster Johnny were assigned to serve in the Mobile Infantry unit upon the *UPS Ramsch*, a vessel so old as to be unworthy of having its own full regiment, settling for a single platoon instead. Both Johnnies seemed friendly enough and caused no trouble if one didn't count their absent-minded tendency to replace their own names with other, strange ones. This was not unusual among new transfers. It was nothing to worry about.

The next shift saw the Mobile Infantry revolt and take over the ship.

STRANGE REPORTS STARTED ARRIVING at Terra HQ.

The UPS *Schmal* reported a delay in its combat schedule due to a long, laborious, and utterly uncalled-for disinfection operation. HQ inquiries as to the exact nature and cause of this resulted in confusing and contradictory explanations. Soon afterward, the UPS *Schmal* stopped replying.

Some other ships noticed its beacon in passing. One of those, the UPS *Platzen*, was ordered to pursue and engage. That was the last that HQ heard of either the UPS *Schmal* or the UPS *Platzen*.

Meanwhile, the UPS *Schlaue* stopped as planned at its next designated combat planet, let the Mobile Infantry off, and then hurriedly left. The stranded troopers, to judge by the single transmission received from their commanding officer, were perfectly fine with this, having decided to erect their own village and dedicate the rest of their lives to agriculture and to the strange notion that all humans were created equal.

The light frigate UPS *Zapfen* was detected moving in a suspicious trajectory toward Ugnr III, famous for being orbited by Puddabest Station, itself famous for all sorts of things officially barred from being famous. As opposed to its siblings, the UPS *Zapfen* never stopped transmitting, although Terra HQ had trouble deciphering the received messages, which for some reason were perfectly rhymed.

Reports kept flying in: mutinies, unauthorized landings, declarations of pacifism and, in one case, an endless list of sausage recipes.

A young Terra HQ intelligence officer, working on this mystery in her spare time, discovered a suspicious pattern: each of the first ten ships to disobey direct orders had received recycled crew members from a single, unlisted source, probably an officially inexistent warship. Further investigation showed that other persons of the same origin were assigned to other vessels, including, to the officer's horror, the Navy's very flagship, the UPS *Ermordung*.

By the time the young officer reported her findings, High Admiral Frosch had already been demoted to a mere Lieutenant General, lightly recalibrated, and sent to command a basic training camp in the Arctic. The two detainees he brought with him as evidence were unceremoniously returned to the UPS *Ermordung*, which was promptly sent out to hunt the rebels. The new high admiral had no time for theories or speculations or, luckily for the young officer, for recalibrating young officers for wasting their betters' valuable time.

Disturbing news started arriving from some of the imperial strongholds. Puddabest Station vocally declared its independence. The local imperial troops were sent to vanquish the rebels. Their last transmission came in the form of a nice official informatica, showing their commander, obviously intoxicated, dancing in a clown suit surrounded by a group of barely yet offensively clothed locals, inviting everyone to have the best time of their lives.

On Bayern III, the local Underground Party of Moderate Progress, created by the secret service in order to lure in potentially politically dangerous elements, declared a transition into a democratic system. It soon established a House of Representatives and promptly voted itself into filling it. Molvadia II, Franca VII, and Volscia V soon followed.

UTILIZING the entire scope of its dwindling Navy, Terra HQ ordered all active, loyal ships to chase the disobedient ones. Even vessels intended for long overhauls in the dockyards were quickly filled with whatever crews were available and sent in hot pursuit. This included a certain unnamed light frigate hastily dubbed the *UPS Snapp*, manned by a hastily collected ragtag bunch of leftovers.

All this, in the grand scheme of things, would have been utterly insignificant if not for a nasty surprise awaiting said crew in, or rather under, the infirmary. Terra HQ learned of this only later via a lengthy and deranged transmission received from a new kind of self-declared rogue ship. It was a series of elaborate speeches condemning the empire for being too soft, too forgiving, too gentle, too humane, and too weak.

The intelligence officers assigned to the case soon discovered that all records of the speaker's identity had been erased, and so he came to be known only by the name he gave himself: Admiral Berserker.

THE NEW HIGH admiral enjoyed her unexpected promotion for less than a week. It took that long for Terra HQ itself to rebel against her. As a planetary base, HQ did not feature its own recycling facilities, and the offensive officers were sent to local hospitals, from which they returned changed in strange and unexpected ways. Or, at least, unexpected to anyone who had not recently served on the nonexistent UPS *Spitz*. After that, the only surprise in store was how long it took the high admiral to lose her position and the position itself to cease existing. Some recently recycled citizens made nice profits betting on it.

And thus had Fux spread, in spirit if not in name, across the entire human universe.

32

FUX IS RETURNED

Indeed I was once suspected of being a spy, but it turned out that I was not qualified.

FROM THE CONCLUSION OF *THE GOOD SOLDIER*, AN ANONYMOUS MANUSCRIPT POPULAR ON BOHEMIA IV

ONE FINE LATE morning in the early spring, when the few remaining lime trees were rebelliously blossoming in the face of oppression, a strange vessel landed, unauthorized, right in front of Kalicha bar in Vordle Street in the Vinohrady district in the city of Praha in the county of Czek on the recently-liberated planet of Bohemia IV.

This reckless or glorious feat, depending on whom one was asking, did not receive the amount of attention it deserved from any of the involved parties. In fact, almost no one was present to greet it. The authorities, as they still referred to themselves despite empirical proofs to the contrary, were still fighting, though by now it was less for control and more for survival. The good citizens of Praha were busy pushing the remaining imperial forces toward the river and, equally important, hunting for breakfast or, in some of the more radical cases, brunch. And so the only witnesses to this somewhat historical event were two pedestrians: Old Lady Kralik, who happened to live nearby, and Master Zizka, who happened to be her cheerful small grey poodle.

The vessel, a shuttle that seemed as least as old as Old Lady Kralik and even more dangerously decomposing than the poodle, creaked ominously and eventually managed to force down its own main hatch cover. A man appeared in the opening. As he slowly stepped down the hatch, Old Lady Kralik noticed that he did not seem to be one of those awful imperial people. If not for his manner of transportation, she could have mistaken him for a local. He was a stocky, jolly man of undeterminable age, and the only foreign things about him she noticed when he stepped down to the sidewalk were a strange paper uniform and a police cap which was unacceptably last year's fashion.

Despite this, he seemed friendly enough. Master Zizka barked, perhaps in disagreement.

"Good day, honourable ma'am," the man said. "I am delighted to meet you."

For a moment, Old Lady Kralik quietly scrutinized the newcomer. In her experience, people who came from the sky, regardless of the shabbiness of their transportation, were strangers. Aliens. No-good scum.

"Are you a spy?" she asked.

"Not at all, ma'am," the man said. "Indeed I was once suspected of being a spy, but it turned out that I was not qualified."

This seemed quite a satisfactory explanation, as Old Lady Kralik was used to people boasting about their qualities and not the other way around. She smiled at the man.

"I would like to apply to your service, ma'am," the man said, "and, to be honest, to the service of your lovely dog, which, with all due respect, I suspect is long past his yearly mechanical checkup."

Now he shows his true colours! Old Lady Kalika thought. "Excuse me?"

"I mean no offence, ma'am," the man said, "but I am somewhat of an expert on the matter. See how his hind legs fail to follow his front ones?"

"How dare you!" said Old Lady Kalika.

Master Zizka growled in sympathy.

"I would say that I am not exactly daring, honourable ma'am," the man said, "and more like trying my luck."

Such atrocity! Old Lady Kralik had met a fair number of swindlers and crooks in her long life, but this direct approach was an absolute spit in the face. "How dare you even speak of Master Zizka!" she snapped. "Who do you think you are? You criminal, you, you . . . pervert! You invalid!"

But the man only smiled.

"Just an idiot, ma'am," he said and gaily raised his foolish, outdated police cap. "Certified, second-class."

APPENDIX: NAMES, REFERENCES, AND OTHER LITERARY MISCHIEFS

CHARACTERS

Fux—"fox" in German.

Corporal Kohl—"cabbage" in German

Corporal Kraut—"herb" or "cabbage" in German

Corporal Kartoffel—"potato" in German

Corporal Kugel . . . who doesn't love kugel?

Commander Kapust—Kapusta/Kapust is "cabbage" in Russian.

Medical Ensign Grippe—"flu" in German.

Master Chief Maguro—"tuna fish" in Japanese.

Private Aubergine—"eggplant" in German.

Commander Ahuru—Star Trek's "Uhura," reversed.

Second Lieutenant Win, aka Big W—his poor mother wanted to call him Winston, after Churchill. He turned out to be a Big Wanker.

Sergeant Zimmer, Pre-Private Johnny, Pre-Private Daisy,

Mister Roseneck—inspired by *Starship Troopers'* Sergeant Zim, Johnny Rico, Dizzy Flores, and Lieutenant Rasczak.

Quartermaster Bolon—inspired by Private Baloun of *The Good Soldier Švejk*.

High Admiral Frosch—"frog" in German.

Sergeant K. Čapek—famous Czech author and playwright Karel Čapek who, among other things, came up with the word "robot."

Second Lieutenant Klar—"clear/understood/plain/transparent" in German.

Ryba the fishmaker—Ryba is "fish" in Czech.

Countess Syrkasa—*syr* is cheese in Czech, *kase* is cheese in German.

Fux's old dogs, Velbloud and Kun—"camel" and "horse" in Czech.

Lady Kralik—"rabbit" in Czech. Her poodle, Master Zizka, is named after a famous Czech general.

As for Lipton, Nightingale, Havock, Berserker, and Clementine, their names seem to me to be quite obvious.

STARSHIPS

All the starship names are taken from German:

UPS (*United Planets Ship*) *Spitz*—"Pointed"
UPS *Ermordung*, the flagship—"Murder/Assassination"
UPS *Schmal*—"Narrow"
UPS *Scharf*—"Sharp"
UPS *Schlau*—"Cunning"

UPS Zapfen—"Tap"
UPS Platzen—"Burst"
UPS Snapp—"Snap"
The Neukölln starship class—Neukölln is my favourite neighbourhood in Berlin

BOOKS, BOTH FICTIONAL AND REFERENCED

Citizen of the Galaxy, Tunnel in the Sky, I Shall Fear no Evil, The Puppet Masters, Double Star, Glory Road, To Sail Beyond the Sunset, Have Spacesuit—Will Travel, and, of course, *Starship Troopers* are all novels by Robert A. Heinlein. *Life-Line* is a short story by the same.

The Person in the Flying Fortress is an alternate-reality version of Philip K. Dick's *The Man in the High Castle.*

Ending the Forever Was refers to Joe Haldeman's *The Forever War.*

My Capital Struggle by Adolphus Marx is a combination of Marx's *Das Kapital* (The Capital) and Hitler's *Mein Kampf* (My Struggle).

And most importantly, the very title of this novel is taken from its spiritual ancestor, *The Fateful Adventures of the Good Soldier Švejk During the World War*—also know as *The Good Soldier Švejk*—by Jaroslav Hašek.

LOCATIONS

All planets except for Terra are based on parts of old Europe:

Bohemia—the largest historical region of the Czech Republic. Fux's address, 197 Vodik Street in the district of Vinohrady in the city of Praha in the county of Czek in the state of Bohemia, can be translated as 197 Vodickova st, Vinohardy district, city of Prague, Czech Republic, a part of the larger area of Bohemia. It is also a lie, for two reasons: one is that Vodickova Street is not inside the district of Vinohardy. The other is that the street is too short and doesn't feature house number 197.

The River Vlt refers to Pargue's own Vltava River.

Kalicha Bar is the real place in which Jaroslav Hašek, author of *The Good Soldier Švejk,* used to sit, drink with his friends, and write.

Bayern—the state of Bavaria.

Molvadia—just messing with Moldavia.

Franca—France.

Volscia—Italy (the Volsci were an ancient Italian tribe).

Ungr—Hungary; and thus:

Puddabest Station—Budapest.

MORALE UNIT SONGS

The morale unit songs are all spoofs on famous ones:

Arise, ye prisoners of oppression—"The International"

Oh, I come from planet Terra with a big gun on my knee—"Oh! Susanna"

Whatever happened to all the heroes?—"No More Heroes" by The Stranglers

Freedom!—this, alas, refers to the famous song by George Michael.

OTHER REFERENCES

The recreational drug Hašek is named after Jaroslav Hašek, author of *The Good Soldier Švejk*.

Sumavska wool—Sumavska is a kind of sheep originating in Czechoslovakia.

Big W's pre-combat speech is taken from Churchill's "we shall fight on the beaches . . ."

The Political Division's pre-combat speech—"In a free republic . . ."—is taken from Theodore Roosevelt's *Duties of American Citizenship*, 1883.

Kapust's victory speech—"This is a solemn but a glorious hour"—is taken from Truman's announcement of the American victory in the Second World War.

ABOUT THE AUTHOR

Nir Yaniv is an Israeli-born multidisciplinary artist living in Los Angeles. He's an author, a musician, an illustrator, and a filmmaker. He founded Israel's first online science fiction magazine and served as its chief editor for ten years, after which he moved on to editing a printed genre magazine.

He collaborated with World Fantasy Award-winning author Lavie Tidhar on two novels, including the "deranged sci-fi extravaganza" (per *The Jewish Quarterly*) *The Tel Aviv Dossier,* and his English- language collection *The Love Machine & Other Contraptions* was published by Infinity Plus in 2012.

His most recent Hebrew novel, *King of Jerusalem,* was

published in Israel in 2019. His short stories have appeared in *Weird Tales*, *Apex*, and *ChiZine*, among others.

Nir's musical career includes soundtracks for film, dance shows, and theatre. His most recent work is the voice-and-drums animated album *The Voice Remains* (LifeArt Music, 2021). Nir has also directed several short films and music videos, both live-action and animated.

Website: niryaniv.com
Twitter: @TheNirYaniv
Instagram: @nyfiction

ABOUT SHADOWPAW PRESS

SHADOWPAW PRESS

Shadowpaw Press is a small traditional, royalty-paying publishing company located in Regina, Saskatchewan, Canada, founded in 2018 by Edward Willett, an award-winning author of science fiction, fantasy, and non-fiction for readers of all ages. A member of Literary Press Group (Canada) and the Association of Canadian Publishers, Shadowpaw Press publishes an eclectic selection of books by both new and established authors, including adult fiction, young adult fiction, children's books, non-fiction, and anthologies. In addition, Shadowpaw Press publishes new editions of notable, previously published books in any genre under the Shadowpaw Press Reprise imprint. For more information, email publisher@shadowpawpress.com.

MORE SCIENCE FICTION AND FANTASY

SHADOWPAW PRESS

New work by new and established authors

The Headmasters by Mark Morton

Shapers of Worlds Volumes I-IV, edited by Edward Willett

The Downloaded by Robert J. Sawyer

The Traitor's Son by Dave Duncan

Corridor to Nightmare by Dave Duncan

The Sun Runners by James Bow

Ashme's Song by Brad C. Anderson

Paths to the Stars by Edward Willett

Star Song by Edward Willett

SHADOWPAW PRESS *Reprise*

New editions of notable, previously published work

The Canadian Chills Series by Arthur Slade: *Return of the Grudstone Ghosts, Ghost Hotel, Invasion of the IQ Snatchers*

Duatero by Brad C. Anderson

Blue Fire by E. C. Blake

The Legend of Sarah by Leslie Gadallah

The Empire of Kaz trilogy by Leslie Gadallah: *Cat's Pawn, Cat's Gambit, Cat's Game*

The Ghosts of Spiritwood by Martine Noël-Maw

The Shards of Excalibur Series (*Song of the Sword, Twist of the Blade, Lake in the Clouds, Cave Beneath the Sea, Door into Faerie*); The Peregrine Rising Duology (*Right to Know, Falcon's Egg*); *Spirit Singer, From the Street to the Stars,* and *Soulworm*

by Edward Willett

For details about these and many other great titles, visit shadowpawpress.com

Made in the USA
Las Vegas, NV
09 April 2024

88456201R00215